KICKING

Paperback Trader
860-456-0252
NOV 26 2012
522 Storrs Road
Mansfield Center, CT 06250

KICKING

LESLIE DICK

A NOVEL

CITY LIGHTS
SAN FRANCISCO

First City Lights edition 1993.
© 1992 by Leslie Dick

First published in Great Britain 1992
by Martin Secker & Warburg Ltd.

All Rights Reserved

The characters and events in this novel are fictional; any resemblance to a living person, or to factual circumstances, is entirely coincidental.

Cover design and photography by Rex Ray

Library of Congress Cataloging in Publication Data

Dick, Leslie, 1954 -
Kicking / by Leslie Dick.
p. cm.
ISBN 0-87286-282-8 : $10.95
I. Title.
PS3554.I29K53 1993
813'.54 — dc20 93-5566
CIP

City Lights Books are available to bookstores through our primary distributor: Subterranean Company, P. O. Box 168, 265 S. 5th St., Monroe, OR 97456. 503-847-5274. Toll-free orders 800-274-7826. FAX 503-847-6018. Our books are also available through library jobbers and regional distributors. For personal orders and catalogs, please write to City Lights Books, 261 Columbus Avenue, San Francisco, CA 94133.

CITY LIGHTS BOOKS are edited by Lawrence Ferlinghetti and Nancy J. Peters and published at the City Lights Bookstore, 261 Columbus Avenue, San Francisco, CA 94133.

My memory is inimical to all that is personal . . .
I repeat — my memory is not loving but inimical,
and it labours not to reproduce but to distance
the past.

Osip Mandelstam, *The Noise of Time*

Death by Drowning

Suicide: Take One

Connie parked the car on Waterloo Bridge, facing south. It was a sunny summer evening. As she was locking the door, and William was getting out on the pavement side, Connie half saw a young man step over the horizontal guard-rail that runs along the edge of the bridge. He stood there for a moment, only a few feet away from William. She was very surprised, thinking this must be some kind of a joke. As she looked, he vanished. He had jumped off the bridge. A momentary pause of disbelief: terrifying. Connie forced herself to go to the edge and look over.

William and Connie held on to the horizontal rail as they leaned forward, looking down to the river below. The young man was bobbing about in the water.

Connie was relieved he was alive. Leaning over, she waved, calling out to him, Are you all right? He looked Chinese, maybe twenty-five years old; he shouted out to Connie and William, I FEEL MUCH BETTER NOW. He was waving to them, he seemed elated, very excited. Connie and William were laughing, very pleased; they were laughing with him, and making gestures of triumph and survival. Connie shouted that he must swim to the embankment, he mustn't swallow any water, she was smiling, with no sense of real danger. This wasn't an emergency, more like some absurd adventure.

Huge sightseeing boats ploughed past. The man in the water began to drift downstream. Connie scanned the river's banks and saw the flight of stairs that runs down from the embankment on the south side of the river to the level of the water. She pointed to it, pointing it out to him, shouting to him to head for those stairs. Everything was all right now. She picked up the pair of worn-out trainers and the red sweatshirt which he had left folded on the bridge; she was going to put them by the stairs for him. Connie and William were laughing and waving to the man in the water. They were all three elated and relieved.

As they started to walk towards the South Bank, Connie saw that the man in the water was having some difficulty swimming. She knew there are treacherous currents in the river. She immediately started to run as fast as she could, to get to a telephone. The sense of relief changed into extreme anxiety.

Running fast, she glanced towards the river; she saw that the man in the water was being carried away downstream. He was moving towards a large metal drum or buoy that floated in the middle of the river. Maybe he could hang on to that, Connie thought, until the river police came to pull him out. As she ran down the steps towards the National Theatre, Connie's last sight of him was some way beyond the drum. She saw his arms wave above his head, like in the poem, and knew he was drowning.

Moving very fast, she went into the National Theatre box-office to make them call 999. She was vehement, insistent. There was some delay, maybe half a minute, because all the telephones were occupied, even the payphones. This was terrible. When she was sure they'd dialled 999, she ran outside again onto the embankment.

She saw a river police launch silently circling around in the water just downstream from the metal drum. They were looking for the man in the water. Connie realised he was dead.

Suicide: Take Two

That afternoon, William had a meeting in town, so they arranged to meet at the ICA, around six or six-fifteen. There was an opening of an exhibition, on architecture, at the ICA, and then afterwards they would go on to meet Edith, and Ruby, and other friends, at the NFT bar, south of the river. They were supposed to be going to Steve's performance, to this avant-garde circus Steve was performing in.

Connie always found it disorienting to change, to dress to go out, at five o'clock, but she'd been to Paris a couple of weeks before, and she'd bought the most beautiful jacket, on sale of course, and she wanted to wear it. She wore her new earrings, clips that resembled crinkled nuggets of ore, crumpled silver foil. They were the other major acquisition of the summer. She put on her striped trousers, indulging a fantasy that the boned and padded pale pink jacket in combination with the baggy striped trousers would recall a Regency dandy, would call this to mind, like a rhyme, a shadow, some kind of echo of *dandyisme*. This idea amused her immensely, since she was at the same time convinced that no one else would see it.

Dressed, she felt slightly more prepared for the scrutiny of the crowds. It was like putting on armour, constructing an image that would impress and seduce, surprise and delight. Again, this idea, this fantasy of being looked at, amused Connie (as she got into the car, gingerly, avoiding the grime), it amused her because she was convinced that no one would see her, see it, that way.

The ICA was packed. William arrived at almost exactly the same moment, they found each other near the door. His meeting had gone well; he was very excited, it looked like one of his many projects might come off. Connie thought he was being more than a bit over-optimistic, and slightly resented being positioned as the voice of reason, or doom. She felt her body soaking up the pressure of William's wishful thinking, but they agreed to discuss it later, and plunged into the throng. One of the exhibits in the ICA show was by the architect who was working with William on an exhibition project. Connie had never met him. Shortly, she found herself standing very straight and still while William talked to this extremely highly regarded, very fashionably dressed, famous young architect. His name was Roland Nicholson. She felt stiff, standing very straight in her new jacket, very much on display. She had nothing to say. The architect's model for the new King's Cross was sublime: it was like a kid's model railway gone completely haywire, with canals and gasometers jostling blocks of flats and giant railway signals and trees and highways. It was great; nevertheless, Connie had nothing to say.

It was partly that the room was so very crowded, everyone

too close to each other, moving in different directions. It was too hot, too noisy, and the white light was very bright. The line between feeling on display, and feeling painfully exposed, in the glare of noise and light, was slowly being erased. As so often, Connie found herself wishing herself elsewhere.

A woman she'd known for aeons appeared amid the throngs with her new boyfriend in tow. They were both brilliant young architects. The boyfriend didn't acknowledge Connie at all. Connie moved from an initial reaction of paranoia (he doesn't like me) to annoyance. Meanwhile she was introducing Dido to Roland Nicholson, and Dido was being extremely emphatic about something to do with shit, undoubtedly making an impression. She couldn't follow what Dido was saying. She wanted to get out of this crowded noisy place, where as always at openings there were far too many people to be able to see the work, and where anyone could appear at any time, suddenly, unexpectedly, and she'd have to somehow cope with a sudden meeting, absorbing or fending off the psychic collision.

There were times when Connie felt not only vulnerable, times when it was more like feeling flayed, and all the amazing jackets, and subtle, understated earrings, and comic, even witty striped trousers couldn't cover her up. She felt the whole surface of her body to be fragile, easily bruised or cracked, and her hold on language tenuous. Anxiety spread through her body, crumbling away behind the careful façade. It was creeping through the evening, an anxiety she tried to dispel with glasses of red wine. She couldn't make out what anyone was saying. She went on standing there, clutching her wineglass, looking at the crazed model of King's Cross.

Finally they agreed to leave. Getting into the car, William and Connie were openly affectionate with each other. They drove around Trafalgar Square with some difficulty, and headed east along the Strand. Still a little jumpy, Connie wasn't sure if this was the best route to take. William didn't drive, and they often had tiny arguments about better and worse routes. As she was diverted in another circle around the Aldwych and back, William asked about the performance. He had strong views on circuses.

As they turned to head south on Waterloo Bridge, the bright sky opened up wide over their heads, with the expanse of the city spread out on either side. It was a Wednesday evening in early August, the sun was shining, long low beams of yellow light, with the blue sky floating high above. It would be light until nine or nine-thirty at night.

Connie parked the car on the left, facing south, half-way across the bridge. There was a small delay, getting out of the car, as Connie reapplied her red lipstick in the rear-view mirror. It was about half-past seven, and as Connie was locking the door on her side, William getting out on his, she half saw a man step over the guard-rail that ran along the edge of the bridge. She was surprised, and perplexed: this didn't make sense. Was it a joke? Rag week? As she froze, her look widened, peripherally, to take in the other kids, students (she half thought) that would be with this man, larking about somehow. He was alone.

The young man stood there for a moment, facing out, towards the river, and then he vanished. She saw him drop out of sight. Or perhaps that's wrong, he fell so quickly it was more like she knew he had dropped out of sight. But this didn't make sense either. The young man vanished. With difficulty Connie understood that he had fallen, he had dropped, he had jumped off the bridge.

That moment of difficulty was also a moment of horror: a mixture of fear and disbelief. It paralysed her completely. She forced herself to overcome this resistance; she moved towards the rail. Within the moment of hesitation lay Connie's research into methods of suicide, her knowledge that when someone jumps off the Golden Gate Bridge, for example, or the Brooklyn Bridge, the velocity of their fall, given the height of the bridge, is so great that hitting the surface of the water is like landing on concrete. It is the fall that kills, not drowning. Believing this, Connie was terrified to look over the edge, reluctant to look at death itself. She said to William, 'You're killed instantly when you jump.'

Together they moved forward and, leaning against the rail, they looked down into the river below. The relief was like a drug, icy and clear, ripping through her body, along her nerves, blowing through her like cold air. The man was bobbing about in the water. Both William and Connie found themselves laughing, smiling uncontrollably. They waved to him, leaning over, looking down into the water, and Connie shouted, 'Are you all right?' Seeing the man looked Chinese, maybe, she imagined that perhaps he didn't speak English. The answer came back, shouted from the river water — an ironic answer that seemed to be replete with implication, a whole narrative, a history, contained in its few words, it seemed — the answer came: I FEEL MUCH BETTER NOW.

To Connie, this sentence confirmed that what she had witnessed was a suicide attempt. Like her, reluctant in the moment of horror, terrified to meet the sight of death and then forcing herself to look, like her, this man too had expected death. He had intended to die. Now he was alive, suddenly, and feeling better, wanting to live. He'd changed his mind. A tragedy had turned into a lark, an adventure, a foolish act: swimming in the middle of the Thames.

When she was sixteen, Connie lived for a summer on the river at Battersea, on a Thames barge that was moored at the bottom of an overgrown churchyard. It was not a houseboat, but a nineteenth-century sailing barge that never sailed; it floated up and down on the tide, settling onto the river mud twice a day. She'd lived there with her sister, after the split, when they left their mother's house. The church was by Wren, and William Blake got married in it, and Benedict Arnold, the traitor, was buried in the churchyard. That summer Connie got to know the river, the wide open space of reflected light, the expanse of water smooth under the wide sky, so quiet in the middle of the city, and she got to know the river police. She used to wake up with the changing tide before dawn, and creep up the ladder to perch on the deck, wrapped in Hilary's thick pink shawl. Sitting half out of the hatch near the bow, watching the light on the river endlessly moving, the river police, or fuzz, would appear, checking her out for drugs or something, no doubt. And Connie would give them cups of tea, disarmingly, and they'd tell her about the river.

This is what she remembered: there are treacherous currents, and the water's so poisoned you have to have your stomach pumped out if you fall in.

Leaning over the rail, she shouted to the man in the river, 'Don't swallow the water!' Nevertheless, none of them sensed the danger. They continued to laugh, and wave, making gestures of triumph and survival. Connie could swim well, she was a strong swimmer. William couldn't swim at all. It was impossible for them to judge how difficult it was to swim in the river.

Looking up, Connie quickly scanned the grey stone embankments on either side of the broad river, and saw the steps that descend from the esplanade outside the National Theatre to the level of the water. Somewhere in her mind was a vague idea of avoiding the police, an idea left over from the past — keep the police out of it, if it's not absolutely necessary. At the bottom of this was a notion that they would punish the poor bloke for jumping off the bridge.

Connie pointed to the steps, pointing them out to him, imagining that the man in the river, like Mao in the Yangtse

Kiang, would swim across to these steps, cutting through the water, avoiding the barges and power boats and pleasure steamers and all the rest of the river traffic. He would swim across the river to the steps, and climb out, she imagined. He would be OK. Connie and William started to walk towards the South Bank.

Connie picked up the man's trainers and red sweatshirt. The sweatshirt was very faded and worn, and very clean. It was neatly folded on the ground just at the point where he'd stepped over the guard-rail. The running shoes were white, and very worn out, with the back of each shoe crumpled, as if they'd been worn as slippers. The pair of shoes, placed side by side on the pavement, next to the folded sweatshirt, seemed imbued with pathos.

Connie's uncle and aunt lived near Seven Sisters, the chalky cliffs on the south coast near Beachy Head, and they'd told her years before that the people who commit suicide from those cliffs always take their shoes off before jumping — as if they were going swimming. They always take off their shoes, and sometimes their coats or jackets, and leave them behind, carefully folded, but the women apparently always hold on to their handbags when they jump.

Connie didn't really want to bring the sweatshirt and shoes, she didn't want to get involved. She wanted to walk away into the sunny evening, laughing with William about their fears and their subsequent elated relief. She wanted to get to the bar and meet her friends. But the practical side weighed heavily: the man in the river would be cold and wet when he got out of the water; so poor, he would need his shoes, his clean sweatshirt.

This sudden momentary resistance, this reluctance to get involved, was real, intransigent, like the fierce hesitation she felt in the first moments after he jumped, the wish not to look, or know, that shock of disbelief and denial. These seemed to be irreducible elements in witnessing a drama or a sudden scene of violence. It was always hard to know how to take part, to measure the correct degree of detachment and help. Connie compromised; she would take the shoes and the sweatshirt, and leave them for the man to find when he climbed out of the water. Connie had no intention of meeting him, or waiting for him to emerge, soaked through and happy, in shock. Hanging around to help seemed too close to a kind of morbid fascination. They were beginning to be late, anyway.

There was this moment, then, that took the place of their initial terror, and their subsequent relieved elation, a moment of calm, almost retrospective, as Connie and William turned away from the railing, to walk towards the South Bank, turning towards each other for the first time, as if to say, phew! what a scene! The evening sunlight filled the air around them, wide blue sky over the wide river, and they were laughing — so very pleased he was all right — and Connie was holding the folded red sweatshirt and the worn pair of trainers on top of it.

Connie was immensely pleased and also amazed that he was all right, and part of this was merely symbolic, as if the young man in the river reflected or represented something to her, something of herself, over and above his existence as a separate person, with a history and a logic completely unknown to her. In some sense, his survival stood in for her own will to die, and the simultaneous contradictory will to live.

Holding these clothes, Connie tried to imagine his predicament. Maybe he was a student, from Hong Kong, Asia, far from home and family, unbearably lonely, with no one to turn to. A foreigner, she thought — as if being a foreigner in London is enough to drive you to suicide. Maybe he was a homeless person, living in the parking areas under the South Bank where the kids used to skateboard, maybe he was homeless, and penniless, and unable to see a way out. His shoes evinced complete destitution: the soles were worn smooth, there were large holes in the nylon fabric, and their backs were worn down. Connie imagined the Chinese man walking all over the city, walking constantly, too poor to do anything but walk all the time. The red sweatshirt was soft and thin, it was so old, but it was terribly clean. She didn't know how you could keep so clean if you were so poor. Maybe he was crazy, not homeless, maybe he walked his shoes to death compulsively, maniacally. His statement, I FEEL MUCH BETTER NOW, didn't sound crazy, but Connie knew from experience, the experience of her suicidal friends and relations, Connie knew how crazed people get before attempting suicide, and how lucid they become afterwards, as if the act could save you from yourself, or as if your craziness, the craziness itself would fall away, shattered and broken by this sudden collision with possible death. As if the act of violence could always draw a line, stop the craziness, put a limit to it.

Walking across the bridge, smiling at each other, this moment, this interval of equilibrium and contemplation, was exceedingly short. As they walked, Connie looked out over the river and saw that the man was having some difficulty swimming. Without hesitation she immediately began to run as fast as she could. It was essential to get to a phone, to get hold of the river police, get them to pull him out of the water. Her estimation of the situation turned inside out in one moment: it was very very dangerous.

She moved completely independently, shouting something to William as she ran. To convey her sense of danger, difficulty, she shouted, 'The water's very cold, it's very cold in the water.' Connie thought the fact that William couldn't swim meant he couldn't judge the extent of the danger, or know what was the correct thing to do. She continued running fast, clutching the clothes, unconsciously.

As Connie moved, running, she looked and saw that the man in the water was being carried away downstream. He was only a little bit closer to the river's edge; clearly the currents were very strong. He was moving towards a large metal drum that floated in the middle of the river. Connie hoped he could hang on to it, until the river police came to haul him out. She imagined a chain or a big rusty ring on the incomprehensible drum or buoy, and him hanging on to it as the huge river poured past, pulling at his body. Maybe he could hold on, against the pull of the tide. She continued to run very fast.

Reaching the steps that went down to the National Theatre, in a glance Connie saw the man was very near the drum, on the far side of it. She hoped that was where the chain or ring would be. As she ran down the steps she looked up again and saw him some way beyond the drum. Without stopping, Connie looked up and out, she saw him, her eyes found him in the water. She saw his arms waving above his head. She had never seen that before, that 'not waving but drowning' gesture, both arms raised and flailing. She knew he was drowning.

Connie rushed into the National Theatre box-office, her voice very shrill, cutting through the air full of fragmented conversations, a thick mesh of sounds and words. Some people were buying tickets, or reading the programmes, and three people were behind the counter, all on the telephone. 'Please can you call 999, there's a man in the river, please, call 999,' she kept saying, over and over, amazed that they didn't immediately interrupt their conversations, cut them off, to dial 999. She was frantic, moving around the small space, back and forth. She couldn't understand these oblivious people: did someone drown in the river every day?

Vehement, insistent, Connie raised her voice to penetrate the layers of cross-talk. As she heard the young woman say into the telephone, 'I really must go, but will I see you later?', Connie moved to see if there was a payphone free. Two people sat on seats in little cubicles, talking.

This nightmare lasted moments, an intolerable delay. When Connie saw that the young woman was dialling 999, she ran outside again.

As Connie came out of the entrance, she faced an expanse of pavement extending to the stone wall that ran along the embankment, the edge of the river. Running across, she saw some people leaning against this wall, people standing there, looking at the river. There was a line of people standing along the bridge, also; she took them in for the first time. What was this, a spectacle? She ran straight towards the river. When she reached the wall of the embankment, she continued running downstream, speaking sideways to William, who was right beside her. 'Where is he?' she said. Connie was still holding the red sweatshirt and the trainers against her chest. She was completely unaware of this. They paused for a moment and a man spoke to them; he told them that he'd telephoned the police, 'as soon as he jumped.' The river was smooth, her eyes scanning, she couldn't find the little figure, distant, she couldn't find the dark shape of his head breaking the smooth metallic surface of the moving water. She saw a river police launch silently circling around a little way downstream from the metal drum. Connie realised he was dead.

Connie placed the red sweatshirt and the trainers on the broad stone wall. Turning away, she burst into uncontrollable, explosive tears and loud crying. She was telling William he was dead, drowned; William couldn't believe it. She was overwhelmed with acute grief for this unknown person, this living thing now dead. Connie saw the clothes and shoes on the wall and picked them up. She was crying so much that people were looking at her. She put the clothes down on a wooden bench, and sat down beside them, holding her face in her hands. Her mouth wide open, she sobbed, wailing.

She said, 'You drown in three minutes.' She repeated this over and over again. It was to persuade William it was true. She had a violent impulse to tear off her beautiful jacket, her ridiculous expensive lovely jacket, and her new earrings, and throw them into the river — as if this sacrifice could bring him back. That's how she formulated it; she felt she would do anything to bring him back.

For the first time the thought struck her that she should have jumped into the river and saved him. She was a strong swimmer. She should have jumped in and saved him, immediately. She turned to William, to tell him this, and together, through her tears, they carefully constructed a justification: No, she shouldn't have jumped into the river, because she could have hurt herself, she could have drowned, she didn't know how to rescue people in big rivers, and anyway, he'd seemed to be OK.

They repeated this, they kept telling each other, reminding each other that he seemed to be OK. William said, 'There's nothing more we could have done.'

A man came up to them, enquiring. He'd seen the guy jump, he'd gone in to get a drink. Bitterly, Connie said, 'He's dead.' The man's response was total disbelief: 'He can't be, he was swimming, he looked like he was all right.' Connie said, 'No, he drowned. You drown in three minutes.' She said it like an accusation, as if she were accusing everyone else of not knowing how easy it is to drown, speaking out her own self-accusation.

Maybe he'd broken something, his arm, maybe, when he hit the water. Maybe he didn't realise, no one realised.

Somewhere in this confusion, Connie was very glad to

know that someone else had phoned the police the minute it happened. She stood up, turning her back on the wide river. She was still crying like crazy. William seemed numb, standing there beside her. Another stranger, surprised by her tears, said, 'What, did you know him?' — as if that would be the only reason to be so upset. 'No!' she said, walking away.

They sat down again further away, on a round piece of stone, like a big grindstone lying flat on the ground. It appeared to be the detritus from some live sculpture event, a South Bank watch-the-artist display. Connie and William were at a loss; they didn't know what to do. Connie went on crying, like an emotional explosion that didn't stop. It was as if she were grieving for all the people who want to do themselves in and then suddenly don't, who change their minds, who want to live, to be rescued or somehow to survive, and who don't make it, by some chance, some malign circumstance. 'He wanted to live,' she said to William.

The man who'd telephoned the police right away approached them, carrying the red sweatshirt and the shoes. He said, 'I don't want to intrude . . .' Connie wiped her face with her hands, wet with tears and snot, unable to look up. The man said, 'Are these his clothes?' He mentioned the police and Connie imagined having to give a statement to the police, she said, 'I don't want to talk to the cops, I won't talk to them.' The man said that was OK, he would talk to them, he'd give them the clothes. So William and Connie told him what they knew, speaking at the same time, Connie crying but trying to be clear and straightforward. She said, 'He changed his mind. He said, *I feel much better now.* He wanted to live.' The man listened carefully, without comment.

It's not possible to mourn the loss of someone you don't know, Connie thought. He can only represent something of yourself to you, he stands in for your own suicide fantasies, your own wish to live. But much more shocking than this, more pressing than the displaced enactment of her own destructive wish, was the simple fact of death: unbelievable.

One moment he was there, the next he was gone. The appropriate word was 'gone'; she wanted to 'bring him back'. The transparent fabric of everyday life was torn through, ripped open, to disclose the constant dark presence, the proximity of death. 'In the midst of life we are in death,' Connie said. It was inconceivable.

Connie and William didn't know what to do. Connie'd agreed with Edith to meet at seven-thirty or eight, in the NFT bar; she remembered saying they'd be there by eight-thirty at the latest. The circus began at nine. She knew she didn't want to go to the circus, now, but she felt she had to go to the bar, if only to tell Edith that she wasn't coming, so they wouldn't wait. Connie and William explained this to each other, and then William said, 'Let's get a drink, anyway.'

Her face wet, still encased in the absurd masquerade of high fashion, red lipstick, earrings, Connie stumbled into the NFT. She felt it was like having a great hole cut in your chest, a great gash through your body, and still being able to walk, talk. One minute he was there, bobbing about in the water, shouting to them, laughing; the next he was dead — gone, absent, lost forever. Nonexistent. She couldn't get over it; she couldn't take it in. It happened so quickly. It was so sudden. She felt like there was a black hole cut in her chest.

Connie paused near the door, reluctant to penetrate the crowded bar any further. Standing there, Ruby appeared, alone, and Connie took hold of her and told her what had happened. She started to cry again. Ruby said, 'Oh Con, how awful, how dreadful, come in, come in and have a drink.'

Then Edith came up, and Connie found herself telling her the story, it was beginning to take form, a story, and Edith was very sympathetic. It was extremely difficult to tell this tale, to give it shape, to bring her shock and the violence of this unknown death to the crowded bar, the group of friends. Edith got her a drink, red wine, and William started downing glasses of rum. It seemed OK, for the time being, to stand there, with her friends, drinking. Robert arrived, her old boyfriend, and she told him about it. He was fantastic, he listened carefully and took it all in, and then without a break he was talking about other things, being normal, and so was Connie, back into life. Talking with him, Connie would abruptly return to the death, and Robert would listen, and then he would carry on about something else. He even made her laugh, her face shiny with dried tears, her mouth pulled out of shape from crying.

It was hard to know what to do, to guess what the right thing to do would be. For a time, standing in the bar surrounded by these friends, talking, drinking, seemed to be the right thing to do. At eight-thirty they all trooped off to Jubilee Gardens, to the circus, and Connie and William climbed the steps up to the bridge, to get in the car and drive home. The river was deep silvery blue, the surface of the water like pewter reflecting the darkening blue of the sky, and the city looked beautiful, outlined in black and grey with all the different lights shining.

At home they ate scrambled eggs on toast and went to bed. Recalling the view of the river, the brilliant city, it was impossible to believe he would never see it again.

Suicide: Take Three

The first suicide that penetrated Connie's world was Marilyn Monroe's suicide in 1962. Connie was seven; she asked her mother what it meant, to commit suicide. Her mother, typically, gave the impression of being slightly annoyed to be asked a difficult question. She said it was when people jump out of the window, when people jump off the roof, when they jump out of tall buildings. It was as if her mother were trying to present a harmless image of suicide, and came up with a stereotype from cartoons in *The New Yorker*, the banker or industrialist ridiculous on the window ledge, the Crash.

They lived in Chicago, then, and there were lots of tall buildings around. It was easy to imagine jumping out the window of one of them. For some years after, Connie associated the death of Marilyn Monroe with this image of sudden, slow falling, this skyscraper death.

Later, when Connie knew how Monroe really died, people said that she'd changed her mind; Marilyn Monroe had taken all these pills and then she'd decided she didn't want to die after all but by then it was too late. Of course, you couldn't change your mind if you jumped off a tall building.

People argued over whether Sylvia Plath had wanted or expected to be rescued, when she put her head in the oven, or whether she'd planned it carefully, timing it so the au pair would show up and the kids wouldn't be alone with no one to look after them. As it happened, the au pair couldn't get into the flat, because the man who lived downstairs who had the extra key had been drugged by the gas seeping through the kitchen floor above, and didn't wake up when she knocked. This would seem to imply rather a large quantity of gas, and the possibility of Plath being revived appears unlikely.

Connie remembered the hot summer day when she went swimming with friends in Sussex, in the River Ouse, near where Virginia Woolf committed suicide. The river was very narrow and silty and slow, and she realised Woolf must have very definitely wanted to die, since it wouldn't be easy to drown yourself in such a river. On the other hand, maybe the meandering river had silted up in the thirty-five years since this death. The name of the river was pronounced 'ooze', appropriately.

Connie's mother always said, 'You drown in three minutes.' She also always said, 'You can drown in three inches of water.' Met with disbelief, or even the slightest whiff of doubt, Connie's mother would insist: 'You can drown in a bathtub with three inches of water in it.' Connie grew up with these vehement statistics, repetitions of the number three, echoing through her childhood. It was the voice of maternal anxiety translated into violent assertion and, finally, threat. Like Connie's mother was always obsessed, it seemed, with the point of a pencil, how it would go in your eye if you ran with it and fell, — or through the roof of your mouth. You mustn't suck a pen or a pencil, or walk with it in your mouth, because you might trip and fall and it would go through the roof of your mouth. You must always hold scissors pointing towards the ground, and walk, not run, when you were holding them.

You must never point a gun at anyone, a toy gun, any kind of gun, because you never know what might happen.

Connie's mother made a habit at one point of giving expensive scissor and paper-knife sets in leather cases to her friends, as Christmas or birthday presents, but she would always make each of them give her a penny or some small coin first, so that technically it wasn't a gift, it was a purchase, like the friend was buying them from her. Because to give someone scissors or a knife implies a wish to cut them, or hurt them somehow. A gift is always a prediction, some kind of wish for the future, like a spell.

Thus everyday objects became a potential source of extreme

violence. Connie's mother would also, more rarely, describe how any sharp object, even something as innocuous as a pencil, could conceivably be used as a weapon if a strange man were attacking you. You could stab him in the throat, for example, with the sharp point of a pencil. Or in the eye. These vivid images reappeared in Connie's dreams years later, glimpses of torn throats and ordinary lead pencils that somehow emanated a vast and uncontainable horror. Thinking about her mother's advice, Connie decided that trying to stab an assailant with a pencil in the throat would probably only infuriate him, and possibly elicit further violence in retaliation. Generally speaking, Connie tended to believe she'd be able to talk her way out of any situation — like she'd talked her way out of being raped by the guy who picked her up hitchhiking that night, the last time she ever hitched a lift — although she knew that belief was unrealistic.

A couple of years before, Connie had decided to study self-defence. She had come to the realisation that she was fundamentally physically frightened of men. This was such a normal part of everyday life she wasn't even aware of it, but it crossed her mind that perhaps it wasn't inevitable, maybe she could learn how not to be frightened, maybe this could change things in some way for her. During the third meeting, the self-defence teacher, a laughing thin young woman who enthusiastically demonstrated the power of Chi energy, taught them how to kill someone. Connie didn't go back again: the class was at an inconvenient time, it was too far away. Later she recognised that she really didn't want to know how to kill someone, even a rapist. She'd wanted to learn how to defend herself. It wasn't a very effective method of killing someone anyway, it would only really be viable if the man were asleep or something, and wasn't fighting back. In New York a while later, Connie was telling this story and a woman friend said exactly the same thing had happened to her. You take up self-defence, you're taught how to kill somebody in the third session, and you never go back. You don't want to know.

The corollary to this of course was not knowing how to save someone's life. One time, Connie was walking quickly down Westbourne Grove, in a hurry to get to the Electric, and she met the eye of a man who was clearly in distress. He was dirty, with long hair and black jeans and a black leather jacket; he looked like a junky, or a derelict, a street person. He was leaning against a parked car and as she walked by he said, 'Please —.' Connie said, 'Sorry,' walking quickly past. She thought he was asking for money, or something else she didn't want to give, and then he said, very quietly, he said, 'Help me.' Connie stopped, she was maybe five feet past him, she was stopped, suddenly, by the simplicity of that demand. Reluctant, shocked, she stopped, and turned. As she moved towards him, the man started to fall over. He was sliding down the side of the car, into the gutter, absolutely silent, and clutching his left arm. Connie knew this was a sign of a heart attack. She held onto him, trying to support his falling body against the car, but he was too heavy, his body in an inexorable descent, until he was half on his side in the narrow space between the kerb and the tyres of the parked cars. Close to his face as she held on to him, Connie knew she had never been near to someone in such extreme physical pain. Finally she let his body go, to rest on the ground, while still touching him, she kept her hands pressed against his rigid body and she kept saying to him, 'Don't worry, it will be all right, try to relax, breathe, don't worry.' She held on to him as if she could become a lightning conductor, earthing all his pain and panic, and keep hold of him, keep him there.

At the same time Connie was shouting for someone to call 999. There was a shop across the road, people in the street, she became frantic, why didn't anyone do anything? Connie guessed this was a heart attack, she had no idea what to do for him. She felt completely powerless. She laid the man's head on the pavement; he was stiff with pain, silent, and Connie looked round, taking in the little audience, the inevitable group of innocent bystanders enjoying the afternoon drama. Furiously, Connie stood up and started shrieking, 'Doesn't anyone know what we should do?' The Pakistani shopkeeper said that he'd called 999; there was no sign of an ambulance. She felt absurd, ridiculous, on the verge of stamping her foot and shrieking, crying out with frustration and rage. This guy couldn't die just because they were all so stupidly ignorant. Connie burst into tears and, amazingly, the little group watching the scene shifted their attention from the man in black, lying on the ground, to Connie, standing beside him. One woman said, 'Don't worry love, it'll be all right.' And someone else said, 'Don't cry, the ambulance is bound to get here soon.' Connie couldn't believe it — they had no idea how to help the guy having the heart attack, so they turned their attention to her, trying to make her feel better. It seemed like they'd been standing there for ages, with this man dying at their feet. Connie didn't know what to do. She stopped crying, and crouched down again, she put her hand on his arm.

Someone saw an ambulance slowly moving down Westbourne Grove. It wasn't the emergency kind, more the kind of vehicle that ferries old people or ill people or people in wheelchairs to and from the hospital. Some of the bystanders waved to flag it down, shouting, but it didn't seem to be going to stop. It didn't slow down. Connie was on her knees beside the man on the ground, staring at him and talking to him and holding on to his hand. Looking up, she saw one of the group run in front of the ambulance to force them to stop. As the ambulance drivers got out and came over to them, slowly, as if to say, this isn't my job, and the bystanders clamoured their sense of urgency, emergency, Connie stood up and walked away, leaving the scene behind. There was nothing she could do.

Going to meet her friend Emily at the movies seemed absurd. But Connie didn't know what else she should do. She was late, she didn't want to leave Emily there, waiting. It's always that way, the drama, the crisis cuts a hole in the day, raw edges, horror, and then there's always someone expecting you, as if that tear, that rip in the fabric, didn't exist.

Portobello Road was busy, with bright fruit stacked on the market stalls, and people laughing, an ordinary afternoon. It seemed like an obscenity, this juxtaposition of terrible pain with the easygoing people down the market. When she got to the cinema, Emily had gone in already; wiping her eyes, Connie went in and sat down at the back. The film was *This is Spinal Tap*. After a while, she found she was laughing like a drain. Back to life.

Some time later William told Connie how he'd been flummoxed by the scene on the bridge, as if he couldn't understand it, he couldn't take it in. Connie was fascinated to discover differences in their recollections and understanding of what happened, although at the time she'd known that the question of being able or unable to swim must make a difference. For example, being unable to swim, William had immediately looked around the bridge for some kind of life-jacket or ring to throw into the water. Connie was impressed; she hadn't thought of doing that. He'd even looked for a telephone on the bridge, an emergency phone; he told Connie about the phone on the Brooklyn Bridge, mysteriously placed just beside the walkway where a suicidal pedestrian could clamber over the fence to get to the edge and jump off. As if you would ring up and tell them you were about to do it, as if there would be a whole apparatus of rescue that would come into operation if you saw someone about to jump and made the call.

There was no such apparatus here, and meanwhile Connie, the swimmer, had mistakenly imagined that the man in the water, swimming, would be all right. William never contradicted this misperception, partly, he told Connie, because he didn't know anything about swimming, and partly because being able to swim seemed to be this guy's only hope.

Connie was amazed to discover that the memory of Chairman Mao swimming in the Yangtze Kiang had also echoed through William's mind. This was the image of strength and hope that they both separately came up with, in that brief moment when it seemed possible for the man to swim across the river and climb out. A Chinese man, in a wide river, wasn't a disaster or an emergency; on the contrary, he was strong and safe, he was like Mao!

Connie hadn't looked for a life-belt on the bridge, and later she'd blamed herself for this. She was pleased to find that William had thought of it, pleased and very surprised, as if her experience of the whole episode had somehow excluded him, as if the crisis had pulled her into a kind of solitude, oblivious to everyone around her. She hadn't expected William to be resourceful in ways that she wasn't.

William told Connie he'd been very shocked by the man's age, but then he thought the man was younger than Connie did, he thought he was about eighteen or nineteen, whereas Connie thought he might be twenty-four or twenty-five. William agreed, eventually, commenting that Chinese people often look younger than they are. Still, he expressed surprise that someone so young should want to kill himself, though he knew that young people bump themselves off all the time. Maybe more kids kill themselves than older people, who knows. The combination of the guy looking so young and being Chinese made the death even more incomprehensible to him.

William said, 'That was the other thing I thought was strange; it seemed strange to me that a Chinese person would choose to commit suicide in that way. I mean, I somehow think of jumping off bridges as being terribly English, a terribly English way to do it.'

Connie didn't feel this way at all; bridges were simply a very cheap and available method, unlike most others, which require some kind of weapon or poison. Bridges were free.

Connie recalled an item she'd read in the evening paper years before, in the *Evening Argus*, about an Indian woman, wearing a sari, who walked into a butcher's shop in Hove and took one of the very large, very sharp butcher's knives and cut her throat on the spot. Connie pictured the collision, what her friend Iris used to call cognitive dissonance; the round pink faces and burly shoulders of the butchers, so very English, blood smears on their white jackets, and then this young Indian woman, her sari bright against the shiny glass counters and white tiled walls of the shop. Bloody meat laid out in stainless-steel trays, every surface wiped clean and shining, this scene of carefully controlled horror invaded without warning by an even more controlled and sudden death. The newspaper didn't speculate on the woman's motives, as if she were completely unknowable, completely opaque: foreign. Connie read the scene as enacting a last-ditch protest against being treated like an animal, to be slaughtered by butchers, but it may simply have been that the woman had no money, and the knives in the butcher's are very sharp and they're free.

Thinking about Englishness, suicide and jumping from bridges, Connie recalled the plaque on Hammersmith Bridge, which she'd discovered by chance when she was about sixteen and very romantic, deeply preoccupied by Keats and Shelley and dying. It is a brass plaque set into the heavy mahogany railing that runs along the bridge, a railing worn smooth by a hundred years of people leaning against it, or running their hands along it as they crossed the river. It commemorates the death of a soldier who heroically jumped into the icy river at midnight, on a date in December or January somewhere around 1917 or 1918. He jumped into the river in order to save the life of a woman suicide, which he succeeded in doing, but unfortunately died himself. He 'lost his life in the attempt'.

Connie could picture this scene too: the late dark night, very cold, and the young woman letting herself into the icy water, knowing her skirts would drag her down. Was this an image from Dickens, maybe? *Our Mutual Friend*? Probably not, but it had to come from somewhere, she thought. In this version, Connie didn't allow the woman to jump from the bridge. She walked or slid into the icy water from the bank on the south side, where there was still a long stretch of tow path running beside the wide, smooth river; a ribbon of old trees and untended bushes, thick grass, overgrown, where in the summer lovers walked or lay, and solitary people would sit, watching the river. Freezing cold, now, dark, midwinter: the woman would be young, and thin, a prostitute maybe, or a housemaid, pregnant, in despair (what book was this taken from?) and longing for death. The young officer on the bridge, his heavy overcoat wrapped tight around him against the cold, the young officer would not hesitate; hearing her inadvertent cry, he would plunge in.

Connie elaborated: he was on leave from the trenches, disillusioned necessarily by the horrors of that war yet somehow retaining a crazed ideal of valour or heroism, some idea of what it was the young men were so endlessly dying to defend, something of value, something possibly symbolised by English womanhood. When Lytton Strachey's claim to the status of conscientious objector was contested, he was asked in court, 'And what would you do if you saw a German soldier attempting to rape your sister?' With only the slightest whiff of irony, Strachey replied, 'I should try and interpose my own body.'

If that were the question, the rape of sisters and how to defend them, then, seeing a woman at midnight in the icy Thames, he wouldn't hesitate. And she would live, and he would die — of what? Exposure, or drowning? Connie couldn't remember. Maybe at an unconscious level he'd wanted to die, maybe he'd had enough of death, too much. More people died in the great influenza epidemic of 1918 than were killed in the war itself. It was the guilt of the survivor; the war over, they dropped like flies. There was the sleeping sickness epidemic around that time too. Connie pictured the whole of Europe in shock, unable to take in the extent of the damage, the deaths, unable to contain the grief, and therefore going to sleep, or dying of flu, some kind of collective self-sacrifice. That's what the scene on the bridge was, the scene on Hammersmith Bridge in 1918, a scene of self-sacrifice, for an unknown object, the anonymous woman. Connie wondered if she'd eventually succeeded in doing herself in, later.

Returning to William, Connie didn't think of jumping off bridges as particularly English. She remembered how she'd pored over Warhol's disaster paintings, the *New York Post* photos of falling bodies; she remembered the great big bridges of America, the Golden Gate, the Brooklyn Bridge, the bridge to Terminal Island. English bridges, or London bridges, were too low for a foolproof suicide, as the scene with the Chinese man on Waterloo Bridge demonstrated. You weren't even knocked out by the collision with the surface of the water, you weren't pulverized like you were supposed to be when you jumped off a really big bridge. You had to drown, but then it wasn't that difficult to drown, it seems.

Connie thought of drowning more as a specifically female mode of suicide, partly because of Ophelia, and her dress, that begins by buoying her up, and later pulls her down to the bottom of the river. Adolescent, Connie would study Millais's painting of Ophelia in the river, fascinated by her friend Ruby's story of how the model, Lizzie Siddal, died of pneumonia after posing for the painting, lying in a zinc bathtub of freezing water hour after hour. Later she found out this wasn't true.

Shelley's first wife, Harriet Westbrook, killed herself at the age of twenty-two by jumping from the bridge across the Serpentine — an amazing feat, considering the little, almost ornamental bridge of white stone can't be more than twenty feet above the lake. It's the bridge where Mrs Dalloway threw a sixpence into the water, one moonlit night; it was another of Connie's favourite views of the city, a view with trees over water. Which is one reason why she remembered so vividly about Shelley's first wife. He'd run off with Mary Godwin, who was about seventeen. She was pregnant, and they'd gone to Switzerland, and then to Italy, with Byron, and Claire Clairmont, who was Mary's step-sister. Claire was madly in love with Byron, and also pregnant. Mary Godwin's first child died within ten days of its birth; she became pregnant again almost immediately. In the autumn of 1816, her half-sister, Fanny Imlay, Mary Wollstonecraft's other daughter, committed suicide; she took laudanum in a run-down Swansea hotel. Then, in December, they received news of the suicide of Shelley's wife, Harriet, drowned in the Serpentine late one night after jumping from the bridge, eight and a half months pregnant with another man's child. All the babies died, or miscarried, and Mary sat down and wrote *Frankenstein*.

Sylvia Plath put glasses of milk beside her children's beds.

Virginia Woolf put stones in the pockets of her long cardigan, to weigh her body down. Harriet Shelley had a baby inside her. It's not difficult to drown if you cannot swim.

Unable to swim, William had no real sense of this danger; not unlike Connie imagining she could talk her way out of anything, even rape, William vaguely took it for granted that he would inexplicably suddenly be able to swim, in an emergency, if he would otherwise drown. Connie found herself returning over and over to fearful thoughts of William's death. She imagined being in the water, the vast, deep ocean, with him, and telling him how to keep his head above water, teaching him to tread water as they waited to be rescued. She wondered if she'd be able to hold his head above the water, to keep him floating beside her there.

This was an absurd image: Connie teaching William how to float, after they've somehow found themselves in the ocean, after their boat has capsized, their plane crashed? Maybe it was reasonable, maybe if someone you love can't swim, you can't help anticipating, imagining what you'd do if you found yourselves at sea. It was part of the role-reversal syndrome, that she should be plagued by fantasies of saving him, and he should be calmly unaware, oblivious to the danger, either real or fantasised, and, it seemed, totally unconcerned with any idea of saving her. William liked her precisely because she could look after herself. He was irritated by her fear of flying, because it so obviously contradicted this impression. As it was, they rarely confronted large bodies of water, except to look at them from a distance. You can drown in a bathtub, her mother's doom-laden voice echoed down the years, resounding darkly in the bright day, but no, that wasn't true, maybe babies drown in bathtubs, if you let them slide under, slip out of your grasp, but Connie couldn't imagine William drowning in his daily, ritual morning bath.

Thinking about it, Connie concluded that she should have

encouraged the man who died, the Chinese man in the river, she should have encouraged him to stay put, to tread water, to let his body float. She should have told him to wait to be picked up, to relax and be patient, instead of pointing to the distant steps and saying, swim over there! It was too far to swim, she should have realised; he jumped at the exact centre of the bridge, and the river was so wide there, a great smooth expanse of moving water. One of them should have stayed with him, talking to him and encouraging him to keep his head above water, to relax, while the other immediately got hold of the police. Probably the fastest way to do that would be to stop a cab with a radio, and get the driver to call. Like using a CB network, use the radio-cab. Faster than running to one end of the bridge or the other.

If they'd done that, the river still would have carried the man away, moving downstream, but maybe he wouldn't have become so exhausted, if that was what killed him. Connie really didn't know what killed him, when he wanted to live so much. I FEEL MUCH BETTER NOW. He was laughing about it, waving his fist in the air, defiantly. Connie imagined it must have been a combination of exhaustion, not being able to swim very well, maybe a broken bone or two, and the treacherous currents and icy cold water of the river that killed him.

Suicide: Take Four

Remembering the suicide, Connie realised the man in the river had met death twice. First, the sudden fall, plunging straight into the endless water, rushing deep, away from the light. And then reaching the point, immeasurable, where the descent slows, and stops, the gentle recoil, as the heavy cold water begins to push the narrow body up again. Moving slowly, and then faster, rising up to break the surface: air, light, sounds. Not dead after all: elation.

And then the second death — drifting, lost. The pull of the water, the shock, exhaustion. People watching from a distance, bright sky so wide and high, isolation. Desperate wish for some help, from somewhere, unimaginable, and no help comes. A hand reaching out, something to hang on to. Arms flailing, lost, and being carried away by the river, carried under, to breathe in the icy water at last.

Connie wept, and then she stopped weeping. She made a decision. Thinking about these literary suicides and parasuicides, and later thinking of her own death, her own occasional longing for death, Connie made a rule, she drew a line.

No messing about with death, no inviting death in and then asking him to leave, after all. No flirting, no fascination, no razors, no pills, no bridges, no gas. Someone walking in with a cigarette could blow up the whole house. No suicide here, no — no white bandages romantically tied round wrists under black leather sleeves. No livid scars up and down her arms, exposed by the gesture of running fingers through her hair, bright bangles slipping along these scarred arms, no chaotic tracery of razor marks revealed. No stomach pumps at the hospital, no body on the tracks. No ocean, no river, no cliff. None of that.

Dream Sequence

Then Connie had a nightmare, a dream that turned into a nightmare.

She was with Michael, out of doors; they were digging something up. Together they found a bunch of dried flowers, or herbs, with a note or label attached to it. Connie knew it was a poem she'd written about Michael, or for Michael, years and years ago. The writing was tied to this bunch of herbs and wild flowers, and Connie was giving it to him, when Mikey said, *why don't you read it through first?* – as if there might be something unpleasant or unexpected. Connie said, *do you think I can decipher it?* She'd forgotten what it was that she had written: she tried to 'read' the bunch of flowers, but she couldn't remember the names: then it was a picture of flowers, with writing on the back. Another woman, Ruby perhaps, was there; they were cooking the ancient ears of corn they'd dug up, boiling them in a big pot of water, and eating the corn, Connie said, *it's been buried – what, eighteen years*, making mental calculations of the time passed. Thinking of Egyptian tomb paintings, she said, *the bouquet will fade now.* But the other two were finding living things inside the corn – a frog, then two frogs, large and dark and wet, squeezed up inside the corn cob, as if hibernating. There was a mouse, their prey, and the huge frogs hopped, plopped slowly away. Ruby said, *and these two mice*, but they weren't mice, more like two beautiful orange and tortoiseshell cats, or kittens, folded up and over each other, sleeping. But when they moved they were long, suddenly they moved very fast, like a streak of colour: *ferrets*. Connie tried to open the door into the house to get away from them, but they rushed suddenly at her, they ran right up the door beside her, where they hung, side by side, clinging with their claws. Connie was terrified. She saw their long bodies in perfect focus, hanging on the door, and sharp teeth and claws and beautiful bright patterns of their fur. She heard someone say, *it's really a typical rat thing*, and she climbed onto a chair, wondering how they were going to get rid of these things, when they clearly weren't going to be able to kill them.

Connie woke up and immediately remembered everything. The dream was like a bunch of flowers, she could tie a thread to each element, and follow the thread to a list of words. Something had been buried for eighteen years; something was terrifyingly alive. She wrote it all down, diligent in her self-analysis. She wanted to know.

A list:

1. Archaeology: to read the events or objects of the distant past, reading meanings into bits of memories. The difficulty of deciphering the past, making connections between then and now.

2. The tag or label was like the blue circle from Mikey's mobile, the one with the writing on it, the one she'd kept.

3. She couldn't remember writing a poem for Mikey, but there was the poem she'd written to Basil – for Basil, or about Basil – Basil with whom she'd been so passionately in love when she was sixteen and seventeen. Basil who'd broken her heart so completely, beloved Basil; she'd written a poem for him relatively recently, although thinking about it she realised it was more than ten years ago, now, she was twenty-three or so, when he'd reappeared, and they'd had this brief affair. (Basil had ended up going out with Hope Lewis, too, eventually; it was amazing how almost everyone ended up going out with almost everyone, eventually.) Anyway what happened was they'd had this little affair a few years ago, to make up for it all, she thought; he'd taken her to bed and made love to her beautifully, as if to compensate for all the pain he'd caused her and the brutality of their clumsy, silent sex, their terrible virginity. In this poem she'd written Connie described herself as a goblin, crouching like a frog in the corner, a goblin of malicious intent crouching in a corner of his life, watching his success, wanting still to break his heart, like he broke hers, and recognising why, she wrote in the last line: because I still want you. Frog in the corn-er.

4. Frogs are amphibian, like the foetus, under water in the womb.

5. In William Faulkner's novel *Sanctuary*, a corncob is used as a penis-substitute, or phallus, in a rape. It is very shocking and violent.

6. Kittens: the description she'd read recently of a child putting her hand on a man's genitals inside his trousers and saying it felt 'like a nest of kittens'.

7. Some medieval peasants thought of the uterus as a frog, which could creep out of a sick woman's mouth into a nearby

brook, and swim around for a while, before crawling back inside.

8. Connie's own 'frog face': her wide mouth, turned up nose, her mottled skin, 'green around the gills'.

9. Among certain circles at St Peter's, 'frog face' was a highly ironic term of endearment, like 'slug-features' or 'fatty'.

10. Connie's current practice of swimming, 800 metres every other day, breast-stroke, kicking her legs like a frog.

11. Connie's frog-like position, as she fucks William, crouching on top of him.

12. In Charlotte Brontë's novel *Shirley*, there are two women protagonists, one of whom leads a completely repressed, retiring life. At one point she compares herself to 'a frog in marble'.

13. P. V. Glob's book, *The Bog People*, which Ruby Powell first showed her when she was about thirteen or fourteen. She'd shown her the photograph of people buried in the bogs of Denmark, people who'd died two thousand years ago. The bodies were dark and shiny, perfectly preserved in the wet bog, the skin like leather, tanned by the bog water. The Tollund Man was found naked, with a little cap on his head, a noose around his neck, and a long leather belt around his waist. He was lying curled up on his side, as if sleeping.

14. When they opened up the Tollund Man, the scientists found his last meal had consisted of perhaps a special gruel or bannock made from the seeds of all the local plants, plants these Iron Age people wanted to return, to grow again in the spring. This meal confirmed the archaeologists'

view that many of the bog people had been sacrificed as part of a ritual that took place in deep winter, a ritual to renew the spring. It seems they were killed and then buried in the bog, the seeds in their stomachs as if planted in the body in the bog.

15. The fertility grave: that's where you bury the sacrificial object, in order to ensure the return of fertility. Grave fertility: that's when the burial site erupts, surging with emotion. Grave fertility problems: that's when you can't find the fertility grave, that's when you're your own sacrificial object, that's when your fertility gets buried, and never comes back.

16. Ferrets: beautiful and violent, vicious. Ferrets are down your trousers, and they're red-eyed and sharp-toothed and clawed, and they hurt things, hunting their prey.

17. Ferrets defy gravity, clinging erect on the door. The violent phallus, again. cf. Freud: '. . . the remarkable phenomenon of erection, around which the human imagination has constantly played, cannot fail to be impressive, involving as it does an apparent suspension of the laws of gravity.' *Interp.*, p. 518.

18. Connie was phobic about rats, it had been severe at one time, crippling, but she was much better now. Nevertheless in dreams it was a way to make her wake up, to bring the nightmare to an end. In the dream the mouse was nearly a rat, but became kittens, then ferrets (worse), and finally the voice clinched it: *rats*, and she woke up.

19. Once Iris Gowing told Connie that she'd seen a rat on Charing Cross Bridge. Connie could never walk across the bridge again without thinking of it.

20. The frogs were inside the corn like the bog people in

the bog and the foetus in the womb, but if that's the case it's a horrible baby, the frog baby is monstrous and frightening. The frogs were hunters, also, like ferrets, because the mouse was their prey. Froggy will a-hunting go – except it was a-courting, wasn't it? She couldn't remember.

21. In *The Bog People*, the woman goddess was represented by a sheaf of corn, an image of fertility. There were photographs of a wooden phallus stuck in the earth, with clay pots around it; the caption said it was an image of the goddess. Thus the ear of corn with the frog inside was an image of female fecundity, possibly, that was also phallic, powerful, violent.

22. The list of the names of wild flowers, the names of the seeds the Tollund Man ate, and 'a scrap cake put out for the goblins', a present-day relic, or trace, of the offerings to the goddess.

23. The problem of calculating distance in time, like Professor Glob proving the Tollund Man was really two thousand years old, and hadn't just been thrown into the bog recently.

24. The more pressing problem of reading, deciphering this poem she'd written that was somehow also a bunch of flowers and the image of a bunch of flowers. When you're learning to read, it's like learning the names of things, you remember the names. (cf. thing-presentations in Freud.) But reading isn't really like that, because language isn't about naming. She couldn't remember the names of the flowers, so she couldn't read the poem.

25. The only bouquet she'd kept was from her sister Hilary's wedding, it was baby's breath, or fog, as Italians called it,

or baby's tears . . . She couldn't remember its proper name: tiny white flowers in a cloud, the bouquet sat, stuck in a decanter, on the dusty top shelf in her kitchen. The poem in the dream became an image of flowers, and she couldn't read the flowers because she didn't know how to, the language of flowers, and then she couldn't remember their names, either, maybe the names would make sense, love-in-a-mist, baby's breath, fog.

26. Fog, bog, Glob, frog, goblin.

Turning the dream, or her analysis of the dream, around and over in her mind, Connie found herself thinking about Michael Stour. She hadn't seen him in years. She wondered if it were possible to contact him, if it would be easy, just call directory enquiries and get his number in New York.

Then she remembered: he was supposed to be dead by now. His father had this bad heart, and Mikey was supposed to have this same bad heart; his father died when he was in his early thirties, and Mikey was supposed to die too, when he hit thirty he was meant to keel over and die one day. Schoolgirls, Hope and Connie would discuss this heart of Mikey's in hushed tones, deeply impressed. His father's death, and his own impending death, lent a gleam of glamour to Mikey, putting his teenage misdemeanours in an epic light. Mikey Stour was very tall, and very thin; he had pale blue eyes and beautiful hands, and he seemed to think that the appropriate line to take was: 'hope I die before I get old', too fast to live, too young to die, etc. He embarked on an unwavering path of multiple drug use and abuse, as if to guarantee the doctors' mythic predictions of an early demise.

Romance always buries death at the heart of love. Romance

loves graveyards, excessive drug consumption, poison. (The day Mikey fell for Connie, they went to Highgate Cemetery.)

When they were thirteen or fourteen, schoolgirls talking, thirty was impossible to imagine, as impossible as their own deaths, and Mikey's bad heart, his putative early death, merely painted a lurid glow of romance along the edge of his presence, like a bright shadow outlining his body.

Like a scar, a limp, like a beautiful Russian sailor with silver teeth, Mikey's mythological 'bad heart' was the flaw in the perfect image, the shine on the nose, the tiny rupture that allows desire to fix and hold.

How old are we? Connie asked. How many years have passed since then? Who's dead and buried, who's buried alive, frozen in memory outside time, who's coming to life again? ('You seem to be killing off all the life that's inside of you,' the trainee analyst said, gently, when Connie told her about the abortion.)

Mikey was dying; his heart, his self-destructiveness, his junk. Then (apparently) Mikey decided he wanted to live. Ruby told Connie about it. He'd cleaned up his act, put on a little weight, got down to work. Maybe he was surprised to hit thirty-five and still be alive.

Death seems so romantic until you get anywhere near the real thing, and then it's only terrible. Maybe, Connie thought, the romance is there precisely in order to veil the terror of the real thing. It's necessary, maybe.

Exhumations

What eventually happened was, Connie'd had this dream about Michael, about all this digging up and finding things alive still, and so she overcame her fears and called him in February, when she was in New York. Connie was only there for a few days; she had a couple of semi-academic gigs to do — she'd been invited to talk about her work on Diego and Pollock and Guston, the Mexican influence. She was staying in a friend of a friend's empty apartment on the Upper West Side, a part of town Connie didn't know very well. And it was freezing cold and snowing the whole time she was there.

The apartment hadn't been lived in for some time; it was dusty and bleak. It belonged to a brilliant and exceptionally charming man whom she hardly knew; he was a very close friend of Catherine's, and he was very ill, though whether he was dying of AIDS, as some people claimed, was unclear. Some time later Catherine told Connie the truth, and then when he finally died some months later, she felt how almost naïve she'd been to hope and even half-believe it wasn't AIDS, a terrible kind of denial, masquerading as optimism. At the time she knew Philip didn't want people to know what was wrong with him, and of course she didn't really want to know either. After his death that reluctance seemed unbearably painful.

In any case Philip wasn't in New York very often; he was teaching at some college in New England, and he came down for weekends occasionally. The flat felt a bit abandoned; for example, the phone bill hadn't been paid, so Connie could receive calls but she couldn't make any. (Connie never figured out if Philip had been too broke to pay the bill, or too disorganised, preoccupied, or simply too ill.) As a result, while staying there, Connie would go out to the corner clutching a handful of change, and with the snow swirling around her, she would try to call people up. It wasn't easy. Iris Gowing for some unknown reason had given up using an answering machine; Connie called about nineteen times and never got a reply. And Michael — Connie was nervous about it, she hadn't seen him in six or seven years, and then only briefly, once, sometime in '83, so she was shy about calling him, but she rang directory enquiries and got his number, and then she called and he answered right away. Michael said, 'Come over whenever you like, this afternoon?' So Connie headed downtown; she went to the big Warhol show at the Museum of Modern Art on the way. She was in high spirits, it was Saturday, and freezing cold, she was knocked out by the Warhol, and very pleased to be in New York. Connie took the subway down to Prince Street, and walked over to Michael's new place.

She felt a little self-conscious, as she phoned from the corner; it was very cold, and she was wearing her somewhat ridiculous, undoubtedly excessive Vivienne Westwood pterodactyl oilcloth raincoat on top of another coat, a woollen one, with bright red woollen gloves and a red shawl tied around her head. It was snowing in a desultory way; minute particles of snow drifted slowly down out of a blank white sky. Connie felt self-conscious when Michael answered the phone, and she said, 'Hi, I'm downstairs, on the street,' and he said, 'I can see you.' Holding the phone to her ear, Connie looked up; she couldn't see him.

'I'll be down in a minute,' he said. They met on the snowy pavement, he suddenly appeared and they embraced, Michael very tall, Connie clumsy in her multiple overcoats, standing in the harsh, icy air, their breath making small clouds of fog as they looked at each other. Then they went in the big door; they walked up the endless staircase, flight after flight doubling back on itself in an interminable zigzag, like in the movies. They were trying to speak and climb stairs at the same time; they gasped out the necessary, preliminary words, broken phrases — where she was staying, how long. And then when they got to the top, finally, Connie stood still silently, taking breaths.

Connie took it in: an enormous space, right at the top of the building, it was wide open, a big oblong with huge sash windows all down one side. She walked across, and looked out: she could see the Bowery below, snow falling, the flat white sky, and the corner lot with the payphone, the dealers and street people, where she'd been. It was very vivid to her, the view of the city from those windows, the snow falling slowly outside, and behind her the incalculable mess scattered through the big rooms. Connie turned to look at Michael, measuring the time passed, looking for signs of recognition.

They drank juice out of long glasses, sitting on tall stools on either side of an enormous work table, and they talked. Michael washed out a glass for her that he'd been using as a vase, containing one dead red rose and thick greenish water at the bottom. He put on some obscure flute-like music from Africa, music of Pygmies, he said. There were two shoeboxes full of cassettes, and a little boombox. There were innumerable heaps of papers, notebooks, drawing books, letters.

There was a Stanley knife, a penknife, palette knife, bread-knife, and one homely, blunt ordinary table knife. Letters, more papers, writing everywhere. Pots of dye, glue, plaster of Paris in open brown paper sacks, clutter, indecipherable to the outsider. Like all studios, the big room insisted on the absolute idiosyncrasy of its chaos; Connie sensed Michael could find whatever he wanted in a moment, the intricate topography of the scatter would be entirely congruent with his gestures and his needs. The enormous table was not only long and wide, but very tall, so he could work standing without having to bend. There was a roll of dark grey carpet, a stove and fridge in the corner by the sink, a mattress on the floor. He'd just moved in, and he was making the place exactly as he wanted it. He was intending to stay.

They talked, and Connie was very moved. It was the first time she'd really seen Michael since he'd cleaned up, and it was like he'd come back, or something. Telling Ruby about it later, she said, 'It was like — there he was again; there were all the feelings and thoughts, all those sensitivities or sensibilities, fluttering over the surface of his face and his body. He seemed so vulnerable in a way. You could sort of sense the delicacy or the fragility of his responses — fragility is wrong, it's not that these thoughts or feelings were weak, more like they were momentary, and evanescent, and multiple.

'There it was, all this inner stuff that had been simply shut down by the junk, it was all alive, and rippling, like the surface of a river. Something like that — I know that sounds ridiculous. But I realised afterwards, when I was trying to describe it to this woman I hardly know — Deirdre Brewer, you remember her; she was at Sedgemoor with him, I think they even went out together at one point; I met her when I was in LA. Anyway, talking to her I realised that part of why I was so moved was because Michael had sort of cast aside his armour, it was like he was allowing things to surface, all this vivid complicated stuff that had been buried so deep, for so long. And it put me in contact with my own past, or our past, I guess. Seeing him opened things up in a way, you know, connecting up with all the stuff inside me that gets shut down for whatever reason. What was amazing to me was he didn't seem ravaged or scarred, he looked incredibly healthy actually. He was wide open, or seemed to be. It was almost as if he'd reverted, again becoming, or at least resembling, how he was when we first met, when we were all so young and spilling over with everything inside. I sensed the distance we'd travelled, and how we'd both survived, somehow. Something like that. Once again I was identifying with him, I guess.'

They talked about things, Michael and Connie, that afternoon; little things, New York, how long Connie was staying, what he was up to, and then she told him why she'd wanted to see him, that she wanted to ask him about the past. She wanted to know what had happened to him, how he made it. Eventually Connie told him about the dream of digging buried things up, and about wondering what it was, precisely, that was buried, and Michael said, 'It's strange, you thinking about burial, and graves, because I went to visit my father's grave, for the first time, just a little while ago, when I was in England at Christmas.'

'How extraordinary,' Connie said. 'So you didn't go to the funeral?'

Michael said, 'Nope — we were too little, or maybe Chas went, I don't think so. In any case, I'd never been to this place, as far as I know, this — what's it called? The family plot.'

Then he told her the story, how he'd driven down to the country, to the churchyard in Dorset, with his brother Chas. It was late afternoon when they arrived, very dark and damp and cold, and Chas wanted to take a photograph of the grave. Michael told Connie how he really wasn't into taking pictures, he just wanted to be there, he said, and he was slightly irritated. And then Chas's camera wouldn't work, so in the end Michael had to take the picture, with his camera. Michael looked up, as if this were the point of the story, he said, 'But I'm really glad I did, because look —,' and he got out two small colour photographs to show her, photographs of the gravestone, flat against the dark sky, with the short grass lurid in the hard bright light of the flash.

It was a very classic, simple stone, with just the name and the dates engraved on its surface. There was yellow lichen growing over the grey stone, bright deep yellow, and this brilliant green grass. Connie was taken aback, she was surprised, for a moment: the gravestone looked so old. It seemed indistinguishable from an eighteenth-century grave, but it was Mikey's father, it was relatively new. Then she remembered that it wasn't new, of course, it was about thirty years old. Thirty years is long enough, it seems, for a grave to settle, for lichen to grow.

They talked about his father, about Michael waking up one day and realising he'd outlived him. It was a shock: he'd never expected to live so long, and it was then that he was able to pack it all in. A new life: no more drugs, or liquor, or cigarettes, no more addiction. Connie suggested that going to visit the grave wasn't only about acknowledging the fact that his dad was dead and buried, but also maybe forgiving him for it, for dying when Mikey was so young. She asked Mikey about his heart, and he said that was all a myth, his heart was fine. He said he'd had every test in the book, and he was OK, and Connie thought, Jesus, he's really looking after himself.

He wants to live, Connie thought. It was hard to imagine — he'd wanted to die for so long. She said she thought he must be basically incredibly strong to have so severely abused his body for so many years, and to come out of it alive. He didn't comment on that. Connie figured he just thought he was lucky.

Then Connie asked him, she said, 'So, what do you think when you look back at that time in Ladbroke Grove, all of us living together in that house?' Michael said he felt it was the beginning, it was like training up for the life of incessant drugs and alcohol that reached full flower only when he left London, when he went to live in New York.

And then later he asked after Ruby, and again Connie felt the most profound connection between them, between her and Mikey, had always been how much they each loved Ruby. It was extraordinary.

He said: 'She's still the most important woman in my life.' Connie was knocked out.

He said, 'Ruby was so beautiful, she was so beautiful, so innocent. When I remember what she was like —'

He said, 'Of course we could never get together again now, nevertheless . . .'

He said, 'I slept in Ruby's bed, recently — in Scotland, you know, it was one of those things where there were too many people in our house, so I went and stayed the night at the Powells'. It was empty, they weren't there, and I slept in her bed. It was so little, and I slept under her thing — you know, her duvet, and it was so small I had to curl up. I cried all night, remembering what it was like, remembering Ruby.'

He said, 'We were so young. She was so beautiful.'

Connie said, 'Yes.'

Ruby Powell had blue eyes, with yellow flecks in them. Depending on the light, the colour of her eyes moved across a spectrum from grey to light blueish green. Her skin was very fair; white, but not dead-white; it was both soft and translucent, revealing muted blue veins along her inside arms, and flushing her cheeks when she was excited, two blotches of pure pink. Her eyes were long and somewhat cold in their regard, as if contemplating the world with a detached fascination, a certain aesthetic or critical distance. Boyfriends compared her to a cat; Hope Lewis always said she was like a lizard, cold-blooded.

Connie knew the rectangular palms of Ruby's hands, her long fingers; the palms of Ruby's hands were covered with an indecipherable net of lines, like a monkey, or some other animal. Walking arm in arm around the playground during break, or holding hands, as they did, being English girls. Ruby's lizard hands were always cool and dry.

At fifteen, Ruby moved through rooms easily, any inner awkwardness successfully screened by her air of detachment, any shyness covered by graceful gesture, her wet red lips pursed in a moue of curiosity and disdain. Ruby wore browns and shit-greens and worn-out blues, to set off her light brown hair, her blue eyes. She stood like a Canova statue, her limbs disposed at gentle angles, her head placed clearly on her long, pale neck, the line of her jaw as she turned her head defining the intensity of her look.

Connie heard a lot about Michael before she met him, about Mikey, the artist, Ruby's cousin. She heard about him at school, from Ruby, and Hope. They were twelve, thirteen, fourteen, then, and Mikey was presented as extraordinary, brilliant, the ideal object, somehow. As time passed, these relations became increasingly murky. It was partly that Ruby was working out her own identification: Ruby was an artist like Michael; Ruby wanted everything Michael represented, or possessed; she wanted Mikey. And Connie wanted Ruby, simply, so she wanted Mikey too — by proxy, so to speak.

Ruby was a painter, and she looked at the world as at a terrible lovely object, to be taken in through her eyes, to emerge again in the careful gestures of her two hands. Connie used to sit for her, when they were at school, and then again later, when they were older, and shared a house. She loved the sounds that Ruby made, painting: the gasp of the brush on the canvas, the muffled thump of the floorboards as Ruby shifted her weight back and forth. Looking up at Connie, her wide eyes stared, as if she saw something quite else, not Connie, and then, turning back to the painting, the movement of her body, her hand holding the brush, moving the paint, marking the surface again. Ruby's look, stripped of defence, was as intense and impersonal as a beam of light. Occasionally during these sessions she would see Connie, recognise her, and react, her face changing; she'd say, 'You all right? You want to stop? Take a break . . .' Connie would say, 'No, that's OK. I'll stop in a bit.' Ruby would continue, losing herself again, absent and present at the same time.

In public, in the world, Ruby was cool as a mousse, her passionate enquiry veiled by languid gesture, eyes half closed in a calm display of ennui. Connie found Ruby utterly seductive, as she moved between detachment and connection, unpredictably. Her mask would fall, without warning, and suddenly there she'd be, Ruby, those burning eyes in that pale face, all there, looking at you as if she understood everything and still wanted more.

Later things got more complicated. Ruby was hurt, damaged by the world she tried so carefully both to seduce and keep at a distance. The shield of cool defiance cracked, she couldn't carry it off, as if her face and body couldn't sustain the mask of indifference that had seen her through the years at school. And then she saved her life. Ruby abandoned plans to go to Oxford, do the usual thing; she went to art college, and there she hung out with working-class kids who took the piss, who cracked brilliant jokes nineteen to the dozen, and wouldn't allow her air of neurotic solemnity the time of day. They'd say, *She's* awfully soulful, isn't she? — right in front of her, and Ruby couldn't keep it up. It just wasn't hip to be so obviously cool. It wasn't any fun anymore, either.

Between the cracks and bruises of real life, and the comic intolerance of others, her whole persona changed, the look virtually collapsed, allowing some of her inner contradictions, the impossible mix of desire and rage, to rise to the surface. She was still beautiful, but differently.

Ruby's vulnerability was palpable, to anyone who cared to look closely. She'd found out about danger, and walked through everyday streets as if she were walking on thin ice, aware of depths, the black icy water just below. Then she couldn't go back, to the safe world of her parents' house; Ruby had to make an entirely other life for herself, to make it up as she went along.

Mikey was doing more or less the same thing, in those days, stepping right outside the limits set by his parents, thinking in entirely different terms. Mikey was going to be a great artist, a famous artist, he was going to go to New York.

In Connie's scheme of things, on the other hand, there didn't seem to be any limits, really. It was as if there wasn't anyone to rebel against, they'd all vanished. At that time, at eighteen, nineteen, Connie had no idea what her parents stood for, she hardly saw them, and to compensate for this absence, she would compulsively imagine what they would say, or think, and then find herself contending with her own guilt or shame. She'd successfully internalised these voices of contempt or disapproval, and so rarely spoke seriously with either of her parents that she had no idea how far the imaginary voices would match reality. When they did talk, Connie persistently mistook her father's tone of perplexed disappointment for unremitting disapproval. In this world it was Ruby, and to a great extent, Ruby's family, who became for Connie the crucial arbiters of aesthetics, politics, morality. Sometimes Connie rebelled, inevitably, turning aside from the true path, but she never stopped adoring Ruby.

After a while Connie got up and looked around the studio, at the work Michael was doing, and she was struck by a particular painting that was hanging on the marked and dirty wall. There were two small paintings, hanging side by side, that Michael had recently made. Connie thought they were very beautiful. They were both made of white wax or encaustic, painted on canvas, with a little phallic figure in the centre. In both paintings the figure was made of the glass part of a weather thermometer, without any of the marks or numbers, just the very narrow glass tube, a bright line of mercury, and the little bulb at the bottom end where the mercury sits. The thermometer was attached to the painting by very thin wire, fine wire wrapped around it at the top and the bottom, and the ends of the wire were brushed over with the transparent wax, so the wire was like traces of four limbs, sticking out at either end. It seemed like a little man, or a phallus, with the glass bulb at the bottom and the line of mercury rising up, or it was like an animal spread out for dissection, against this translucent waxy surface.

These two paintings reminded Connie of the Cycladic sculptures in the British Museum, the ones in white stone, small figures, with very flat face and body, a completely minimal triangle for the nose, arms lying flat across the body, a chiselled line to mark the vagina. Like the best of Michael's work, the two paintings had this edge of the archaic, like an invocation of ancient forms within a kind of minimalist aesthetic. Connie remembered he'd been to Egypt, a few years ago, with Solveig, and she'd also been, the year before, at Christmas, so they talked about that. But she was immediately completely taken with one of these paintings, although the two of them were very similar. She felt elated looking at it; she told Ruby after that it reminded her of a painting Ruby'd done, years before, a painting that was almost black, with a white X in the centre.

Also Connie was thrilled, simply, to see Michael alive and well and working, making a living, making good work. She was terribly happy. In retrospect Connie recognised, thinking about it she was forced to recognise, that both she and Michael were a little over-excited, exalted, perhaps, that icy afternoon in New York. They were carried away on a swell of emotion, passionately talking, remembering the past, reconstructing a narrative, a sequence of some kind.

Later Connie told Ruby: 'It seems as if it's all too easy to see one's past, or our past, I should say, as *mythic*, almost . . . you know what I mean? Like a place of beautiful youth and innocence — in fact its almost impossible not to see it like that, especially when this abyss of horror separates the present from that lost time. But that's not right, it really isn't.'

'No,' Ruby said, staring absently at her glass of wine. 'We weren't innocent, exactly, in those days. I mean, we were teenagers. Which means, we were tormented, confused, cruel, selfish, and miserable. The difference is that we didn't know then what we know now, we didn't know what would become of us.'

Connie paused. 'Yes, I think that's right. I always remember Beata talking about finding this photograph of herself at about sixteen or fifteen, and realising that she knew now exactly what happened to that girl, she knew what happened next, so to speak. It's really only in that sense that we could be called innocent, I think.'

'Yes, it's technical, like a structure of suspense,' Ruby said. 'The audience (us now) knows something the protagonists (us then) don't know. We know they'll find out, eventually, but at this stage they're in the dark. They inhabit a realm of potential, in which anything could happen.'

Not so now, Connie thought; our paths are fixed. Nothing can erase the years of junk in New York, no matter how healthy Michael may be now. Nothing can wipe out that pain, it cannot be undone.

A day or two later, on Monday, Connie finally got through on the phone to Iris, and Iris said she'd come to Connie's gig that night. She didn't show, Monday night, but Michael did, and he was very enthusiastic about Connie's paper, coming up to her afterwards, Michael told her he thought her work was terrific. Connie was terribly pleased, smiling like crazy.

They were standing together at the side of the room, as the audience of around twenty people was breaking up, chatting, putting on their coats, the folding chairs shifting out of their rows. Standing talking there, clutching the jamjar of Stolichnaya that always got her through such occasions, suddenly Connie said, 'I want to buy that painting, you know, the small white one, but I haven't got any money.'

Michael said, 'Which one?' — because of course there were two. Connie said, 'The one on the left.' And Michael said, 'Oh Connie, I wish I could give it to you, but —.' She interrupted him, she said, 'No, you absolutely mustn't give it to me, I don't believe in that. We can't give each other our work —

but think about it, think about how much you'd be willing to accept for it.' Michael said he'd really like her to have it, it was wonderful when the work went to friends, to people who really liked it. Connie told him she'd phone him about it the next day.

There was a young girl that came up to her then, tall and skinny and blonde, and she reminded Connie of herself, oddly, in the way she introduced herself, saying how much she liked Connie's work as they walked down the street, and all the time interjecting these lines, sotto voce: 'Terribly shy! terribly shy!' she'd mutter quietly, and then carry on talking. Connie was completely charmed. They were heading down the street to some strange English bar, a New York bar pretending to be a pub, and Connie was elated, and distracted, the centre of attention, surrounded by these friends. They sat around a long table, and everyone talked at once. Looking down the table, Connie saw Michael talking to two women she didn't know very well, artists; she was pleased he knew people there to talk to. She didn't get a chance to talk to him very much, and later all she remembered about the scene in the bar, the thing that struck her most deeply, was the fact that Michael didn't drink.

It was amazing, really. He didn't drink, or smoke, or do drugs, Michael, who was never without a cigarette, always ready for a drink. Never again, it was over.

Connie remembered it so clearly: the cigarette stuck between the fingers of his right hand, the cigarette held deep between the index and middle fingers, his hand making a loose fist. The cigarette hovering, as his fingers lightly shift its position, in some kind of perpetual play. The cigarette in his teeth, gently biting the filter, as he lifts something with both hands. Sitting still, his hand curved around the glass, cigarette between his fingers, his arm resting on the table, his long hand comfortable around the smooth pint glass. The sudden intake of smoke before he spoke, a wry smile as he looked up at you, eyes narrowing, defiant, the slightly sorrowful glint of transgression in his eyes. The box of matches, tapped, turned, examined. The shot glass, knocked back. His flat white face, blotto, smashed, gone; eyes half closed, dead to the world.

It was breathtaking, when she remembered.

Downtown

In September 1975, Connie was twenty, and she'd never heard the word Tribeca, maybe it hadn't yet been invented. Connie described the place where Michael was living in New York as 'way downtown', on the third floor of an industrial building in a narrow street full of enormous Mack trucks, and noise, and sagging cobblestones. As a joke, Mikey described the area as So-what, after Soho. He was sharing the loft with a woman called Hannah; they didn't sleep together; it was her place, really, and he had the back room, or space, and slept in a little enclosed bridge that ran between two buildings, high above the alley.

It all seemed terribly appealing to Connie, who was staying for a week or so with Iris Gowing way uptown, up near Columbia, en route from London to study for a year in San Francisco. She'd known Iris for years, since they were kids in Chicago; they went to school together and then, when Connie left, she and Iris corresponded, fitfully. Later Iris would appear in London, during school vacations, passing through on her way to Paris, or Rome, on the way to visit her mother. Now she was studying at Columbia, living on Riverside Drive, and going to the opera a great deal.

Connie thought the whole downtown scene was too perfect, absolutely what she wanted, where she wanted to be. She would get on the subway and plummet south to Chambers Street, to go and hang out with Mikey and his friends. Connie used to come and visit her grandmother in New York, when they lived in Chicago, before her parents moved to London, but on those childish occasions she never went south of 57th Street, except maybe to visit the Museum of Modern Art. The Village was a disappointment, full of tourists in coffee shops, looking for Bob Dylan, or something, but Canal Street was a revelation.

Mikey'd been living in New York for just over a year, and things seemed to be all right, despite the inevitable money troubles. As Connie wrote in a postcard to Ruby: 'Mikey doesn't *seem* to be doing a total self-destruct routine.' That first afternoon Mikey took her up onto the West Side Highway; the deserted motorway was like a vast minimal sculpture, the archetypal contemporary ruin. There were people jogging, and pushing prams, and riding bicycles, avoiding the sudden jagged edges where the concrete had simply fallen away. There were people walking, watching the orange sun set, the concrete underfoot still hot from the long afternoon. She could see the Statue of Liberty, and the World Trade Centre, another monument to minimalism. It all seemed spectacularly beautiful.

Early every evening Mikey'd go to the dark, narrow bar near his place, where you could play pool, you put fifty cents on the table and played the winner, and quickly Connie found herself comfortably perched on a red vinyl barstool, buying Johnnie Walker Black with beer chasers, flirting wildly with Mikey's friends. It was a real scene. Mikey's friends were all artists, and most of them were men, and they all wore torn white T-shirts and black jeans, they were irresistible. Connie was enchanted: this was like something out of a book, or an opera, *La Bohème;* this was perfect.

One night, after eating in Chinatown, Michael and Connie sat together in the bar and got blind drunk. At one point Mikey was busy playing pool, Connie repeatedly putting quarters in the jukebox, she was trying to enjoy being rather aggressively chatted up by a self-proclaimed ex-junky, ex-alcoholic, a guy who described himself as 'thirty-five and wasted', when suddenly, without warning, Connie burst into tears. Mikey came over and put his arms around her, smiling at her he said, 'You don't understand, Connie, you don't cry in New York.' Connie wiped her nose on the back of her hand, laughing. They decided that could be the title of their book, *You Don't Cry in New York*, the opposite to that other one, *By Grand Central Station I Sat Down and Wept.* Connie's hair was so short it was like velvet on her skull; Mikey stroked the back of her head, hard, feeling the bone beneath the silk. They went on drinking.

At four a.m., when they could barely walk, they lurched out of the bar and up the stairs to Mikey's place, where they somehow managed to hurl their bodies gently up the ladder into Hannah's platform bed (she was away, out of town for a week) and lie down together. Their limbs entangled, lips pressed to hot skin, Connie and Michael half heartedly attempted to make love. It was very hot, very late at night; when they started to feel something they felt sick. This was something they'd never done, never intended to do. They persisted, however, almost overwhelmed. At length their bodies separated; they slept.

Connie woke up in the morning, drained and anxious, hungover, feeling beaten to a pulp. She got up and out silently, and hitting the street, decided to go and take a look at the Brooklyn Bridge. She walked out into the brilliant morning, wide empty streets and the sky filled with light, she went to find the bridge. It wasn't far away. Maybe it was luck, or else a vestigial memory of some movie or a photograph, but she found the wooden walkway across the bridge, the walkway she hadn't known existed, and crossing the river she was so excited, buzzing on the hum of the wires, the hiss of the cars on the metal surface underneath. Connie was smiling wildly; she felt blank, spaced out, elated, watching the sun glinting on the wide river, distant boats moving across the water. When she got to the other side, Brooklyn, she turned around and walked back. Then she went home to Iris's place, and went to sleep. Later that evening she booked her flight to California.

The next day she called Michael and asked him to meet her at the Empire State Building. The sign said: UNLIMITED VISIBILITY. Mikey was preoccupied and polite, and stood on the observation platform saying very little. Then he left, he said he was going back to work. Connie succumbed to ennui. She fled uptown to Iris's and spent the evening reading *The Wild Palms*.

Connie went back to the bar with Michael the following evening, and as they sat down she said to him, 'Look, I don't expect you to sleep with me.' This cleared the air somewhat. They drank all night, Connie buying, and then (precisely) slept together, exhausted, from five in the morning until one p.m. When they woke up, hungover, they embraced, briefly, lying naked in bed together, exchanging desultory kisses, both feeling drained. Michael's long body seemed unspeakably beautiful, beautiful beyond words. Connie draped her arms around him, sleepily, sensing his heavy bones and warm skin. Eventually they went out for breakfast at the local diner, eggs and sausages and toast, reviving, smiling at each other, vaguely, and then Connie scooted off to spend her last day in New York with Iris, who was in crisis over a haircut. Connie was amazed.

In the late evening, Connie's last evening, she returned downtown, it was like a magnet pulling her back, and she got drunk, one more time, with Michael. She kept talking about Ruby, she said, 'Ruby is so beautiful.'

She said, 'Ruby is so beautiful, how can you leave her?'

She said, 'Ruby is so beautiful, and so alone.'

They kissed passionately in the noisy bar. They were drinking like fish, and wildly attracted to each other, all over again. Connie was dancing to the records on the jukebox, too loud to talk, until finally Mikey said, 'Connie, you better go home.' So she did, she got into a taxi, careening up Eighth Avenue, drunk and wiped out. The next day Connie left town, reading *The Golden Notebook* on the plane.

A week later, from San Francisco, Connie wrote to Ruby, telling her she'd slept with Mikey in New York. Her letter implicitly put forward the somewhat confused view that she'd slept with Mikey because she loved Ruby so much, or because they both loved Ruby so much, or something. She was scared to death, imagining Ruby's reaction: a shrug, or a scream, or what. In the event Ruby said she really wasn't angry; when she wrote back, she said, these things happen, and yes, if she were having a drink with Connie's ex-boyfriend, she'd expect Connie's presence to hover around a bit too. As for triangles, she said she really didn't see it that way, but maybe that was because she wasn't feeling very claustrophobic these days.

Connie was relieved. Ruby's response to this transgression seemed like yet more evidence of her extraordinary understanding. As usual Connie felt the whole incident had been more about her relationship to Ruby than anything else.

Dear Ruby —
I'm in San Francisco now, trying to find a place to live, wandering the streets all day figuratively and literally, feeling like such an outsider, a total stranger, with my too short hair and my black black dress and my flat Chinese shoes. I'm staying with old friends of my mother, people I don't know, total lap of luxury, very kind to me and somewhat naïve-seeming. They attend church on Sunday, staggeringly, and try to discipline their seventeen-year-old son by rationing his use of the car, viz: 'Can I borrow the car this weekend, Dad?' 'Not until you do your homework!' Real summertime blues stuff. Needless to say I throw numerous spanners into these works, by expounding all my theories of independence, how I left home at sixteen, no one ever told *me* to do my homework, etc. etc. They all (incl. the son) listen in horror, eyes and mouths agape, and then go back to their familiar routines. Clearly I'm not an example they would want to follow! After breakfast every day I set forth again, pounding the streets, trying to find something remotely simpatico, a room, a household, somewhere to *live.* School starts next week, so I better fix this soon.

I slept with Michael when I was in New York. I feel I have to tell you this, although I'm scared and unhappy at the pain it could cause — but in a way it felt like it was all to do w. *you* — I mean, that's the link, *you're* the link, so obviously in a sense it could be seen (or could be) a betrayal, but in another way it was a confirmation of our relationship(s). Does this make any sense? It's all so triangulated: I remember horrible Edward Denham telling me I ought to take up trigonometry, and this does seem rather to underline that tendency — .

But it was *weird* (I should say, of course, that we were paralytically drunk and sexually completely inadequate, so to speak) — it was weird, sitting in this dark little bar talking nonstop, it was like your ghost hovered, really, your presence was felt. I realised I loved Michael much more than I'd ever allowed myself to recognise, yet in a way it was just another route back to you. It's terribly painful for me to talk or write about this, partly because I'm terrified you'll hate me for it. I hope you don't mind too much. I'm terribly *ashamed*, on the one hand, and yet it all seemed relatively inevitable at the time, I suppose. Do forgive me. I know he misses you more than words can tell.

As I do, here, now. It's funny, wandering around the Mission, I keep thinking of you coming through here whenever it was, in '73, I picture you in your backpack and boots, all independence and freedom of the road. Of course I don't feel free at all — I feel anxious and lonely and confused, constantly wondering what the hell I'm doing here, so many miles from home. I loiter in bookstores, hoping someone nice might talk to me. In a self-service café the other day, a man in the queue told me I looked like Jean Seberg. I was terribly pleased, of course, and told him it was nonsense. I'm not blonde for a start. Still, it's an improvement on total strangers staggering up to me to tell me they went to school with me somewhere in Indiana or Delaware. I've gradually been forced to face the absolute fact that literally *everyone* with very very short hair looks *exactly* the same. Still, I'd rather the association was to *A Bout de Souffle* than third grade, needless to say.

I must go — hope you're well — do write to me, tell me what you're doing, etc. — I send love to you.
C. XXX

At Christmas, Connie came back to New York.

This time she was staying with Mikey, sleeping on a narrow slab on the freezing tiled floor, her clothes hanging in a row above her on a sprinkler pipe. It snowed continuously, and the loft was extremely cold. They tended to sit in the front part, Hannah's part, where she'd built her platform bed, and the kitchen things (the cooker, the sink) stood in a row beside the door, with the huge dirty windows running along two walls around the corner of the building, making a broad strip of icy light.

Mikey and Connie had corresponded somewhat, since September. Michael was trying to get a green card, a legal residency, and he needed to marry an American. He couldn't leave the States, he couldn't go to England to see Ruby, for example, until he'd sorted this out. When he told her about it in September, one late night in the bar, drunk as skunks, Connie didn't hesitate: 'Jesus, I'd marry you, Mikey,' she said. Michael smiled, terribly polite. 'That's awfully kind of you, Con,' he said. They left it at that. It was a slightly ridiculous proposal, in that Connie was an American who lived in London, most of the time, while Mikey was English and wanted to live in New York. Nevertheless, a while later, in San Francisco, Connie received a letter saying, 'Would you really? I know it's a lot to ask . . .'

Connie was amused; it seemed too ironic, the idea of marrying Mikey after all these years. She couldn't help wondering what Ruby would think. Nevertheless, she called him up, to say, yes, why not, and then suddenly wondered how this marriage might affect *her* status, as a resident alien in England. It could only benefit both of them, surely? After getting her sister Hilary to do a little research, it turned out marrying Mikey was probably unwise; Hilary sent a telegram from London: 'DO NOT MARRY STOP TAX CONSEQUENCES LOUSY STOP LOVE.' Whereupon Mikey admitted that the fact they didn't even live in the same city might look a bit suspect to the INS. Apparently the punishment for a fraudulent marriage with intent to obtain a green card was permanent exile. This seemed awfully risky.

Meanwhile Connie wrote to Ruby and asked her what she thought, suggesting that her primary motivation in all this was to bring Ruby and Michael together again. More triangulation: if she, Connie, made this supreme sacrifice, Michael would be able to come back to London, to see Ruby, sooner rather than later. Ruby wrote back, very clear about it, saying she found the whole idea repugnant and certainly this project did not have her blessing. Ruby suggested there were zillions of women in New York whom Mikey could marry, why did it have to be Connie? Plus she wanted Connie to know she wasn't in the least bit happy with the idea that Connie thought she was doing it as a favour to her, Ruby. Connie took this in.

Then, finally, after persistently searching her heart, Connie came to the tentative conclusion that she might someday want to marry Mikey for real, however unthinkable this seemed, and this remotest of possibilities, this figment of an unknown future, was something that would be precluded, or even jinxed, by a false marriage now. So they didn't do it, after all. She didn't tell Mikey, or anyone else, exactly why.

When she came to see him at Christmas, again they spent a lot of time in the narrow little bar down the street. Mikey compulsively played pool while Connie drank. One night she met a guy Mikey did carpentry and decorating work with, a guy called Nick. He was Polish, he had very white skin, and black hair, with a dark little beard, and he was very sadistic and very seductive. He was an artist, of course. Connie found herself terribly attracted to him. He gave her his phone number, and in the morning she called him and they arranged to meet.

That night she ended up getting drunk and going back to his place; another somewhat dismal industrial space, with the regulation high white walls, enormous dark windows and broken-down furniture. It was very cold, very late at night. They sat on a collapsed sofa and kissed, and then occasionally he'd pause, taking time out to insult her for a while. He asked about her family, what they looked like; Connie told him her mother looked like Patricia Neal. Nick was scathing: '*My* mother looked like Ava Gardner.' Connie just wanted to fuck him and leave.

They kissed some more. Then he showed her an eight by ten black and white glossy photograph of his girlfriend, the woman he lived with, who was out of town at the moment. The young woman was naked, you could see her small breasts, her thin ribs, she had extremely short dark hair (like Connie's), and she was pulling on her underarm hairs, her skinny pale arms bent at an acute angle, pulling out the underarm hair to show it off. She had very long dark curly hair under her arms, and long thin fingers plucking at the hairs; she had a wild, ironic look in her eye, and a small crooked smile, her head held at an odd angle, staring straight into the camera. 'It's a self-portrait,' Nick said, terribly impressed.

Connie felt totally outmoded; it was all too depressing. She figured she would never be hip enough to make this scene. Nick placed the photo on the floor at their feet, and they went on making out. Then he picked it up again, contemplatively, and fixing her with his nasty smile, he said, '*Her* name is Constance too.' Connie found this hard to believe, but nodded solemnly, wishing she wasn't so drunk and so turned on.

Later, at around two or three in the morning, Nick decided to shave off his beard, and Connie watched as he took scissors and razor and soap, standing in front of the bright mirror, smiling at himself. Connie hated beards; she was pleased to find Nick looking much younger, and much more vulnerable, without it.

In the end, however, Nick refused to fuck her. Connie spent the night with him anyway, what was left of it, sleeping for a couple of hours on his foam mattress on the dusty floor. She left very early in the morning, feeling like death. Mikey would be annoyed with her. She felt she'd made a fool of herself, again, which she could bear, another sexual rejection, basing her rather contorted notion of self-respect on being brave enough to be uncool, to be humiliated, or rejected, or abused, on her ability to crawl away, bloody, bowed, but with the inexpressible dignity of a victimisation that's self-chosen.

Nevertheless, she hated the idea of Nick saying condescending things about her to Mikey, while they hammered in nails or whatever. She didn't want to sink in Mikey's esteem, finally, and she didn't want to embarrass him either. Falling into bed, or onto mattress, with his downtown New York friends probably wasn't such a good idea. Connie decided to avoid seeing Nick again. When she ran into him in the bar a couple of days later, he seemed slightly remorseful. Defiantly, Connie overlooked this, as if nothing whatever had happened.

A month or two later, back in California, Connie wrote in her notebook: 'My vision is to get skinny grow my hair and become a walking talking replica of Patti Smith.' Then she wrote: 'Replica, the word replica will always remind me of that evening with NYC Polish Nick and the ghost mirror image "Constance".' These images functioned as models of what she ought to be like, how she ought to look, how wild or crazy she should be. Whatever she was wasn't good enough, that was clear.

The same day Connie had her date with Nick, she'd gone out in the late afternoon with Hannah, and Hannah's girlfriend Roz, to acquire a Christmas tree. It was snowing and windy: the three women each had scarves wrapped around their heads, thick gloves, and they placed their feet firmly on the slippery sidewalk, stamping slightly with each step. They were laughing, taking swigs of Irish whiskey from a little bottle in Hannah's pocket. Connie felt shy, she didn't talk much, walking along grinning in the cold air.

Christmas trees were being sold on a vacant lot nearby; Hannah bargained with the man successfully, flashing her teeth in a sudden flirtatious smile. It was getting dark, and the lot was deserted. He wouldn't have any more customers that night. They walked back in a line, bearing the bound tree triumphantly up the stairs, and managed to stand it in a white enamel bucket full of bricks. The tree was about seven or eight feet high, and very broad. Hannah spread an old sheet under it, making folds in the white fabric in a conventional imitation of snow. Every element in this replication of tradition seemed wildly romantic and exciting to Connie, as if she were taking part in some superb subversion of the patriarchal Christmas. They decided to decorate the tree the next afternoon. A while later Connie went out to meet Nick.

The following day Connie felt terrible: she hadn't slept, she had an appalling hangover, and she imagined everyone condemned her (failed) attempt at seducing their friend. Unspoken disapproval seemed to fill the air. Connie writhed in agony for a while, but later in the day she took real solace in joining the others to make decorations for the tree. Her body ached all over, her mind quivered with self-loathing, yet it was comforting to sit in Hannah's big room, quietly working together; it was comforting to hang out with this lesbian couple, laughing at silly jokes, after such a classically heterosexual hellish night. What Connie'd imagined was silent disapproval turned out to be more like unspoken solidarity, as Hannah and Roz quietly but firmly made her feel better.

Mikey came in as they were making bread dough; they were going to roll the dough into long worms, like plasticene, and form it into shapes to bake in the oven, to hang on the tree. At first they made little figures, like gingerbread men, and Connie watched Hannah make a vagina, gently placing the outer labia, and then the delicate inner lips, and then laughing as she put a raisin where the clitoris would be. It came out of the oven swollen and perfect.

Connie found that if she rolled the strips of dough thin enough, she could form words in a continuous script. *Happy xmas*, she wrote, experimentally, taking the needle and thread to make loops to hang the baked words on the tree. Then she wrote *Connie*, sticking the dot on the *i*, wondering if it would come out. It worked. She put a loop of thread through the *o*, and one through the *e*, and hung her name high on the tree. After that, elated, Connie laboriously wrote the only line of poetry she could remember, *my heart aches, and a drowsy numbness pains my sense*, hanging the words in sequence on the thick branches. Mikey was busy making quirky little shapes to bake, motorcycles, TV sets, a Kalashnikov, and wandering around the room, hanging whatever found objects seemed appropriate on the tree.

Sometimes elaborate constructions simply collapsed in the oven, but generally each attempt surpassed the last, as they became more ambitious and more skilled. Hannah had bought two boxes of silver tinsel to drape, and yards of sparkly fairy-lights. By the time they were finished the tree was monstrously laden with kitchen implements, baked words, sex organs, strange replicas of everyday objects, and all kinds of shiny trash. At last they switched off the neon overhead lights, and turned on the lights on the tree. It was sublime, really beautiful, they were terribly pleased with each other and with the tree.

Later that evening, they were planning to go to a party down the street, where a disparate bunch of exiles (all men) from London, South Africa, Belfast, and the Midwest had taken possession of two enormous floors of another industrial building. The street was riven with hives of artists, all illegal, all very cheap. Recognising that Nick would inevitably be part of the group, Connie unobtrusively made an excuse and stayed behind. She was utterly exhausted anyway, and she felt like reading a book.

Connie had an extreme relation to reading, a neurotic relation: books saved her life continually. It was as if the emotional uproar she inhabited, the voices of self-accusation and defensive despair that clamoured in her head, the sheer noise and confusion of it could be silenced only by the soothing structure of narrative. It was like a drug. She turned to books in desperation, voracious, needy; she regarded them as simply giving her another world. It was all she wanted, at times, and then she had to have it: the absolute obliteration of this world in an elsewhere constructed solely of words. Not spoken words, not remembered words, nothing personal, but silent little black printed letters, inky bits containing within their quirky shapes this inexpressible wonder: the ability to superimpose an altogether elsewhere on her here and now, blotting it out entirely. It was intensely private, and perfect, limited to the encounter of her own eyes with the rows of words on the page. Nothing could undo this pleasure.

Some time later a boyfriend told her about his other friend (the other woman he was seeing at the time), a young woman who apparently had always gently masturbated as she read, quietly rocking back and forth, and who subsequently attributed her fascination with literature to this practice. Connie was surprised: masturbation was so intrusive. She used books to disappear herself, to vanish; it was a different order of pleasure.

Now in her weariness she craved it, like a wolf craves bloody flesh; she was currently reading *Bleak House*, a thick, heavy paperback intended to provide real ballast for her Christmas visit to New York. She would read, by herself, tonight, and recover.

So Hannah and Roz left with Mikey, to go over to Adam's place, and Connie was left alone. She poured herself a glass of red wine, and took her shawl, and settled down in the only comfortable chair. It immediately became apparent that there wasn't enough light to read by. Connie desperately looked around the room for a lamp. She was right on the edge, any minor setback was a crisis. She'd decided that she couldn't bear to turn on the fluorescent overhead lights, she couldn't face the enormous room flooded with cold even light, the desolation of it. Connie was shaky with tiredness, after her ordeal; she felt angry suddenly: 'Don't any of these people read?!' They probably didn't, she thought; they probably liked the neon lights.

Connie spotted a cheap clip-on lamp with a round aluminium shade, attached to a shelf on the platform bed. She unclipped it, to attach it to the windowsill nearer the comfortable chair, then she moved the chair over towards the lamp. Foolishly, she stood still, holding the plug in her upraised hand, looking around for some place to plug it in. There seemed to be only one socket in this end of the huge room; it had numerous electrical adaptors sticking out of it, like a grotesque plant form growing out of the wall. Worst of all, it was behind the Christmas tree. Connie was determined. Taking the lamp's wire in her hand, she crouched down, to stretch behind the tree. It was very difficult, she was on the floor, arm extended, leaning sideways, trying to force the plug into one of the adaptors.

Suddenly, without warning, the tree fell. It toppled over, crashing onto the floor.

Devastation: without drawing breath, Connie wailed, tears forcing themselves through her screwed-up eyes. Her mouth opened wide as more sounds came out, sobs and jerking cries. On her hands and knees, whining, pressing her hands painfully against the cold floor, Connie couldn't stop crying. The tree was like a living thing shattered, its multitudinous decorations scattered across the tiled floor, mixed up in terrible confusion. Connie was paralysed with despair and shame.

Some time later, she picked herself up off the floor, and turned on the neon lights. Then she went to the phone, where they'd left the number in case she wanted to join them at the party. Connie asked to speak to Hannah, still crying. She told her what happened, and Hannah said, 'Don't worry, don't worry about it. I'm sure it's all right. Do you want to come out?'

Connie realised with a kind of bitter disbelief that they were having what's called a good time. 'No,' she said. 'I think I'd better stay here and clear up some of this mess.'

When she hung up the phone, Connie took a breath and faced the destruction. The tree looked like a broken animal, lying crooked on its side. The first thing she did was to unplug the multicoloured fairy-lights, which were still somehow bravely shining. Then she tried to stand the tree up again. This proved extremely difficult. After many attempts, wrestling with the bricks and the bucket, she managed it, and then sat down to rest, sinking into the low chair, her face dry and shiny from tears, her whole body empty and shaking inside. She surveyed the scene: chaos and desolation.

Connie got up out of the chair, and began to gradually retrieve the fallen and scattered decorations. There were things all over the floor, and what little remained on the tree was confused and hanging askew. The vagina had slid under a kitchen chair, the tinsel lay in sorry heaps, yet slowly she put it back into some kind of order, strewing the tree's branches with fallen strings of beads, untangling the tinsel, piecing together her line of Keats.

Her eye fell on her own name, *Connie*, broken into three pieces. Again she began to wail, as if this perfect last straw was more than she could take. Then she wiped her eyes, and went on picking things up. After an hour or so, there was nothing left on the floor. The tree looked a little the worse for wear, its initial glory lost, but maybe you wouldn't even notice it if you didn't know, if you hadn't witnessed the scene of destruction. Connie was amazed to discover that the only thing irretrievably broken was her name. The resounding crash of the falling tree seemed a disaster, but she'd made it good, an act of reparation, and nothing was broken except herself. Connie placed the fragments of her name carefully on the grimy windowsill and turned out the lights to go to bed.

The next day Mikey was sitting in his great empty room, on a straight chair beside the huge window, near the heater. He appeared both glum and idle, though Connie imagined he was probably working, or thinking, at least. It was about six in the evening.

'Do you mind if I come in?' she said.

'No, that's OK.'

Connie sat down on the other straight chair, facing Mikey, about fifteen feet away from him across the dirty tiled floor.

They sat there separately and together, under the harsh fluorescent lights of Michael's studio, as the evening darkness intensified. It was very cold, snow was falling outside. Connie lit a cigarette, and then spoke, nervously gesturing with her pale hands.

'I wanted to apologise, well not apologise exactly, but I felt really terrible about all this drama — you know, I feel like I've been forcing my little melodrama down everybody's throats, and I kind of wish I hadn't.'

'I don't know what you mean, really,' Michael said calmly.

'Oh you know, all this fucking Nick and then knocking Christmas trees over, it's all a bit much, isn't it? Crying my eyes out, all that. A bit nauseating, I think.'

'You always seem to be wishing you hadn't done something.' There was a note of deep irritation in Michael's voice. Connie persisted, wanting more.

'Yes, I don't know why that is.'

'I must say, I find it incomprehensible.' Michael pronounced the word slowly, syllable by syllable. Connie started to panic.

'I guess it's all to do with my family and stuff, all of that. But I suppose that's just going for the sympathy vote, as they say.' Connie attempted an ironic smile.

Michael started again, and then stopped himself. 'It's just that — oh I don't know if I want to go on with this.'

'Oh please, say what you think. I want to know what you think, really,' Connie said.

'It's just that — you're so out of control. All over the place.'

Connie was silent.

Michael continued, 'I don't understand what you do all day.'

'What do you mean?' Connie said.

'I don't know — it seems as though you come here, make a mess of things, get hurt, or hurt yourself, or whatever you want to call it, you freak out, and then you go shopping with Iris, and you sit in bars: I mean, don't you have any work to do?'

Connie was devastated.

'No,' she said. 'No one in my family has — it's congenital, none of us knows what we want to do . . . with our lives.'

'It's so bourgeois. If you don't mind me saying so —'

Connie looked up. 'No, no, go on,' she said dully. 'I want to know what you think.'

'It's just that I look at you, totally scattered, all over the shop, literally ruled by your emotions (or so it seems), and I think, God, it's all so fucking bourgeois.'

Connie was silent, taking this in.

'All this *emotion*. You're always going on about what happened in the past. I don't know if you're aware of it, but it's as if the past is the only thing that means anything to you. Emotional regurgitation. It's so fucking sentimental.' Again his mouth emphasised each syllable. 'I'm glad I've left England — I'm really glad I got away with it.'

'But Mikey, I really miss England. It may seem pathetic, but I really miss Ruby, and Hope, and everyone.' Their eyes met.

'Please don't call me Mikey,' he said calmly. 'Mikey is a baby name.'

'What?' Connie said.

She was shocked rigid. For Connie, to use the name Mikey was to signify her intimacy with the whole scene, with Ruby and Mikey and Chas and everybody, it proved to herself and to the world that she wasn't an outsider here.

'My name is Michael. Mikey is a baby name, a nursery name. It's what my mother calls me, for Christ's sake.'

Connie didn't know what to say; she felt rubbed out, erased. In desperation she resorted to bathos.

'I'm not surprised you find it all so contemptible,' Connie

muttered. At this word she started to cry. Michael made a gesture of revulsion, almost imperceptible; it seemed he couldn't stop.

'What I don't understand is the emotional indulgence of it all. I really don't,' he said. 'I mean, all this wallowing in pain — whether it's self-inflicted or not, seems completely irrelevant. I keep thinking, do something with it. But without any work, there's nothing for you to do, it seems, but go over it, over and over, until all you're doing is rolling around in your own shitty feelings. It's so self-indulgent, don't you think?'

'Yes, I know it is.' Connie's face was flooded with tears, her nose running, her mouth pulled out of shape. 'But I don't know what else I can do. Nothing's any good. Nothing works out. My parents —'

Michael interrupted her. 'This endless harping on parents, it's so unnecessary.' Again each syllable was stressed. 'Your life is such a mess, Connie . . . All these men, one crisis after another, your fucking family, what happened to you when you were fourteen — can't you shove it all to one side? Can't you forget about it for one minute?'

Connie paused for breath, and then she plunged in, unhesitating, joining Michael in his condemnation. 'Look,' she said, 'don't think I don't agree with you, I do, I agree. This is all too familiar, you know?' Connie sniffed loudly. 'I mean, this is basically what I call the emotional blob routine: people are constantly sitting me down and telling me I'm nothing but an emotional blob. I mean, like total strangers. Or a sponge, that's another one, a sponge soaking up emotion. So don't think this kind of thing doesn't happen to me at regular intervals, although —' Here Connie ground her teeth, pathetically stifling a sob. 'Although I fucking wish it didn't, I mean, I wish I wasn't, like this.'

Michael seemed completely detached from Connie's tears.

He sat there, smoking, watching her coldly. Then suddenly the phone rang, and Michael went to answer it. It was Iris; Connie went to the phone, wiping her nose.

Iris said, 'I'm just calling because I just talked to Elena, and I mentioned you, you know, I said you were in town, et cetera, and anyway, she said, oh, tell her I really liked her Proust paper. It was brilliant. So I thought I'd call and pass on the message.'

Connie was silent.

'Connie?'

'Yes.'

'Was this the paper on Odette, the one you were talking about?'

Connie sniffed, gulping air. 'Yup, Odette.'

Then Connie mustered a note of ironic detachment, a you've-got-to-be-kidding-me air, saying, 'Did she really say brilliant?'

Iris was cool about it. 'Yup.'

Connie took a breath, thinking hard. 'Iris, listen, I'll call you back,' she said. 'I'm just in the middle of talking to Michael, I'll call you later, OK?'

Connie's tears were dry. She went back into Michael's room, and sat down on the same hard kitchen chair.

'Michael, Michael, look. You don't know everything. You think – I mean, I know, I'm a complete fuckup, and I let everyone know that, I know, I mean, as I said, I shove it down everybody's throats, I don't know whether I'm coming or going, but look, I'm living all by myself in San Francisco, right? I mean, I'm not sitting in London surrounded by all my nearest and dearest, whimpering. Like I've been doing for the last however many years. And I do have work. OK it's academic work, but I don't give a shit. That was Iris on the phone; she knows one of my teachers, this brilliant woman, Elena Grosz, and — she said my paper was good. Actually she said it was brilliant. My paper on Proust.'

Michael's eyes opened, he sat up in his chair, slightly. Connie went on. 'So maybe I am at the mercy of every emotion that sails through me, or — haunted by my family, or whatever, completely confused about everything. Irredeemably bourgeois. But it's changing, also, maybe, I think.'

'Here, have a cigarette,' Michael said, offering her the packet. Connie took one, snorting deeply. She felt deluged by tears, snot, saliva, too many emotional liquids. Michael spoke: 'Do you want to go for a drink?'

'OK,' Connie said, smiling, and wiping her eyes with the back of her hands. 'I'd better fix my mascarfuck.' This was a name Connie gave to what she otherwise commonly called 'my fucking mascara'.

As they walked down the dark street to the bar, bending forward against the freezing sleet, she said, 'I wish I didn't cry so much.' Michael laughed.

'I wish you didn't either,' he said.

The next morning Connie moved out of Michael's place; she went to stay with her godmother, Harriet, uptown, in a posh apartment with central heating and wall-to-wall carpets and an enormous refrigerator full of luxury food. She escaped.

A day or two later, Connie wrote to Ruby, describing her time in New York, delineating the crisis she'd survived. She wrote:

> It still freaks me out though when I think of how STUPID I was with that guy Nick — agonies of retrospective embarrassment. It's all so awful. It was an impossible predicament, you know — bourgeois is

the word, je crois, and very right of Michael to have produced it. Rather worrying. I don't know what to say about it, except that I find myself thinking of the bourgeois predicament as essentially retrospective, a compulsive return (in fantasy only) to the scene of the crime. I said to him, yes, you're right, there's no real work, just extensions of family relationships. I don't know if that's really true. The whole time I was there I felt in that funny mood of justified awkwardness, I mean a condition of terminal self-consciousness which cannot be sidestepped or disguised. Which in my case is seemingly *always* accompanied by the compulsion to draw attention to it, an irresistible urge to tell the whole story, or to confess, to justify myself, to *exhibit* this appalling self-consciousness. You see how I squirm, going over and over the humiliation. Sitting now on a seat on a pole on Lexington between 62nd and 63rd . . . and the whole thing is very worrying in the sense of being *trapped* — & eating French fries — & a cheeseburger. I'm so far away. I guess feeling trapped and/or far away is bourgeois too. Too nauseating. But I went back, finally, yesterday afternoon, back downtown, and I left a blood red butterfly (in a box) for Hannah, and a tiny lead motorcycle for Michael, and I was glad I'd gone back, because I met Michael by accident in the street on my way, leaving, and we hugged and said goodbye and No Hard Feelings. You know the scene.

When Ruby replied, Connie felt released.

Dear Connie,

Thanks for your letter. Needless t'say I find your accounts of NY, Michael, SF, etc. endlessly fascinating, if a bit agonising to read. I wanted to say a few things, or write them, though, bec. you really seem to have been going through it — and it makes me angry, it does, all this 'bourgeois' wheeze. I can't help thinking, as you would say, What *is* this shit? If being un-bourgeois means not having any feelings, then it's no good to me, or you, or even Michael in the end, *I* think. It's this 'let's all be butch in New York' scenario, toughing it out, and Michael can't stand your vulnerability bec. — what? bec. he's vulnerable too (dare I even suggest it?) and refuses to allow himself to be. The flight to the Big City is what he's done — and of course the city, NY, is *the* mythic big city, the big ART city, the big CITY. It's almost a bit Dick Whittington-esque, you know what I mean? Coming from somewhere else, i.e. Nowhere, Arizona, the provinces, right? And demanding something, some kind of recognition or success, from the centre, the City Itself. I mean, we're all supposed to be like that, bowing down in homage to the Great City, amputating our various pasts, cutting out the bits in us that might feel pain, or anxiety, or loss. Unquestioningly.

But if Michael wants to cauterize his emotions and forget his past in some possibly vain attempt to become a successful artist in NY — God, it's really too clichéed for words. It's about as BOURGEOIS as you can get, this absurd, ancient dichotomy between how you were *before*, and how things are now — before and after, what's missing, what's been jettisoned. Feelings go first, then the furniture.

But the thing from where I stand (or sit) that seems most striking (and outrageous) is the part about telling you how bourgeois *you* are. Bec. no matter how distant you may feel fr. the backwards romance that Michael's gone in for (I mean, the romance of deprivation and solitary triumph, the romance of New York), still, that bit penetrated, *bourgeois*, it's like some kind of sharp seed planted there in you. (And I think we are none of us so distant, really, from the seductions of being butch in the big city — I mean, possibly I'm protesting too much, a bit, though lately it's becoming more and more of an issue for me to place myself *here*, in England, or London, now, 1976, and not simply jettison all history, culture, etc.) (I mean (I think) that *I don't want to go be an artist in New York*.)

But what I wanted to say to you was, this accusation, this what amounted to a reprimand, this 'you're so fucking bourgeois', is finally just another example of them (I mean men) telling us what to do. That we ought to be different, like, something *else*, please. It's just *more of the same:* not quite right, not there yet, get rid of that part, how about trying a little harder? Not quite free enough, not quite confident enough, not quite sexy enough . . . or what? Not independent enough. Not successful enough. ETC. *Too vulnerable.* That's it, that's all I wanted to say.

Things are looking up here. School's fantastic, amazingly, and I've met a soulmate, which has swept me off my feet, somewhat. I hope things get better out there. Courage!

Love, Ruby

Connie sent a postcard the day she received Ruby's letter. In tiny writing, it said:

Dear Ruby, I saw *Blow Up* last night, it looked extraordinary, terribly dated, o'course, you know it was the first X movie I ever saw . . . but I was reminded by yr. letter, there's this amazing line David Hemmings says to one of the aspiring models: 'GET RID OF THAT BAG — IT'S *DIABOLICAL*.' Enunciated w. total contempt. And you identify w. him, not her, you can't help it. I thought, Ruby is right, it's just *more of the same*. I love you — C. XXX

Dies Irae

The next day, Tuesday, Connie had her other New York gig to do, in the evening, at Dia. It was much more official, in the sense that they were paying her much more, and she anticipated the audience wouldn't be mostly made up of her old friends and acquaintance. She was leaving New York early Wednesday morning, so Tuesday daytime was Connie's last chance to see Iris. She'd finally got through on the phone, and arranged to go round to her place Tuesday afternoon, to the flat Iris had been living in for ages, in Little Italy. Connie guessed Iris was angry with her — because she'd been in New York since Thursday night, and she hadn't managed to fix to see her sooner.

Iris was terribly thin, and Connie could feel her bones, her shoulder blades, and each individual rib almost, as they embraced: it frightened her, a little. Still, she looked great. Iris was quite tall, and very skinny, with small bones, and her heavy blonde hair was cut short, as if in defiance of prevailing expectation. She wore blues and greys, to bring out the colour of her eyes; she wore her grandmother's grey suede jacket, and beautiful battered shoes. Iris's aetiolated body always made Connie feel monumental by comparison, although she tried to salvage an acceptable self-image, a woman in a painting, perhaps, with heavy marble-white arms and legs, a proper eighteenth-century belly. Statuesque was the word Connie sought, to account for her seemingly massive form, next to Iris's delicate concavity.

The first thing Iris said when Connie arrived was how she hadn't been able to come to Connie's gig the night before, because her friend Beth had to go to the hospital, to the emergency room, and Iris went with her. Then she said, there was nothing really wrong with Beth, in fact.

Then Iris said that she couldn't come to Connie's gig that night either, because she simply had to go to her Spanish class. She'd missed three weeks in a row; in fact she never went, hardly, she said, so she really must go tonight.

Connie bowed her head, figuratively speaking. She was disappointed and as usual when she was disappointed, Connie didn't protest, instead she silently castigated herself for expecting something else. Connie thought, naturally Iris wouldn't want to come to my gig. Connie thought, I can't expect that of her, that she would come, for my sake, to please me. Connie sank down on one of Iris's enormous orange sofas, and stared out of the window at the snow, while Iris disappeared into the tiny kitchen.

The walls of Iris's living-room were covered with a kind of chinoiserie wallpaper, bright orange and green shapes against a black ground; there was a beat-up Persian carpet on the floor, many pictures on the walls, and innumerable books in glass-fronted bookcases and piled up on the floor. The decor was idiosyncratic, a seemingly arbitrary mix of slightly battered antiques retrieved from her grandmother's attic, and quirky treasures of one kind or another. Among the pictures was a Cocteau drawing that Iris's grandmother had bought in Paris in the forties, hanging next to various other drawings and prints, unframed exhibition posters, postcards tacked up, and one large painting by Robert Ryman, which Iris had inherited from her mother, Elizabeth.

In the kitchen Iris was engaged in the production of extremely strong coffee, and calling out to each other, indirectly, the two women began lunch negotiations. Connie wanted to go out, to the Japanese across the street. Iris was vehement: Afghan bread spread with tahini and honey, the perfect lunch. Connie protested, she offered to buy her sushi. Connie explained she was still jet-lagged, and craving protein. Iris was adamant; she didn't want to go out. No, no, no, she said. 'Afghan bread spread with tahini and honey,' she said, lingering lovingly over the words. 'And maybe we can have a nice long nap afterwards.'

Connie looked across the room as Iris came in, carrying the tray of coffee; as she approached, Connie felt the aggression emanating from Iris's thin body. It was like sheer, undiluted hostility, pure and bright, veiled by the heavy languor of her limbs. It felt like Iris wasn't even aware of it, of the intensity and brightness, like distilled rage.

The scene seemed very familiar; Connie felt she'd been set up, again. It was as if Iris were saying, no I won't eat sushi with you, no matter how much you want your protein. I will insist on bread and honey for lunch. I will flaunt my wish, unapologetic, what — sensible food, a proper meal? Not for me! And no I don't really want to *see* you, even though you're only in New York for a few days. Of course not, it goes without saying that I want to go to sleep!

At the same time Connie busily persuaded herself that she was over-reacting: in reality Iris's insistence wasn't quite so extreme. Nevertheless she felt set up, by Iris, to be the voice of maternal reason, the one who said, don't you think you should —? Don't you think we should — eat? And so Connie abdicated this position, she refused to play, as if by passively submitting to the bread and honey, she was denying Iris the pleasure of a fight. 'OK, OK,' Connie said. Connie'd been through this movie before with her, and she bowed her head. They'd known each other for more than twenty years, and Connie liked to think she was being a good friend, overlooking Iris's foibles, her demands. Connie thought that not intervening, not protesting was being nice, kind. Connie figured there couldn't be very many people in the world who would put up with it. She was making nice.

The Afghan bread was sweet and heavy. Connie wasn't surprised by Iris's recipe for a nap; Iris was always tinkering with her bodily responses. She would eat sugar and then fall asleep (this was called sugar shock), or she'd avoid all sugars, even fruit, and careen around on an energy rush for weeks. A great deal of the time Iris ate nothing at all. It was as if Iris knew precisely what effect each food would have on her chemistry, or at least she believed she knew, pretending to a scientistic accuracy in this, a pseudo-rationality that Connie saw as a residue, a leftover from her drug-taking years: the fantasy of total control.

Iris took all kinds of drugs as a teenager, and indeed she was still taking drugs, these days — prescription drugs, antidepressants. She told Connie, as they chewed slowly through the heavy bread and honey, she told Connie she'd been taking something day in, day out, for a year or so, and then the drug doctor suggested she change, go on another, so now, Iris carefully explained, she was taking both.

Connie remembered that Iris hated the drug doctor, because he himself had never tried any of the drugs that he doled out to people like her. When she'd challenged him on this, the doctor told Iris that since he wasn't mentally ill, it would be inappropriate for him to take these drugs. Iris despised him for that.

Connie said, 'I don't understand. Surely if you're changing

from one drug to another, one regime to another, shouldn't you stop taking the first one?'

'Yes, that sounds likely, doesn't it. I don't know. I don't understand it really either,' Iris said, looking up. Connie asked what these drugs were, and Iris told her their names, slightly condescendingly, as if to say, you won't have heard of them, why ask. Connie immediately forgot what they were called. Then Iris said, 'Apparently, the new one is the only drug they've found that gives any kind of solace to crack addicts coming off crack.'

'Jesus Christ,' Connie said.

Iris seemed rather pleased at the effects she was producing, munching away on her bread. Connie felt Iris found it rather impressive that the chemical composition of her brain apparently caused her distress comparable only to crack addicts kicking. Once again Connie felt at a loss.

Iris's mother, Elizabeth, was dead; she was killed in a car wreck when Iris was twenty-two. And to complicate matters, Iris always thought her father wasn't her real father; she was convinced he'd married her mother when she was pregnant with another man's child. Iris called him 'my mother's husband', or 'my stepfather', for short. She'd had nothing to do with him since her mother's death. Iris had no idea who her 'real' father might be, although she indulged the occasional fantasy, constructing alternative escape routes from the family.

So there was a whole set of reasons, or excuses, for her misery, her paralysis, depending on your point of view. Iris didn't see it that way, though; she didn't make the connection. It was true that Iris had been persistently doing drugs since she was twelve or thirteen, long before Elizabeth's death. Iris insisted it was a built-in predisposition, peculiar to her, nothing to do with her mother.

Connie remembered when Iris was on heroin, she used to

say, 'Maybe it's my metabolism, maybe I need it — maybe my body just doesn't produce enough endorphins naturally, it needs some help from outside.' Iris still seemed to be thinking in the same terms, as if some innate lack or disturbance of the chemical equilibrium would justify her paralysis. And as if this trouble could be put right by ingesting the appropriate drug, or the specific, special combination of drugs, that would fit exactly, would fill the gap, or fix the short circuit in her chemical composition.

It was legal, these days; it was prescription drugs Iris was taking, instead of heroin — relatively risk-free, at least to acquire. On the other hand, she'd liked heroin, she'd enjoyed it, at least, whereas these ghastly regimes didn't seem like much fun. It was all about finding something she could take for the rest of her life, something that would allow her to function relatively normally. Yet she'd never tried lithium, which Connie always thought of as the classic rest-of-your-life drug. Maybe it's gone out of fashion, Connie thought. In any case, it was all part of the same syndrome, Connie felt, an ideal of control inscribed across a spectrum of varying intake: from Afghan bread with tahini and honey, to the drug doctor's latest scrip, it was all about ingesting specific chemical combinations in order to adjust her bodily sensations, and thus control her state of mind.

Connie tended to see all of Iris's problems as somehow tied up with Iris's mother and the idea of control. This reductivist attitude was, no doubt, symptomatic of Connie's own need to keep things in line, under control. Iris was excruciatingly thin, but she'd always been terribly thin; in this as in other things, it seemed to Connie that Iris's mother's death merely exacerbated an already extreme pathology. Elizabeth hadn't paid much attention to Iris when she was alive. In fact, Connie always thought Elizabeth had been staggeringly self-absorbed. It was as if Elizabeth saw Iris as some kind of malevolent mirror of herself, years younger, as if Iris had only one function, to upstage her. Elizabeth seemed determined to prevent this; she accomplished this aim by ignoring Iris almost completely. When they did coincide, they fought bitterly. And then, suddenly, Elizabeth was simply, unbelievably, dead.

Pursuing this analysis over the years, Connie developed strong views on junk, and mothers. As she explained to Ruby late one night, 'I don't know, but it seems to me the figure of the mother is really central to all this shit. Back when Iris and Michael were both being junkies, in '81, '82, I spent a good deal of time thinking about it, and I ended up thinking it should be called breastfeeding. Junk, I mean. It seems to me that it's all about presence and absence, like the mother's physical presence or absence that really means everything for the tiny baby. Don't you think? And it's about longing; everything is always too early, too late. And it's all about control: too little, not enough, too much. It's breastfeeding! Then (what one imagines to be) the sheer bliss of it, the plenitude, the unutterable abolition of lack that ensues: junk really seems like a reenactment of this first, infantile drama, this struggle with the mother for food.'

Ruby listened in silence as Connie rushed on. 'You could even argue that the baby must sometimes feel like it's dying, or like it wants to die, as it repudiates the missing mother. Fuck you, it says, if you don't come back I'll starve. Fuck you, it says, I'm dying. With junk, the classic scene of "too much" is the overdose, supposedly a risk taken in pursuit of pleasure, but perhaps more profoundly the final accusation against the mother: you gave me too much, you forced it down my throat.'

Iris didn't shoot up; she smoked it, chasing the dragon. It was much more elegant, needless to say. Yet it was Connie's belief that Iris was sensible, ultimately. Connie didn't think

Iris actually wanted to die. She wanted to destroy her life, though, Connie thought. Connie knew a bit what that was about. She remembered once when Iris tried to get her to do it, to chase the dragon. It was in 1983, in New York, in her living-room. Connie remembered how shocked she was by Iris, by her vehemence, as if there were an unquestionable (and unquestioned) code of conduct that required everyone to try everything at least once. Connie didn't feel that way. She was scared of it, simply; she was scared of liking it too much. It seemed like it would have been so easy to take that path, and Connie didn't want to. But also she thought putting pressure on someone else to take a drug of any kind was totally un-hip. Connie was shocked.

In those bad old days Iris was really proud of the fact that she wasn't addicted. Like so many junkies, she'd smile as she proclaimed: 'I can stop whenever I want to.' But it seemed to Connie, as she watched Iris, that kicking was as much a part of being a junky as lounging around in some beatific state, nodding off. It was structural, so to say.

Iris had an iron constitution, and a will of steel, and it was true: she'd stop, cold turkey, and survive the sweats and terrible aches and pains and groans, and all the wild reflexes, tossing and turning and kicking. She could stop whenever she wanted to, just to prove she wasn't addicted. She'd straighten out, for a while: a citizen, as Louis used to say.

It was here, in this kicking scene, that the profound sado-masochism of the breastfeeding scenario seemed to be playing itself out. Connie saw it as a kind of refusal, the infant finally saying no, the infant saying: I don't need you, I can control my hunger, endure this pain. I can separate, I can wean myself. I can abjure this dependency. Only to return eventually, as the infant returns, to the breast.

Iris would stop, and then start again. Connie always remembered one time when Iris let on she was at it again, and Connie replied, 'I know.' Iris seemed surprised, she said, 'How did you know? I don't seem any different, do I?' And Connie smiled, and she said, 'Of course you seem different, my dear, but the real giveaway is when I come in and see the roll of tin foil on the coffee table.' Iris laughed, Connie remembered.

With this history behind them, Connie really hated feeling set up, even over something as insignificant as lunch. She felt manipulated, at the mercy of Iris's explicit and implicit demands. And Connie felt intensely anxious about the drugs Iris was taking, she was terribly worried about the drug doctor, the analyst, all these fucking scrips. She didn't know what to do. Connie felt like a reluctant stand-in for the disapproving parent — Iris's dead mother to be precise — some poor sap left wondering, and guessing, and fearful.

Connie had consistently tried to sidestep this position, but it was a struggle; over and over again she was left wrestling with the ethics of intervention and inaction. Straightforward stuff, like, if Iris is starving herself, should Connie try to get her to eat? When Iris was on junk, she did intervene, in the end, quite dramatically. Iris behaved appallingly to her, Connie thought. She slept with an old boyfriend of Connie's, 'an old phlegm' as Hope used to say, whom Connie had herself been intending to seduce, and for once Connie couldn't pretend it was all OK, she couldn't pretend nothing had happened.

At that time, Connie finally sat Iris down and she said, 'I can't be friends with you as long as you're doing drugs.' They talked for a long time. Iris presented all the usual arguments as to why it was really perfectly all right; she seemed to think that Iris on heroin was Iris at her best, simply. Connie contradicted her, she said it wasn't so. Connie argued with her. Iris was an equal match for Connie, and they argued seriously, each attempting to convince the other of her point of view.

Connie said, 'You seem to think that the place to draw the line is at addiction, as if that's the limit, that's the line you won't cross, the place where you'd become dehumanised, or out of control, or self-destructive. An automaton. I don't think so. I think all that automaton stuff comes into operation with the transformation of your everyday sense of yourself, when you start thinking of yourself as someone who needs heroin to feel reasonably all right . . . I don't think you have to be addicted to really fuck up, I think it's already a total disaster area.'

Connie said, 'What's so amazing, is how people are actually most out of control just when they're living out a fantasy of total freedom, or transgression, like when you give yourself over to some drug, you think you're free, or something like that. Like this woman I met recently said to me, she said, if I were a psychopath, I could do whatever I wanted to. And actually it's the opposite: if you're psychotic, you can only do what your psychosis makes you do, what it forces you to do or what it allows you to do. I mean, you think you're choosing this drug, that you're in control. Actually you've given up completely, you're subject to heroin, something completely beyond you. You only imagine you're in control.'

Connie said, 'It's like turning yourself into a machine, trying to control everything inside you, by controlling the intake, turning euphoria on or off. Turning pain on and off. It's no good.'

Connie said, 'I think all this must have a lot to do with Elizabeth's death, and your father; I think maybe you must want to cut out, to cut that out of yourself. Though I expect no doubt it's much more complicated than that.'

Connie said, 'You see I think all that self-destructive stuff happens when you're on junk, it only gets *worse* when you're addicted.'

Connie said, 'All addicts kick. It's part of being on junk. Kicking doesn't mean a fucking thing.'

Connie said, 'What's so interesting about the whole process of kicking, is that it's like turning pain on again, for a while, after this intense period of turning it off, this phase of painlessness.'

'You're not addicted, you can kick whenever you please, but look — you're still on junk,' Connie said.

Then Connie said, 'I can't be friends with you when you're on junk. It's that simple.'

Then Connie said, 'What about going back into analysis?' And she went on saying those things all afternoon.

Connie was pleased, she was gratified when Iris stopped. Because she did stop. She stopped, and she found another analyst, and she seemed better. (Iris had plenty of money from her mother's family, so running her life around psychoanalysis five days a week wasn't a big problem, practically speaking.)

But Connie was out of her depth, she'd always been out of her depth, because now, here they were again, six years later, at the same impasse. Connie was almost as angry and almost as hurt, and Iris was almost as insistent on the damage done, as if her emaciated body were a walking talking demonstration of the damage done to her, as if the time when she was on junk was just one of the more melodramatic versions of this non-stop display, this endless performance of damage and disorder.

Connie still couldn't take it, and it was a foolish pretence to think she could, that she could weather these storms, keep her head down, and get out without having to respond, or engage, or perhaps without having to take responsibility, for Iris, one of her oldest friends, someone Connie really loved.

Ladbroke Grove

The house in Ladbroke Grove was mid-Victorian, substantial, and very ordinary. An untended lump of privet marked the boundary between the wide pavement and the little area of front garden where everyone left their bikes. There was a bay window at the front of the house, overlooking Larry's big black Norton and Mikey's BSA. The heavy front door on the right opened into a little tiled vestibule, where a second door, partly glazed with narrow strips of red and blue stained glass, hung permanently open, revealing the wide hallway, high ceilings, the bare floorboards and bicycles inside.

The big house echoed continually with noisy footsteps, feet thudding in a sudden rush down the stairs; there were no carpets, the pale floors were sanded and varnished, with loose floorboards and amazing amounts of dust. The walls throughout the house were painted brilliant white, and gradually acquired the smudge-marks of shoulders and boots as time passed. Music sounded behind various closed doors — Joni Mitchell, David Bowie, John Lennon, Loudon Wainwright III — as if each room housed a separate world.

When they first moved in, late September '72, it was very

different. It was impossible to tell how many people, or families, had been living there before them; it had been a rooming house of some kind, probably. The ancient patterned wallpaper was filthy, there was one outside toilet, no hot water, no bath. The house was freezing, the floorboards black with dirt. A smell seemed to emanate from the damp and grubby walls; a trace of the previous occupants that might have been food, or bodies, or smoke. Chas and Mikey and Connie moved in, originally, and Connie was pleased with the view from her curtainless window, the white porcelain sink in the corner of her room. She placed her bed in the middle of the room, so she wouldn't have to touch the icy dirty walls.

During the previous summer, Connie had suddenly found herself with nowhere to live. She'd finished school, she'd done her exams, and in the process she'd become extremely ill. Connie had hepatitis, and her sister Hilary decided she couldn't cope with looking after Connie and dealing with her new boyfriend, what with Connie being so very ill. So Connie had to move out of the tiny flat they shared, at least for the foreseeable future. Connie was seventeen, she'd just finished school.

Connie's mother Helen was in the process of moving back to the States, she was busy dismantling the house outside London where she'd lived since divorcing Connie's father, since Connie and Hilary had moved out. Against her will, powerless to contradict the doctor's orders, Connie went to stay with Helen for a couple of weeks, to be looked after. She found this fate impossible to accept. Connie didn't speak to her mother at all for the first three days. She didn't speak to anyone. It was more than she could bear, the prospect of sleeping under her mother's roof for more than a night or two, and feeling so ill, and knowing it would take a month or six weeks before she could function properly, and her mother going on and on about her life, what she was going to do next; Connie felt like she'd been run over by a truck. She was desperate: too ill to do anything except recline with a book, she knew she couldn't stay there.

Characteristically, the Powells saved her: they were going to Scotland for the month of August, Connie could have their cottage in Suffolk if she wanted it. Connie spoke to Ruby on the phone daily; Ruby was worried about her, worried about this situation with her mother; Ruby talked her parents into giving Connie the cottage, and eventually a set of instructions folded around one unmarked key arrived in the post.

Connie persuaded Helen to drive her down to the country, to leave her alone in the Powell's tiny cottage with a good supply of food, cigarettes, matches, coffee. The cottage lacked a telephone, a bath, the toilet was an Elsan in the shed at the bottom of the garden. Connie was without a car (she couldn't drive, anyway), and the cottage was two fields away from the nearest lane, a mile down the lane to the road, and five miles to the nearest town, where there were shops, a chemist, etc. There was a newsagent about two miles away, where one could buy bread and milk. There were a couple of old bikes, however, and Connie intended to cycle into the little market town, to buy food, and other necessities. She had no qualms, imagining such solitude would be undiluted bliss, after the time in her mother's house.

Upon departure, Helen put a half bottle of Smirnoff in the glove compartment, protection for the two-hour drive. Connie was trying hard to be friendly on the way down to Suffolk; she sat back in the front seat, watching green fields flashing past, trying to take her mother's mind off things. Connie knew she'd won. When they arrived, driving across the fields to the little house, surrounded by green hedgerows and blowing trees, Helen was devastated. This gesture of Connie's — implicitly stating: I'd rather be stranded, alone in the middle of nowhere without transport or a phone, than be ill in your house, submit to your ministrations, listen to you talk, — unquestionably marked the lowest ebb in their already lousy relations. In later years, Helen referred to this period as the time when she and Connie 'got divorced'.

Connie felt nothing but relief to see the beautiful little house again, but as Helen walked through its few rooms, her voice rising hysterically as she took note of every detail, every sign of difference, Connie shut down her responses.

'My God, they have gingham curtains on the windows, — you know and I'd have to have chintz. And look, she's got three knives,' Helen pointed to Mrs Powell's magnetic knife rack, the three knives neatly pointing upwards, 'and of course I'd have a drawer full. I would never know what I'd need, what I'd want, would I. Oh God. I never know what's enough, do I?'

'Don't over-react, Mum. They only come for weekends. I mean, it's not a proper *house*, you know.

'Still. This is what you like, isn't it —?'

'Mm,' Connie said, emotionless. 'I think it's nice.'

'But when I look around, I mean, is this it? This is it?'

'What do you mean?'

'Aren't you scared? I think you're insane. I think you've flipped. Aren't you scared? The idea of being here, all by yourself, in the middle of fucking fields, without a phone! Ill! Have you gone crazy?'

'I'll be OK. Really, it'll be OK.'

Connie was beginning to wonder when her mother would ever leave. Connie was hanging on to the bitter end, knowing it would be over soon, trying not to fight, not to respond, knowing Helen would have to go, soon, knowing she'd long since forcibly deprived her mother of the authority to forbid her to stay here, alone in the little house. Helen would leave, and then Connie would take possession of this heaven, this beautiful place. Helen raved on, tears in her eyes, she asked Connie to reconsider, but Connie was immune to such parental melodrama, she just let this hurricane run its course. And then Helen pulled herself together, she made herself a sandwich and a large bloody mary, and finally she got into her car and drove off. Connie put this painful scene out of her mind; she feared the extent of the damage she'd wrought, the pain she'd caused her mother, but it was compulsive. Connie felt she'd had no choice.

Connie wasn't alone long, only about three days, in fact. This was fortunate, since she really was too weak to cycle to the shops on a regular basis. She only did it once, and it wasn't any fun. Connie wrote a bunch of postcards, saying, come visit, I'm on my own, and her friends did, their impending arrivals announced by telegram, delivered (by bicycle) across the muddy fields.

Very quickly there was a semi-permanent household. The first to appear was a friend of Connie's from St Peter's, Dido Smith, and her baby, whose name was Clara, but who was called Baby, or Tiny, most of the time. Tiny was nine months old, and Dido, like Connie, was seventeen. Dido was inscrutable, a real oddball, with shiny straight black hair and dead white skin. She'd left school to have the baby, and found herself stuck in a little flat with her mother, trying to make some money doing graphic design and illustration work from home, and mostly just tied to this impossible child, her very own unimaginable consequence.

Then Hope Lewis came for a weekend, and while she was there, Chas and Mikey Stour showed up, unannounced; they swept in, two very tall young men climbing out of a beat-up little VW. They'd seen the Powells in Scotland, briefly; they'd heard Connie would be in the cottage, so they came to tea, and stayed. They were at a bit of a loose end, Mikey was getting ready to start art college in the autumn (he'd failed to get in to the Slade), and they were trying to find a house to buy in London, a house that the family trustees would approve. The Powell's country cottage proved the most congenial place to hang out while the contracts were exchanged, and all the legal business was taken care of.

The most important thing was the car, Chas's VW: it was this that made the summer possible. They would all pile into the back seat, Hope and Dido and Connie squashed together, with Tiny scrambling around in Dido's arms, the two tall boys in the front, and they'd plummet into town, The Mothers of Invention live in concert blasting away on the cassette player, very loud, with Chas and Mikey singing along in a semi-recitative, word perfect, their mouths exactly shaping the sounds of electric guitars, wow-wow pedals, without mistake. 'We are *not* groupies!' the girls would cry, in unison, from the back seat.

Once the Stours decided to stick around, so did Hope. Various crushes developed: Chas fell for Dido, and the baby, simultaneously; Connie fell for Mikey, in direct competition with Hope, and the ghost of Ruby, an almost forgotten presence in the house. Connie languished through the summer, too ill to take action, almost overcome with the intensity of her fantasies. In the end, nothing came of it, except at the end of August, when they were all leaving, the Stours invited her to share their house in Ladbroke Grove.

That summer Ruby was hitching around southern Italy with a friend from Holland Park. Connie dreamed about her once, very vividly: in the dream Ruby was sunburned, her skin glowing orange-red. She was walking with them, like a visitant; Connie and Hope and Mikey and Dido and Chas were walking together, along a path through broad fields, Chas was carrying Tiny in his arms, and Ruby was there beside them somehow, walking with them, and yet not part of the group. When they saw each other again in September, Ruby's skin had indeed changed colour, the effect of six weeks out of doors in baking sun; she was reddish-brown, like in the dream. Connie told her about it, and Ruby said, 'Yes, there were a couple of times that I visited you, in my mind. I would think of you all there, you and Mikey and everyone, I would picture you all in the cottage, I'd try to imagine what it was like.'

Other friends and acquaintance came and went, mostly staying one or two nights, throughout August. At one point eleven people were staying in the little house, which was bearable only because the weather was so hot, everyone could sit in the garden most of the day. In the morning, Connie would get up before everyone else, and she would walk across the dewy grass to the bench at the bottom of the garden; she'd sit in the early morning light, wrapped in one of Mrs Powell's shawls, reading, drinking china tea. Gradually people would surface; one morning Connie heard herself cry out, 'Do have some Lapsang!', and immediately caught herself in this moment of affectation, wondering what it was about. Caught in the act: who was she trying to imitate, who was she trying to impress? At this time, Connie used to tie up her hair in a loose knot, fixing it with a pencil or biro or small paintbrush shoved through; she wore layers of loose cotton dresses, always avoiding definition, eschewing the hard edge. (It was the following year that Connie cut her hair short, and never looked back.)

She was reading Dostoyevsky, *The Idiot, Brothers Karam, C & P.* Connie buried herself in these immense novels, so that she didn't have to think. One long Saturday afternoon Hope translated the chapter about taming the fox from *Le Petit Prince* for Connie, to show her what she meant about friendship. Dido and Tiny would periodically retire to their bedroom and have tantrums; Tiny would cry uncontrollably, and Dido would end up shrieking back, as if to drown her out, as if to say, I can scream too, listen! No one intervened, amazingly, no one went upstairs and rescued Dido; no one went upstairs and said, 'I'll look after the baby for a bit, why don't you have a cup of tea, or something.'

No one intervened, because no one felt they were in a position to make judgements on anyone else's behaviour. It was taken for granted, their detachment, and it was this that Hope found perplexing, Hope with her elaborate ethics, her sense of commitment to things. Hope seemed almost to believe that friends were responsible for each other (that's what the chapter about taming the fox was all about), Hope didn't think they should simply ignore each other's crises, overlook each other's cries for help, however obscured. Still, even Hope was more interested in 'helping' Mikey, than in giving Dido a hand.

Evidently Mikey needed help; he seemed to be dependent on a cough mixture that you could buy over the counter, a cough mixture containing morphine, among other things. Every time they drove into town, Mikey would go to the chemist, and buy a couple of bottles. Then he would down a whole bottle at once, and space out. One afternoon Chas and Dido and Tiny had gone for a long walk, with a picnic, and Mikey asked Connie if she'd like to accompany him into town, in the car. Connie was shocked: Mikey didn't have a driver's licence. Wouldn't Chas mind? Mikey wasn't bothered, he figured Chas wouldn't care, so they got into the car together, and drove to the chemist to pick up some more of the lethal mixture. On the way back Mikey told Connie he couldn't understand why people went to all the trouble of scoring dope, when you could buy this stuff legally. Connie didn't comment. Then Mikey said he thought the chemist knew precisely what he was up to, but he sold it to him anyway.

It was quite expensive, as cough medicines go. Mikey seemed wired and down on the way; he was smiling on the way back, describing the look on the chemist's face as he handed over the bottles. He said, 'You can't do it too often at the same place, because they do end up refusing to serve you, eventually. But in the country it's pretty easy, really. Too easy.' Connie said nothing. There was nothing to say.

While they were living in the cottage, Mikey made a series of site-specific artworks: using rat poison to burn a circle white as phosphorous into the field beside the river, outlining the walls in the living-room with invisible fluorescent paint that glowed pale green in the darkness. Sitting up late at night after everyone else had retired to bed, Mikey would explain to Connie how he never had a father because his father died, and then his mother thought she should be both father and mother to him, so he never had a mother either. He gave Connie his battered paperback copy of *Our Lady of the Flowers*, and she read it through one long afternoon, while Mikey did a drawing of her sitting in the sun outside the little house. He borrowed Dido's 2B pencil and her eraser and Stanley knife (unlike Mikey, she was making drawings every day), and he drew the house, the tiles on the roof and the smoking chimney and the little casement windows with the honeysuckle creeping around them and the big trees behind, and Connie, wearing Mrs Powell's big straw hat, a loose smock, her arms and neck bare, the little book in her hands. It was a perfect English pastoral scene. Mikey wrote at the bottom of his drawing: '*Connie reading Genet, August 1972.*'

When they were leaving, Mikey pinned the drawing to the wall above the fireplace, as a gift to the Powells. When Ruby saw it, she was annoyed: how dare Mikey stick his drawing on her wall? The overlap between family intimacy and sexual relations was intolerable. She took it down immediately, but

Mrs Powell put it away in a portfolio, she kept it carefully: Mikey's gift.

When they first moved into Ladbroke Grove, they would take baths when they went to visit a friend. It was pleasant, to undress in various houses, a funny kind of intimacy forced on all sorts of different relationships. Connie got used to saying, as she sat down at someone's kitchen table, 'Do you mind if I have a bath?' Within a few months, the builders came, to knock down walls, build a bathroom, a downstairs toilet, to strip the wallpaper and sand the floors, coating every wall with the soft brown of lining paper, installing radiators in every room. The house was unrecognisable.

Mikey's sister Jude went to jumble sales and church fêtes in the country and bought innumerable large plates in miscellaneous patterns, heaps of cutlery, a plethora of battered pots and pans. They found the big kitchen table in a junk shop in Kilburn, and the ancient gas cooker on the pavement outside someone's house; it was huge, in creamy enamel. An extraordinary variety of kitchen chairs appeared, to gradually loosen under the strain of a household of tall people constantly rocking on the back legs. They all collected ashtrays from bars and cafés, they stole salt shakers and pepper grinders, pint glasses, teaspoons, whatever was easy to take, producing each stolen item like a treasure salvaged from a hostile world.

The kitchen was at the back of the house; it was a large, long room, an irregular shape, made up of two smaller rooms knocked through, with a door leading to steps down to the back garden. Two old black and white TV sets sat one on the other on top of the fridge, facing the big table: one TV for sound, the larger one for vision. An incredibly worn sofa was placed at an angle beside the tiny tiled grate, while detritus of every kind collected on the little mantel shelf above it. There were ashtrays everywhere, mugs of cold Nescafé, a mess of old evening papers, *Time Out*, and a mountain of washing up that was terrible, completely overwhelming, in anticipation.

Five people lived in this house, at first: Chas, Mikey, and Jude Stour, Connie West, and Larry Geist, who was Chas's American friend from college. After about six months, Blot Watkins moved in, a woman Mikey'd known vaguely through friends at Sedgemoor. There was always something going on in the kitchen, some scene: friends would drop in, and sit around the table interminably. People endlessly came to stay; Iris came, on her way to India, and again later; friends came for a night, or a few weeks, depending.

The disorder was permanent: there was never any food in the house, never any quiet. Each one of the inhabitants had a record player in their room, each one had friends, lovers, whatever, constantly coming and going. When someone wanted a bath, a cry would go up: 'Is it all right if I have a bath?!' Mikey would come rushing down from the top floor, stairs shuddering gently under his feet, and negotiations would be entered into. Chas was the responsible one; he would calmly go downstairs and adjust the thermostat, to make sure there'd be enough hot water. The bathtub was six feet long. Connie was five foot ten and she could lie down completely flat in it, washing her hair. Chas and Mikey had insisted on this sarcophagus of a tub, which, like the kitchen counters and sink, was designed for their height. It was their home, they could have it exactly as they pleased.

Each person had a big room, and Chas had a tiny study as well. Mikey had the whole top floor. He got the builders to knock down all the walls up there, and then he installed a door on the stairs, a sloping door that opened upwards, like a trapdoor. There was no attempt to share food expenses fairly; whoever happened to be around would go out to the corner shop and bring back milk or butter or bread when they ran out. Connie ate bread and cheese, and Weetabix, and sometimes, for a treat, she would buy little Bird's Eye frozen chicken pies which you put in the oven for half an hour. Jude made leek and potato soup; Mikey always insisted on cutting up the leeks. He said it gave him such a thrill. Larry made eggs in his extraordinary way, beating them with a fork after they'd started frying. Blot didn't eat.

Larry had been a US Marine, he'd fought in Vietnam. He'd volunteered. This was incomprehensible to Connie, completely beyond her understanding. All the young Americans she knew were terrified of being sent to Vietnam, they were outraged by the war. Chas was very close to Larry, and when Connie asked him about it, Chas explained that in the context of Larry's liberal family, joining the Marines was the most outrageous, the most rebellious thing he could do. Still she couldn't imagine it. She took it for granted that Larry was against the war, now.

Then one night Larry told her about the time he drove the family car into the ocean. It was in California. Connie pictured a huge American station wagon, the kind with fake wood panels down the side, sinking into the wet sand as gigantic waves pounded into it. A beach at sunset, Larry drunk out of his mind, laughing, and the car slipping sideways in the water. This incident with the car stood in for any more detailed description of Larry's teenage years. She got the impression it was meant to convey how crazy Larry was, at seventeen, how wild he was, and that wildness somehow included joining the Marines. It wasn't until much later that Connie wondered if she had missed the point; maybe he'd been trying to kill himself, driving the car into the sea. Maybe he'd been trying to top himself, going off to war. It was the early sixties, anyway; it was another world. Now Larry was twenty-eight or twenty-nine, much older than everyone else. He wouldn't talk about the war.

By comparison to Mikey, or Chas, Larry came on like a real man. Chas loved him like a father. Connie slept with him sometimes. Mikey became obsessed with motorbikes with him; it was Larry who reminded him that BSA stands for British Small Arms, laughing. Mikey adored Larry's Americanism, it was like something out of a movie, the way he talked and joked. Larry took liberties, and Mikey let him; Larry was the only person in the world who called him Mike.

Chas told Connie, in confidence, that in Vietnam Larry had volunteered, over and over again, to carry out the most dangerous missions, parachuting alone into the jungle — to do what? Connie wondered. Chas wasn't sure. It wasn't very clear precisely what Larry had done — just the compulsive, suicidal risk-taking, the intensity of the danger and the solitude. Chas was obviously deeply impressed. He made Connie promise she'd never let on he'd told her about it. She was mystified, but she really didn't want to know more. She could forget about it most of the time when she was with Larry; anyway the whole point of the house, the implicit, unspoken foundation of this anti-family, was that no one ever criticised anyone else, ever.

They were orphans, figuratively speaking, the inhabitants of the house in Ladbroke Grove; Chas was twenty, Mikey nineteen, Connie turned eighteen just after they moved in. Jude was sixteen or so, and still at school in the country, boarding school, but she soon left, and came up to live in London. So it wasn't that surprising that Larry got to play father figure to the rest of them. Most of Connie's friends were still living with their parents; their laundry got done automatically, dinner appeared. It was a different world. Connie's parents weren't around; her father had moved to

Paris, her mother had remarried and gone back to the States. Connie went to the laundrette every other week; she mostly ate sugar and alcohol, at odd hours. Connie appreciated this good fortune; she was lucky, to be able to get so far away.

Once when she was out with people she didn't know very well, one of the men told Connie it sounded like she lived with a bunch of hippies. Connie was bemused, that didn't seem quite right. 'No,' she said. 'No, not hippies, more like artists, bohemians.' When she got in that night, late, Connie went up to the top floor, to visit, to say hello to Ruby, who was lying naked in bed with Mikey, their clothes scattered across the freezing floor. Recounting this incident, this question of social identity, Ruby objected, vehemently; she said *she* wouldn't mind being called a hippy. Ruby always evinced a great deal of respect for all that. She thought 'bohemian' sounded pretentious.

Talking with them, Connie's eyes fell on a beautiful drawing of an erect penis, come spurting out, on the wall beside the bed. It was drawn in white chalk on the old wallpaper, and to Connie it seemed both comic and transgressive, celebratory evidence of what she imagined to be sexual delight. She silently attributed the drawing to Ruby, her rapacious visual curiosity, her desire to take possession of all forbidden images. The penis was perfectly delineated, the tulip-like head, the sensitive mouth, the bulge of a vein traced along its length, and the come spurting was drawn like a loud noise in a cartoon, three quick strokes across the wall. Connie fondly pictured Ruby drawing the penis from life, so to say. It was the kind of thing she meant when she told the stranger they really weren't a bunch of hippies, exactly.

Larry wasn't a hippy at all; he was always trying to figure out a way to make money; he talked about opening a bar, in London; he'd say, 'The economy's fucked, but even when people haven't got any money, they still drink.' Like everyone else in the house, Larry drank a great deal.

One time, leaving the pub, Larry was driving Chas's VW and they were stopped by the police. Everyone in the car sat tight, quaking, watching in amazement as Larry was handed the breathalyser device (recently introduced), watching Larry cracking a joke as he blew into it. There was a moment of confusion, and then Larry was back in the driver's seat, saying, 'Do you think we've missed the movie?' They roared with delight. Driving away, Larry said he'd taken very short breaths, blowing from the top of his lungs, that he'd used two breaths to blow up the bag. Connie couldn't believe it; she'd seen him pour a glass of rum and a pint of Guinness down his throat, only a moment before; Larry was like a magician, relying on good luck, persistence of vision, wit, to get by.

Iris once asked Connie if Larry had a small penis. Connie was shocked rigid; it was true, he did have a small penis. Nevertheless she felt protective of him, of this apparent vulnerability; she felt she should not expose this man she slept with to derisory eyes. Connie said, 'No-o-o-o,' thoughtfully, as if to say, well, I wouldn't exactly call it *small*. Iris laughed out loud, she looked at Connie, and said, 'I just thought he was the kind of guy who might —.' Connie thought about it for a minute; she realised Larry did indeed live his life like a guy with a small penis. It was all bikes and cars and jokes and hard drinking, and a lot of male bonding, buddy stuff, a loud voice and stocky body. Larry was a guy with something to prove, and maybe also a guy who wanted to die, or to risk death at least. In any case, that old seductive cocktail, the weird mix of masochistic machismo and subterranean violence, permeated the atmosphere at Ladbroke Grove.

The girls in the house in Ladbroke Grove were not immune to this scene, they bought into the myth, trying hard to be one of the boys. They weren't deeply into women's liberation, then, but they were into David Bowie, and they found themselves virtually competing with the men they knew as to who could most archetypically live out (at least at the level of style) the lost cowboy, tough guy, James Dean routine. Under the influence of Bowie and Lou Reed, the ambiguity of femme boys and butch girls became *de rigueur*. Jude and Connie and Blot all had very short hair, the classic fifties cut, standing up on top, *en brosse*, with a duck's arse at the back. They wore men's clothes, with a difference, and aggressively picked men up at parties, dropping them without a qualm before breakfast: 'No, you don't understand,' they'd say. 'This is a one night stand, nothing more.' It was revenge, or something; it was boystown, or unleashed aggression, or a walk on the wild side, or liberation, or something. Mikey was allowed to be passive; Connie and Jude and Blot were allowed to pursue, to reject, to wield power over strangers. They slept with anybody, just to prove they could.

Back home, back at the ranch, they could laugh about it together, holding their victims in contempt, amused by the pathos of phone calls late at night, Jude or Connie calling out, 'If it's David, or Ed, or Paul, I'm not here!' They were protective of each other, in some strange approximation of sibling solidarity, and as a result there was almost an unwritten rule of the house: no sexual power games here. The broken hearts lived somewhere else, as if the household was sacrosanct, as if the incest taboo made sense. No one was supposed to hurt another's feelings here, no serious crush, no knife in the back. Like kids, together, Lost Boys, or Babes in the Wood, maybe, they were in cahoots, with some sort of unspoken agreement not to fall in love, not to take anything that happened between them too seriously.

Once Larry asked Connie to marry him. Not really, not in so many words, he didn't really ask her, but since it was the only proposal of any kind that she ever received, she cherished it fondly. What he said was, 'If I asked you to — if I asked you to stay with me, um . . . you wouldn't, would you? So there's no point in asking, right?' Connie was terribly surprised, moved, even flattered. 'Right,' she said, hugging him.

They first got together in the darkroom, in the basement. He was teaching her how to develop pictures, how to print. Larry kept telling jokes, making her laugh. Connie was always subject to this kind of verbal seduction; any time a clever man paid attention to her, she succumbed. But it was never a romance with Larry, more like friends who sometimes slept together. She used to get out of bed in the night, wrap herself in her thirties dressing-gown, and creep down to his bedroom to slip into bed with him. Sometimes someone else would have beat her to it, Jude, or later Blot. So much for the small penis argument.

Larry would offer Connie kleenex, to wipe up the come, after he made love to her. She would always refuse, as if she enjoyed lying there all wet and sticky. Larry seemed slightly disgusted, he'd say, 'Jesus, you're the only woman I've ever known who doesn't want to wipe herself off afterwards.' Connie would say, 'I like it,' thinking, this is sex, I'm supposed to like it, even this bit.

In the hierarchy of glamour that Connie still more or less subscribed to, Michael and Charles Stour were, so to speak, unassailable, right up there, on Mount Olympus, with Jude almost honorarily, due to her sibling proximity, close behind. Larry occupied his own unique position, based on his jokes, his cynicism, the cars, the motorbikes, as well as the absolutely foreign, frighteningly exotic quality of his past. Meanwhile Connie was Ruby's friend; she was implicitly accepted into this group, she always felt, at least partly on that basis. Ruby and Mikey were soulmates, and lovers.

Blot appeared out of nowhere and stayed. Blot was nobody,

she didn't pretend to any place in this scheme of things. She didn't subscribe to Connie's hierarchy; she was irreverent, even amused. Blot was little and skinny, with short hair, and bright dark eyes. Connie never held her in very high esteem, and she was surprised when Blot applied to do English and Anthropology at London University, and got in, and used to come home from college holding forth about structuralism and Lévi-Strauss. Connie found it hard to take Blot seriously, although she liked her well enough.

Connie never dared ask Larry directly about what he'd done in Vietnam. Or what had happened to him there. She was cowardly, she was fearful of disagreement or conflict, fearful of a violent refusal. The one time he mentioned it was when Iris was going on about the baby airlift, when the Americans were flying hundreds of babies out of Vietnam, to bring them to the States for adoption. Connie and Iris were wild with disapproval. Larry spoke out, for the first time. He said, 'You don't know anything, you know nothing. You don't know about these people, the Vietnamese, they just abandon their children by the side of the road. They just leave them to die. You don't know what you're talking about.' The two women were silent: finally Connie said she didn't want to argue with him.

Blot, however, wasn't scared of Larry, or Mikey, or Chas. She'd ask Mikey about the drugs he took, or the artworks he was making, totally oblivious to the invisible walls of fearful discretion that silenced everyone else. Mikey occupied an unquestioned position in the house, a role he exploited to the hilt. He was the creative genius, the artist; as a result, he mustn't be questioned, or pursued. No demands could be made on him, no invasions of his privacy, no comment made on his drug intake, his sudden disappearances, his apparent misery. It would have been unthinkable to offer comfort, even, unasked. Connie occasionally loaned him money, for this he was grateful.

In the house in Ladbroke Grove there was a certain kind of mutual ignorance, an overlooking of pain. Everyone was allowed to get on with whatever they were doing, without interruption or interrogation. No one made moral or political judgements on anyone else. No one made rescue attempts or even critical comments. They'd go to the movies together, or go looking for drugs, or a party, or sit around the kitchen listening to records and playing games, or snorting coke, but when you retired to your room, no one bothered you. Unless it was after midnight, when someone might come knocking on the door, asking for the simple comfort of physical contact.

Blot didn't think of Michael as some kind of genius, unapproachable. She wasn't impressed. So it wasn't very surprising when she ended up not only sleeping with Larry, occasionally, but also sleeping with Mikey. Connie was amazed, however, still putting Mikey on the old pedestal, the most desirable object, infinitely fascinating. Why would he be interested in Blot? She figured he wasn't, really; he'd just succumbed to Blot's insensitivity, he'd passively given in to her wishes without thinking. He didn't care.

One afternoon Connie and Jude were sitting in the garden at Ladbroke Grove, sitting in the sun, reading books and talking about Michael and Ruby. They expressed perplexity, commiserating over Mikey's seeming inability to come clean, to deliver the goods, talking about his emotional blocks, his necessary isolation. It was pathological, they agreed.

Connie said, 'The horrible truth is, I feel guilty about Mikey.'

'You *do*? Why?' Jude gasped.

'I don't know,' Connie said. 'I think — I remember how he opened his heart to me, you know, when we were fourteen or whatever we were. He offered me love — I mean, he said, I love you, *constantly*, it was amazing. No one's ever done that since! And I just rejected it, outright, absolutely. It was a real kick in the teeth — I mean, he was devastated, at the time. And I think, how horrible I was, and I wonder what difference it might have made, if I hadn't been so — cruel.'

'God, Connie, I had no idea,' Jude said.

'Well it was ages and ages ago, we were so young, but somehow remembering how young we were only seems to make it worse. What I did, I mean.'

'I don't know, Connie, I mean, Mikey's a mess, but I really don't think you should hold yourself responsible. I mean, really, not.'

'I was perfectly foul to him,' Connie stated.

'I know. But it happens to everybody — *everybody!* Everyone has had their heart broken. I have, *you* have.'

'Sure, but —'

Jude interrupted her. 'Everyone gets through it, sooner or later, and you survive, you know what I'm saying? Everyone's heart gets broken, usually when you're fifteen or something, or sometimes not until later, which is a disaster actually, because then you're really unprepared for it.'

'Mmm,' Connie said.

'Arguably it's better to go through it sooner — younger . . .'

'I guess you're right,' Connie said slowly, 'I never really thought of it that way, as something everyone goes through. I guess I was too involved with casting myself in the leading role, as they say.'

'I don't think that's so, Connie. To tell you the truth, I don't think you should castigate yourself for fucking Mikey over, and then immediately castigate yourself for *thinking* you fucked Mikey over totally!! Really, Con, you could let up for a second.'

Connie sensed Jude's impatience, her near irritation. All this stuff about Mikey was dodgy territory. She felt Jude resisting the myth, the idea that Mikey was so very exceptional, that he was too sensitive to bear a broken heart, or have a girlfriend, or be an ordinary person. Yet Connie knew Jude adored him, she just couldn't stomach the deification routine as perpetrated and perpetuated by people like Hope, or Connie, even. Simultaneously Connie felt relieved by Jude's words of wisdom, absolved of her responsibility for Mikey's dysfunction. What Jude said made sense, it happened to everyone — everyone. Still, the image of Mikey's vulnerability, shimmering beneath the cool façade, prevailed.

These were the conversations that took place in the house in Ladbroke Grove: amazing anecdotes, and true confessions. Sooner or later all the women told all the other women the story of their lives, to the last detail. None of the men did; they tended to talk about cars. No one *ever* talked about art.

The only one Blot didn't sleep with was Chas. Connie didn't sleep with Chas either. He was out of the running, somehow. He was too straight, too sensible, too hardworking. Connie and Blot and Jude were wild women, free as the wind. Chas wanted a proper relationship, not a sporadic series of one night stands. Chas wanted a girlfriend. Michael had one, apparently: Ruby. They were star-crossed lovers, they were made for each other, they were madly in love. They would fuck all day and all night, and then not see each other for a week or two. It was incomprehensible to everyone else. Connie was particularly confused, but she kept her mouth shut. She ignored it, overlooked it, like so much else that went on in the house in Ladbroke Grove. Both Mikey and Ruby cultivated detachment, masking vulnerability with an impenetrable glamour that only compounded their special isolation. In a sense, they remained on their pedestals, as if that built-in distance provided real protection. Ruby always seemed so enigmatic, so hypersensitive, Connie didn't feel she could simply ask her what she thought, or how she felt about things, like any other person. Connie was wary of Ruby's intense stare, deeply critical, Connie was scared of her sudden disappointment or irritation, her dark moods. It was so easy to hurt Ruby's feelings, inadvertently.

Much later Ruby told Connie she hadn't really enjoyed coming to Ladbroke Grove; she didn't like the way you never saw anyone alone there, she didn't like the scene. There were always a million people around the place, always people coming and going. Even when she and Mikey would go upstairs and close the trapdoor behind them, she didn't feel like she was really alone with him. Connie thought it was almost as if Mikey were using the house against her, the whole motorbike bit, Larry and all that, to make sure Ruby couldn't get through to him. As if he was hiding behind this barrage of drugs and people and constant, pointless activity, to protect himself against the intensity of his feelings, or her feelings. Ruby tried to see him outside the context of the house, his siblings, Connie, Blot, but it was hard to extract him from the scene. Ruby had no interest in riding around on the back of Mikey's motorbike. Maybe she wanted love, not some kind of pop song, some tacky movie image of excitement and romance. Mikey didn't know what he wanted, when it came to love.

Blot

It was some months after Michael had left London for New York that Connie told Ruby about Blot. This revelation was inadvertent. They were sitting together outside a pub. It was early spring, 1975, and both women were wearing thick woollen coats, scarves, gloves, sitting outside in the pale sun of spring, drinking halves of lager and eating crisps. Ruby spoke of Michael, the difficulties of going out with him, of knowing where you stood. Connie emphatically agreed.

'Yes,' she said, 'there's a way in which he really didn't seem to know what he was up to, like with Blot.'

Ruby paused, looking directly at Connie as if to bring her words into focus. 'How do you mean?' she said.

Connie was oblivious. 'Oh, I don't know, he was always so inscrutable, you know. I never felt I really understood most things he did.'

'But Blot?' Ruby asked.

'Yes, well, Blot. I never quite saw it, you know what I mean?'

'*What* about Blot?' Ruby asked, an edge of urgency entering her voice.

Connie misunderstood completely. 'I just meant them falling into bed together all the time. I didn't mean there was anything more to it than that, I mean, I'm not implying that there was anything serious going on or anything like that . . .'

Ruby was silent. Connie looked at her face, questioning. She took in how pale Ruby was, her wet lips pursed slightly, clear red against the white skin. Connie still didn't know what she'd done. She went on:

'It's just that he did rather plummet in my esteem, but maybe that was just some kind of loyalty to you, or maybe,' Connie laughed, 'maybe I was envious, who knows.'

Ruby remained silent. Connie said, 'And I never knew what you thought about it . . .'

'I didn't know.' Ruby spoke quietly.

Connie was shaken, she repeated Ruby's words: 'You didn't *know*?'

'No. I didn't know,' Ruby said.

'Jesus, so — what? So you just found out now, from *me*?'

'That's right,' Ruby said, smiling bitterly as she drank her beer. Connie felt panicked; she was in the wrong, she'd said something wrong, she'd hurt Ruby, she'd exposed Michael, she felt the swarm of self-accusation envelope her like a black cloud of stinging bees. There was no possibility of making good this offence, no way to undo it, to take back this poisonous gift. As always, she felt responsible, and therefore guilty, as if she, not Michael, had wronged Ruby.

'Ruby, I had no idea, I thought you knew. I took it for granted that you *knew*. I'm *so* sorry.'

Ruby paused before she spoke. 'So they slept together a lot?' She was very calm.

Connie ransacked her memory, hoping to come up with an answer that was truthful yet wouldn't simply compound Ruby's pain. 'No, not a lot,' she said. 'It's hard to say, really.'

'You said "all the time" before,' Ruby said.

'That was, you know, hyperbole, you know what I mean. I really don't know how often they . . .'

'But it was an established thing, I mean, it wasn't completely unusual, or surprising . . .' Ruby looked at the trees in the little square before them.

'I don't know,' Connie said. 'I never felt there was any serious attachment between them —'

'No,' Ruby said.

'I always felt it was sheer laziness on Michael's part, as if Blot just happened to be there.'

'Don't feel you have to try to make it better, Con.' Ruby said. 'He's in New York now anyway, I mean, it's not as if we're together, or something.'

'No.' Connie said. She was terrified of saying the wrong thing, she was at a loss, as if she had no idea what anyone knew about anything, as if anything could happen. She was relieved when they got up to go.

A couple of weeks later, when Connie saw Ruby again, Ruby made her position clear.

'You know all that about Michael and Blot, what you said . . .'

'Yes,' Connie said.

'It's really not that I mind about that, really, you know. What's painful is that he didn't tell me.'

'Yes.'

'That's what's painful: that he didn't tell me, you know. I didn't *know*.'

'Yes.' There was nothing more to be said.

One time Blot gave Connie a leopard skin jacket that she'd been given by a friend, who'd found it in a junk shop. It was ancient, and very soft, and rather worn, and very beautiful, and Connie loved it absolutely. There was something so straightforward about the way Blot gave it to her, as if she saw that Connie ought to have it, unquestionably. Connie was knocked sideways; she hadn't even dared covet the jacket, it was so desirable, so perfect. She wore it constantly, over black crêpe dresses, over her pale puce thirties suit, over jeans. The best black crêpe dress, of this period, was another gift, from Jude. It was very simple, quite long, and cut on the bias; it hung from two spaghetti strings that tied at the neck, leaving her shoulders and back bare. It was made by Ossie Clarke. It was stunning.

These treasures, gifts, the leopardskin jacket, the black crêpe dress, were compensatory, in a sense, since Connie was constantly lending Blot and Jude her clothes. She found it obscurely flattering, that other women wanted to wear her clothes. Connie never borrowed clothes, she was too insecure, driven by her sense of the crucial importance of idiosyncratic style. In a way, she felt sorry for Blot and Jude, wanting to wear her clothes, to look like her. As a result, they were pleased to offer up the only things she did want, though she never said, never would have asked for them, the black dress, the jacket.

This kind of constant exchange was symptomatic of the women's relations, this sympathetic identification, this lending and giving. Like the unacknowledged household taboo on criticism, they were living out what was probably best characterized as a hippy ideal: no one ever said no.

The summer of 1974 was the summer Connie referred to much later as the summer of cocaine. It was also the summer that Mikey had his first real show. He made a series of photographs, big glossy black and white prints, and no one saw them until the afternoon of the opening, when he put them on the walls of the alternative gallery space in the East End. The work consisted of photographs of himself seductively draped across a divan, wearing the black crêpe dress that Jude had given Connie, wearing the leopardskin jacket that Blot had given Connie, wearing Connie's black jet necklace, three rows of glittering black stones that barely encircled his neck. He wore makeup, in the photographs, and looked straight into the camera. It was very well done, this masquerade, it almost persuaded.

Connie's first thought was that Mikey must have come into her room while she was out, to find the clothes. She was surprised, or shocked, thinking of the transgression of privacy that this work represented. She imagined him looking through her wardrobe, going through her box of what she referred to as her jewels, her heaps of glass beads, diamanté brooches, her clip-on earrings. Sidestepping more complex and possibly threatening issues of sexuality or aesthetics, she wondered *when* he'd done it, precisely. She wondered when he'd stolen her clothes.

Connie remembered a time shortly after they'd moved into Ladbroke Grove, when Mikey came to her room holding two LPs, *Hunky Dory* and *Ziggy Stardust*, and he'd said, 'This is really amazing, you must listen to this.' It was November, or December, 1972. He left the records, and she put them on her record player, one after the other. She read the words on the inner sleeves, she looked hard at the pictures on the album covers, the girlish boy with his long hair falling forward, the peroxide queen in his silver spacesuit, she listened intently to the songs, and she was convinced, a convert, sudden and complete.

A few months later, under the influence of letters from Ruby, Ruby in voluntary exile on the West Coast, Ruby discovering the Women's Liberation Movement circa 1973, Connie bought a paperback copy of Kate Millet's *Sexual Politics*, and read it, and she was convinced; she thought, this explains everything, all my anger and all my misery. This explains *everything*, she thought.

The summer of '74 in June, Martin, her pal from college, turned Connie on to cocaine. He'd said, 'You must try this, it's really amazing.' He'd said, 'Have you got any money?' Connie always had some money. (Once she had a ten pound note pinned to the wall of her room, as a joke. It looked nice there, a kind of comic artwork, a little homage to Warhol. When she came home in the evening, it was gone, replaced by a piece of Kleenex with a pencil sketch of the Queen and the appropriately baroque design of banknotes, and a little caption: 'THINKS: WILL SHE NOTICE?' It was Mikey, of course.) That night Martin took her on the back of his motorbike to see his friend, the dealer, whose name, impressively, was Sly. He was a white boy, ex-public school, terribly good-looking and laid back. They bought a gram and a half of coke, for £30, and she rode home after midnight in the freezing wind, high as a kite, elated and excited and clear as ice. That was the beginning of the summer.

No one commented on Mikey's photographs, except to say they thought they were amazing, they were great. No one said, wow, but you're wearing Connie's clothes! Or, more accurately: you're wearing Connie's and Jude's and Blot's clothes. And Connie didn't ask Ruby what she thought of this dramatic self-presentation. She imagined it couldn't have been very easy for her. As usual everything remained unspoken, as if they could only go on together, as if they could only keep this house of fatherless children together, if they didn't talk about anything, if they pretended everything was perfectly understood.

That summer they would sit around the kitchen table for hours, Connie's grandmother's mirror flat on the table, lines laid out, razor blades gently licked, with the TV on, silent, the afternoon wrestling broadcast in fuzzy black and white, and Bowie's *Pinups* blasting away on the record player. Larry wasn't around, he was in the States, maybe that was one reason things got so out of hand. Chas didn't do drugs, he tried to ignore the endless sequence of indulgence, hangover, and time-consuming pursuit of dealers, a schedule that everyone else, Connie and Mikey and Jude and Blot, were allowing to shape their days. Ruby rose above it, as if she had better things to do. Jude ended up taking a plane to South America.

Iris was in London that summer, for a week or two, and she seemed right at home, sitting in the big kitchen in Ladbroke Grove writing her application to NYU, as the elaborate domestic scene unfolded around her, revolving as it did around cocaine, speed, dope and alcohol. It was like Connie had finally joined in, though of course she could never really catch up with Iris in this department.

Connie remembered: they were going to the movies one night, she and Iris, they were nineteen years old, and they were high on cocaine — that familiar, easy energy (speed), that wild smile, with the inevitable sour taste at the back of your throat, a taste Connie always associated with the rush of cocaine.

They were late for the movies, running up the long escalators in Piccadilly Circus station, smiling and jumping two steps at a time. Leaping up the escalator, Iris tripped, and fell, a great gash in her knee, where she'd hit the metal teeth of the escalator step. Blood was pouring down her tanned leg, dripping onto her pale pink suede platform sandals. Iris looked annoyed. Connie remembered they were in Piccadilly Circus: the all-night chemist in Piccadilly.

Iris wanted to get to the movie; Connie persuaded her. The pharmacist sat Iris down on a straight chair where ordinarily junkies waited for their prescriptions to be filled, and he crouched down and cleaned the rather dramatic wound. As he poured antiseptic down over her knee, he kept saying, 'I'm afraid this is going to hurt,' and Iris kept saying, 'It doesn't hurt. Can't feel it. Doesn't hurt.' Eventually her words sank in, and the chemist paused, looking up at her face. Connie thought, ninety per cent of the people he deals with are probably either in agony, or else they can't feel a thing.

They went to another movie in the end. It wasn't very good. Some years later in New York, Connie reminded Iris of this scene, and Iris said, 'Yes, I really should have had stitches; I should have gone to the hospital and got them to stitch it up. The scar is really ugly; you know which one it is . . .' Iris lifted her dress to show her the white shiny zigzag on her right knee.

'Edmund always used to complain bitterly about the scars on my legs,' Iris said. 'That one was the worst of the lot.' Connie was surprised; Iris always seemed so proud of her scars.

Some weeks after the escalator incident, on Carnival weekend, Connie finally took so much cocaine that she made herself really ill. It was then that she decided to stop; Connie saw the road ahead, the absurdly generous allowance her family provided; she saw she'd always be able to buy drugs, there was no limit to how much she could take. She saw herself sitting around, lazy, sad, and gloomy because nothing was any fun without coke. She saw long afternoons, longer evenings passed trying to get some drugs, so they could have some fun. She decided to stop, because the alternative was too grim. Anyway the summer vacation was over; it was almost time to go back to school.

In September, when Mikey announced that he was leaving, he was going to New York, to live, Connie was stunned. Mikey didn't think he'd be coming back, ever. He left a couple of weeks later. As they were standing on the doorstep, with everybody clamouring goodbye, Connie suddenly thought of something. 'Wait one minute!' she announced, and leaped up the stairs to her room, to return, moments later, clutching the leopardskin jacket in her hands.

'Here, Mikey, it's for you.'

'No, no — Connie, I couldn't!'

'No, you must. Blot gave it to me, and now I'm giving it to you.' Blot looked very happy, standing there with the others.

Michael slipped the jacket on, holding his cigarette between his teeth as his long arms slid down the satin-lined sleeves. He looked very pleased. Then he left for New York, wearing the jacket, carrying one small hard suitcase, which contained some clothes and a notebook or two. He'd destroyed most of his work in a bonfire in the garden over the weekend. Mikey vanished, virtually empty-handed, leaving almost nothing behind.

Nearly four years after Mikey's departure, in the spring of 1978, Connie talked her father into giving her the money to buy a flat in London. They talked long-distance, as always, on the phone. Her father was living in Rome, now, with a woman Connie liked better than the previous one. Somehow the transaction made economic sense (although this aspect was beyond her, outside of Connie's frame of reference), a decision was taken, and the family trust duly disgorged a lump of capital, to be turned into a place to live.

Connie bought a three-storey flat above shops on Kilburn High Road; all day long the 28 and the 31 bus rumbled past, making the sash windows shudder, loose in their frames. The building was tall, and narrow, made of brick darkened by a century of London air. Her flat had lots of rooms, and the top floor had been knocked through, to make one long room, reminiscent of Michael's space in the house at Ladbroke

Grove. (That house had been sold two years before, as the Stour siblings and their friends went their separate ways.) Connie's anxiety of ownership was overwhelming; she took possession of the smallest room in the house, a room just big enough for a bed and nothing else, and dedicated the big studio room on the top floor to communal projects and entertainments. The house would be a feminist collective, no one would pay rent, they would split the bills equally, they would work together and play together, without conflict or rivalry. The fact that Connie owned the house would be obscured, obliterated to the point where everyone would forget this built-in inequality. Vron, Connie's friend from college, moved in immediately, and Ruby was due to move in also, as soon as she finished art school. In the meantime, while there was still chaos, builders, no furniture, blank white walls, bare floors, before any pictures went up, before the house settled into any kind of routine, various people came to stay. One of these visitors was Michael.

Michael had figured out his visa status, finally, and therefore he could risk a visit home. He moved into the empty room that would eventually belong to Ruby, his notebooks and papers spread across the dusty floorboards, next to the narrow mattress on the floor. The phone wasn't yet connected, so everyone was constantly coming and going, crossing the street to use the payphone in the Indian shop, trying to get things done. Most of the time the doorbell didn't work; friends would shriek up, keys would be thrown out the window. During this period Connie veered between despair and elation without warning, yet it was a real pleasure for her to see Michael again.

Then Michael's sister Jude and her sidekick Candy appeared; Jude had been living in Los Angeles for a year, she and Candy were a team, inseparable. They were very skinny and very funny, like something out of a thirties movie, fast-talking, speedy, surging with electricity. They arrived, surrounding themselves in a force-field marked by endless cigarettes, mini-performances, shrieks of laughter; they unpacked enormous shocking pink zipper bags, scattering innumerable outfits throughout the house, then they rushed out to buy Krazy Kolors, and took over the kitchen to dye their hair. Candy ended up with white blonde spikes with pink highlights, Jude bright purple and blue. Watching their double act in the kitchen, Connie felt about a hundred years old. At twenty-three, she was past the point of no return. When Jude turned to her, to say, 'And you? why not!' Connie ruefully suggested that it might be just a little too too mutton dressed as lamb, no?

Suddenly the empty flat was full of people, Jude, Candy, and their various hangers-on (some famous, some merely adoring). It was a real scene. Michael was around a lot; occasionally even Ruby showed up, though generally speaking she avoided scenes like this. There was constant activity, echoing feet on the stairs, people in every room, and Connie recognised the atmosphere: it was just like Ladbroke Grove. No one ever had to be alone with anyone else, no one ever had to be alone. There was always somebody to hang out with, always someone to take the edge off everything.

The first thing Michael did was buy a television. It was tiny: the TV was about the size of a book, and the black and white screen on the side was the size of a large postage stamp. He also bought a book-sized Sony cassette player, which he plugged into the stereo system, making his little black box fill the big speakers with noise. The tiny TV was always on. Michael borrowed someone's super–8 camera, and shot a bunch of stuff; he went to a gun shop in Praed Street and shot the salesman showing him a Kalashnikov, he shot people in the street out the window.

Connie remembered watching a western once on Michael's

tiny TV. Michael brought a little heap of books from the not yet unpacked boxes in the living room, he piled them up on the kitchen table (so the screen would be more or less at eye level), and as they ate lunch one afternoon, eggs and toast and bacon, Connie and Michael were completely gripped by a John Ford movie, watching almost imperceptible figures gallop across Monument Valley. Connie saw it as a demonstration of the fascination of narrative; for Michael, it was mere delight in the latest technology, despite the almost indecipherable image.

The Red Brigades had kidnapped Aldo Moro; Joe Strummer appeared at a Rock against Racism free concert wearing a T-shirt with the words BRIGATE ROSSE blazoned across his chest; Michael came straight back and made a stencil, dug a black T-shirt out of his bag, and produced his own BRIGATE ROSSE T-shirt, using thick red paint. He wore it everywhere, unwittingly managing to upset the Italian owners of the Blue Sky, the cafe that Ruby frequented in Westbourne Grove. In May, Moro's body was found in the trunk of a car, exactly half-way between the central offices of the Italian Communist Party and the central offices of the Christian Democrats. Late one night, Connie expounded her various theories of terrorism, terrorism as political action displaced, political action at the level of representation, only, as they sat around the kitchen table drinking whisky and beer, just like old times.

One morning Connie came downstairs to find the National Front monogram written on the white painted wall beside her front door. She immediately rushed back upstairs, to grab a magic marker, and reappearing, she added an R and drew a horizontal line, transforming the fascist initials into the sign of the RAF. Connie didn't really support these groups, the Red Army Fraktion, the Brigate Rosse, Baader Meinhof, but they were undoubtedly interesting. In this context, punk was understood as a form of 'cultural terrorism', and the intensity and inverted glamour of punk almost served as a kind of validation of terrorism itself. At the time, the symbolic obliteration of the letters NF by the letters RAF was a case of extremes meeting, virtually cancelling each other out. When Connie saw RAF initials scrawled over the escalator walls in the underground, or on the advertisement hoardings by the bus stop, she could have no idea whether this was written by RAF 'supporters' (she pictured ruthless men and women, kitted out in chains and leather), or by other well-meaning types like her, trying to undo the much more prevalent NF graffitti. She figured most people didn't know what the initials RAF stood for anyway. This gesture seemed a measure of confusion, yet she felt this confusion, this conflict, was preferable to the fascist certainties of the National Front.

When Michael went back to New York in June, he made a series of works concerning the media representation of terrorist actions. Then he became a junky, and Connie went into reverse. Ruby and Mikey finally gave up, again, after a disastrous two weeks together in a cheap hotel in New York (*very* Sid and Nancy, Connie said). Connie stopped going to the States, and Mikey didn't come to London. In the end it was another five years before their paths crossed, before Connie laid eyes on Mikey again.

Triangulation City

After lunch, Connie phoned Michael from Iris's flat; she said, 'Listen, Michael, I want to buy that painting, you know the one with the thermometer, have you thought about what you'd be willing to accept for it?'

He said, 'I really want you to have it, Con, so why don't you tell me what you can afford.'

Connie said, 'God I don't know, Michael. I wish you'd say, I mean, I don't want to make you do anything you don't want to.'

Iris was sitting on the other sofa, obsessively filing her nails. Iris's living room was dominated by two long orange sofas, at right angles to each other, an arrangement that allowed two people to lounge unobstructed. Iris always used to bite her nails, but these days she tried to file them instead. Connie went on talking into the white phone, as Iris stared at her fingers.

Connie said to Michael, 'I haven't really thought it through very clearly, because in theory I can't afford anything at all! But I'm getting paid five hundred dollars — for this gig I'm doing tonight. And I think the minimum amount that would be fair to offer you is five hundred dollars. I mean, I know very well you'd get much more for it, in any other circumstances. So I don't know what to think.'

He said, 'No, I think five hundred, actually that's what I was thinking, I was thinking five hundred would be fine.'

Connie said, 'Really, you're sure? You're sure you're happy with that? I don't want to feel —'

He said, 'No, it's fine, it's really OK.'

Connie said, 'Really? I'm so pleased, I can't tell you.'

Michael said, 'You're leaving tomorrow?'

'Yes,' Connie said, 'at dawn. But I'm at Iris's now, which isn't that far.' Connie looked out of the long window; she saw tiny bits of snow swirling around in the thick light.

'You're at Iris's,' Michael said slowly. It seemed as if he was remembering who that was.

'Yes,' Connie said.

Michael said, 'That's not so far, why don't you come by? I can wrap it up for you and you can take it away with you when you go tomorrow.'

'Great,' Connie said. 'Fantastic. What if I come by around five, how does that sound?'

He said, 'Yes that's great.'

Then she said, 'Hang on a sec, Iris wants a word with you.'

Iris had been gesturing at Connie, her face registering a series of indecipherable reactions to what Connie was saying to Michael. Anticipating nothing, Connie handed over the phone, turning back to the window as Iris said, 'Hi, Michael. How are you?'

Connie couldn't hear his side of the conversation, only Iris's low voice, her carefully punctuated words. Connie sat there, looking out at the snow falling, as they spoke. Iris went on talking, and Connie's jaw literally dropped, as she heard Iris say, 'I suppose you can't have forgotten that you owe me five hundred dollars.'

Connie suddenly remembered; it came back to her in a horrible flash, like a blow. It was true, Iris had lent Michael five hundred dollars, back when they were both into heroin, she'd loaned him the money, five hundred dollars, knowing very well he needed the money for drugs. They'd been in cahoots, in those days, outsiders together, all that. Iris knew he was desperate, then. Iris knew he'd use it to buy junk, or to pay for junk he'd already used.

Then Connie remembered Iris telling her, as Michael became more successful as an artist, how she felt he owed her a drawing, at least, in recompense. Connie remembered Iris saying this a number of times, over the years. Connie thought of her painting, the painting she was buying from Michael.

Then she heard Iris say, 'Well you know it's *such* a long time ago, how many years? Six, or seven years . . .'

For an instant Connie's heart leapt, she thought Iris was going to say, forget it, let's forget it. Connie really thought she was about to say, it was ages ago, we were crazed drug fiends, now we're not (thank God), so don't worry about it.

Instead Iris went on, 'You know five hundred dollars was worth a lot more then than it is now.'

Silence. Connie was reeling; she couldn't believe it, she was stunned.

Iris said, 'Well, a drawing, perhaps.'

Again there was silence, as Michael spoke.

Then Iris said, 'And the interest, that really must be quite a substantial amount.'

Silence.

'Well it could be double, it could have doubled the amount, over six or seven years,' she said.

Silence.

'Maybe it's eight years, I don't remember,' Iris said.

Silence.

Iris said, 'No, I don't know how to calculate the interest, but I could make a couple of phone calls, I know people who do, who would know.'

More silence.

Connie was in shock, partly because of what Iris always used to call cognitive dissonance, the appalling clash between Michael's extraordinary generosity to Connie, almost giving this painting away, and Iris's lack of generosity to him. As if one utterly negated the other. Connie's careful transaction seemed in the process of being transformed into something else entirely, something ugly and mean. Connie found herself thinking of Iris's money; she had tons of money, more than enough for the rest of her life, trusted up in various forms; *trustus americanus* as William's friend Alexander used to say, like some kind of living dinosaur of the ruling class. Then she heard Iris saying, 'So you're willing to have Connie simply write the cheque to me.'

Connie froze. Triangulation city, Connie thought, as she turned to Iris, saying, 'I want to speak to Michael.' Iris gave her a look as she passed the phone across.

Connie took a breath and then she spoke into the receiver. 'Michael, hi. Listen, are you sure about this?'

He said, 'Why, you think I shouldn't?'

Connie said, 'That's right.'

He said, 'What, you think because Iris has so much money she won't miss the odd five hundred dollars, whereas I . . .'

'Precisely.' Connie said. She was speaking in code; she felt very close to Michael, very passionate about him, as if plunged by this accident into an unanticipated intimacy.

Michael paused for a moment. Then he said, 'I know what you mean.'

Connie said, 'Also the painting . . . I'm just not sure what to do.' She was distressed to think that she, Connie, would end up with the painting, and Iris would end up with the money, and Michael would have nothing whatsoever.

Michael said, 'But you want the painting.'

Connie said, 'Yes. Yes, very much.'

Michael said, 'Well, I think it's OK, I think it's probably the right thing to do. I mean, it's OK with me.'

'I really don't know,' Connie said. Iris's spidery hand was waving, wanting to get back on the line. Connie handed her the phone.

'Hi,' she said. 'So if Connie gives me the money, then —'

Michael spoke.

'But that's not it, Michael,' Connie heard Iris say. 'Of course I want the five hundred dollars, but I also think you owe me at least a drawing as well. To cover the interest.'

Connie was horrified. She got up and went into the bathroom, closing the door behind her. Connie felt she couldn't listen to any more of this conversation. She sat on the toilet and pissed, holding her face in her hands, thinking fast, and almost immediately she came to a decision: Connie decided she wasn't going to play. She wouldn't do it. Her transaction was with Mikey, with specific reference to their own shared past. She would not let Iris's poisonous history with him interrupt or obstruct this seemingly straightforward exchange.

Connie returned to the big room, and she said to Iris, 'I want to speak to Michael.' Again Iris passed her the phone.

Connie said, 'Michael, I'm not going to do this.'

He said, 'What?'

Connie said, 'I'm not going to write a cheque to Iris.'

Looking up, Connie saw Iris there, reclining on the other orange sofa, looking perplexed and furious.

Michael said, 'Oh. So what happens next?'

Connie said, 'Look, it's perfectly clear, you can do whatever you please with the money, you can throw it away, or give it to Iris, or put it in the bank. You can endorse the cheque to Iris right away, just give it straight to her. But that's between you and her. I'm not interested in that, it's none of my business. I'm just buying this picture from you. That's it.'

'I suppose you don't want to talk about it, with Iris there,' Michael said.

Connie said, 'I'm not going to write a cheque to Iris. You can. I won't.'

Michael said, 'It's OK Connie. Don't worry about it.'

Iris was livid. Michael said to Connie, 'Let me speak to her again.' As Connie passed her the phone, Iris looked fiercely at her, saying in a terribly calm voice, '*Why* are you doing this?' Connie said nothing, cowardly.

Michael talked to Iris for a while. Then Connie heard her say, 'So when is Connie coming over, about five? OK. I'll come too, and you can give it to me then. Fine. See you later.'

Connie's heart sank, again. That was it, she'd been set up again. Connie wasn't pleased. Indeed, as she described it later to Ruby, she was ready to strangle Iris, and yet there she was, stuck, with no place to go, no retreat, except maybe a coffee shop, no alternative but to hit the street in the snow. At the time that didn't seem to be an option. A familiar paralysis crept over her, an unutterable passivity in the face of emotional distress. Now Iris was intending to accompany her to Michael's, so Connie's delicate, loving exchange scene, and Iris's ancient revenge would be all mixed up and mingled together. Drug money, fuck that, Connie thought.

Hanging up the phone, Iris said, 'What *is* all this about?'

Connie looked away, saying, 'I'm sorry, really, it's just I can't do it, I won't.'

'Jesus Connie,' Iris said. 'You *know* I've been waiting years to be paid back, you *know* if you give this money to Michael I'll never see it. What is this about? What is the problem?'

Connie would have liked to make her position clear, but

she was scared of Iris, of her anger. In the account she gave Ruby, later, Connie was forced to recognise how she'd always been frightened of Iris, of her temper tantrums, or the possibility of a real fight. It was really quite pathetic, how familiar this scene was.

Finally Connie said, 'This is what I think. What I think is, people who lend money to junkies, that money's *gone*, it's lost, it's lost and gone forever, water under the bridge. It's a foolish thing to do, ever, and having been so foolish, you're unbelievably lucky if you ever see any part of that money again.'

Iris let out a sigh of impatience.

Connie went on talking. 'What I think is, it's a write-off. That's it. It's like, you have to recognise, later, how lending money in those kind of circumstances is really just like giving it away.'

'I'm not sure I agree,' Iris said.

Connie said, 'Look, I've lent money to friends in the past, various different people, in different circumstances, you know, and sometimes they gave it back to me, and other times they didn't. And after a while I developed a rule, a basic rule, which is, never lend money to anybody unless you're perfectly willing to never see it again. I mean, of course, you'd rather see it again, you hope to get it back, but fundamentally you feel you won't be shattered if you don't. Otherwise it just ruins the friendship. Which it probably does anyway, actually.'

'I can't say I was ever really *friends* with Michael,' Iris said.

'No,' Connie said. 'I was.'

Iris said nothing. Connie went on, compulsively expounding her position. 'It's just that, I think, if that's even remotely a principle of lending money to friends — that one ought to think of it virtually as a gift, that it's best to think of it that way, something you don't really expect to get back — then lending money to a fucking junky, that's all the more reason to kiss it goodbye.'

'Maybe,' Iris said, 'but that's not the situation. I mean, Michael's got the money now, you're giving it to him this afternoon.'

Connie thought for a minute. 'Still, I don't know,' she said, 'I just think — this is my transaction with Michael, and that's yours, and I don't want them mixed up like this.'

'What, you don't want yours tainted with my seedy past?' Iris said.

Connie said, 'I don't know if that's it.'

Iris said, 'But you *know* he'll never give me the money once he's got it. I don't understand, why do you want to help him rip me off? You're my friend, why can't you just write the cheque to *me*?'

Connie said, 'I don't know why, exactly. I know I don't want to.'

'I *don't* understand.' Iris was beginning to look blank, like she was cutting out. She seemed terribly hurt, as well as totally exasperated.

Connie's body was rigid with anxiety; she hated this, being so angry, making Iris so angry. She couldn't stop it.

Connie said, 'You see, I think this situation is absurd. It's completely crazed. You asking for this money, after all these years, and then asking for interest on top of that — it's breathtaking. I find it hard to believe.'

'I don't know what you mean,' Iris said. 'I've always wanted one of Michael's drawings, you know that.'

It was an impasse, complete deadlock. They both felt betrayed, yet they went on, masking their anger in apparently rational justifications, elaborate expositions of their differing positions, until finally Connie said she didn't want to talk about it any more. She said she'd made up her mind, there was nothing more to say. Iris looked petulant and bemused, her frustration dulled by unhappiness. She got up and walked across the room.

Again Iris vanished into her tiny kitchen and brought back huge bowls of strong coffee for both of them. Connie felt strung out, very tense and weary, and the coffee made her feel sleepy and jumpy at the same time. And then they changed the subject: they paused, briefly, sitting silently together, drinking coffee, bright specks of snow blowing around in the darkness outside the window. Then Iris, astonishingly, got out some political flyers and leaflets to show Connie. It was very graceful, or gracious, the way she turned their attention to another topic. She was working for a Latin American support group, as a volunteer, and she began a long, elaborate account of her work with the Guatemalans, incorporating a number of anecdotes starring people Connie didn't know. Connie listened, asking the occasional question, feeling drained. She was filled with dread at the thought of the rest of the day; to Michael's with Iris, quel nightmare, then to Catherine's for takeout, and then to Dia for her gig. From the vantage point of Iris's sofa at four in the afternoon, the evening seemed almost beyond her.

Highgate

No cemetery near London can boast so many natural beauties. The irregularity of the ground, rising in terraces, the winding paths leading through long avenues of cool shrubbery and marble monuments, and the groups of majestic trees casting broad shadows below, contribute many natural charms to this solemn region. In the genial summer time, when the birds are singing blithely in their leafy recesses, and the well-cared-for graves are dazzling with the varied hues of beautiful flowers, there is a holy loveliness upon this place of death, as if the kind angels hovered about it, and quickened fair Nature with their presence, in love for the good souls whose tenantless bodies repose there.

William Justyne, *Guide to Highgate Cemetery*, 1865

After the dream, after analysing the dream, the dream about digging things up, Connie suddenly remembered where they'd first met, so many years ago. Old emotions never die, they just get buried, she thought. It was at Highgate Cemetery, when she was fourteen. When you uncover the grave, the site of that burial, the old feeling, half-decomposed, leaps out at you, grabs you by the throat, alive and kicking. Connie was struck by the irony of it: she'd met Michael for the first time in Highgate Cemetery, on a Sunday afternoon in 1969. This wasn't true, quite; it wasn't absolutely the first time. Hope Lewis brought him round to Connie's house a couple of weeks before that, they'd sat on the enormous sofa in her mother's living-room and talked. Connie remembered Hope's friends from the country were there, those two posey girls, swinging their long hair as they turned their heads, letting it fall forward and then hurling it back. They were all crazy about Mikey, it was more than a little ridiculous.

Iris was in town, just passing through as usual, on her way somewhere. She was there too, that afternoon, sitting on Connie's mother's yellow ochre carpet, smoking cigarettes and telling stories, Connie's outlandish friend from Chicago.

And then Connie remembered they'd also seen each other the night before they went to Highgate, she and Michael, or two nights before, Friday, at a party somewhere in North London. Still, that was where they met, properly, where they spent the afternoon together. That was where she and Michael fell in love, almost, in a graveyard, in Highgate Cemetery. She hadn't thought of it for years, the afternoon they spent trailing around the vast overgrown necropolis, Highgate, in the old days, when they still let you in.

It was a Sunday, in May or June, probably. Connie couldn't put the different parts of memories together, she couldn't figure out the dates. Maybe it was insignificant, May or June, but it seemed important to her, what kind of weather it was, how much her memory may have intensified what was possibly March or April weather, the sun of early spring, giving it an imaginary warmth, a deeper shadow.

Reconstruction: Michael had just been thrown out of

school. She didn't know that then. And she was still in school, of course, still going to school every day. It was a weekend. It was just after the Easter holiday, so it was late April, in fact. They'd met at her house, briefly, and then they'd seen each other, literally, at a party two nights before. Ruby had been at that party; Connie remembered Ruby and Louis, their arms draped around each other. She remembered dancing alone, and Michael leaning up against a wall, smoking cigarettes and watching. She was fourteen, he was fifteen. Connie thought it must have been late April, or early May at the latest.

Highgate Cemetery seems limitless. It spreads out across a steep hill in North London, and on a clear day it affords, from certain positions, an extraordinary view of the city below. Landmarks make sense of the vast scene: in the east, the clutter of skyscrapers that signifies the City, framing the dome of St Paul's; to the west, Battersea Power Station, massive, with glimpses of the silvery river snaking between them; the Post Office Tower, sticking up, like a strange relic of 1960s optimism; and in the distance, the hills gently rising again south of the river. Sometimes one can make out the two great television broadcasting towers on these hills, at Crystal Palace, standing like enormous beacons, surrounded at their feet by the undifferentiated and indifferent little houses of the South London bourgeoisie.

The view twenty years ago was very similar, except the buildings in the City weren't quite so high. The cemetery is divided into two parts, and most people tend to visit the east side, where Karl Marx is buried. In 1969, the east side seemed less intriguing, partly because it was still in use, and therefore maintained much more like an ordinary cemetery. It was very simple to walk in to take a look at the Marx tomb, not far from the entrance, and then cross the narrow street, to penetrate the west. While the east side is full of Victorian monuments and funerary sculpture, it lacks the luxuriant undergrowth, the crazy brambles and wild roses and ivy and holly and wild flowers, the proliferation of trees and saplings; all that was kept back, or down, more or less. The west side, by contrast, had been closed to further burials for some years, and was almost entirely given over to wilderness.

White stone statues of mournful angels stood overwhelmed by ivy, or lay broken, almost invisible in the excess of patterned green leaves. Obelisks stood crooked, leaning towards a little mausoleum, a ten-foot pyramid or tiny temple. Flat Victorian gravestones presented a text picked out in yellow lichen, and this disorder (for no pattern was decipherable) was like an illustration of Victorianism, or Empire: the grandiosity, sentimentality, the rapacious appropriation of images from elsewhere, and of course, the inevitable decline into ruin. These expensive, ostentatious monuments were broken now, cracked and damaged by the wrack of time. Huge slabs of stone were split, graves had been robbed, broken into with fires lit to crack the stone, pickaxes to lift the broken pieces. The cemetery represented the relentless passage of time: a statue fallen as a result of a tree's enormous root pushing slowly through the earth, a tombstone crazed by frost, or covered in ivy, a vault opened by thieves; it seemed part of a natural process of disintegration.

Natural decadence, Connie thought; it was a hippy ideal. There were birds and some butterflies at Highgate, she remembered, wild flowers. It was like a strange kind of nature conservancy, easy to imagine moonlit foxes running between the rows of gravestones while leaning angels stood over them, their carved faces blurred and worn with a century of weather, an expression of sorrow in their stance, pale hands clasped together in supplication.

It was strange to remember that time. It was much more like a *fin de siècle* than things are now, Connie thought, with a real delight in decay, in loss, in a sense of evanescent grandeur. She remembered buying black lipstick at Way In, made by a company called Your Mother Wouldn't Like It. Connie aspired to the profoundly unhealthy, ecstatic look of Pre-Raphaelite paintings, or Biba posters. It was evocative, blurred around the edges, visionary. It was a drug culture, certainly, and that aesthetic, that experience seemed to bleed through the usually impermeable walls between the risky edges and the mainstream, tainting even schoolgirls with an opium sheen.

Connie was fourteen; unlike most of her friends, she didn't do acid, she didn't do dope. She didn't even smoke cigarettes. She presented herself as if she took it for granted that if it was cool to do these things, it was even cooler to feel free to choose not to. The image was of some kind of freewheeling Victorian maiden, pure in mind and body, wild in spirit, and she felt she could get away with it only by perfectly approximating the look. Tuberculosis and Twiggy merged in her fantasy of an ideal body. Connie read Swinburne, she loved Burne Jones and Rossetti, she lingered lovingly over the word phthisis. 'Her phthisic hands', she read, in Thomas Wolfe, and wished for paler skin.

Connie wore 1930s chiffon tea dresses that came to her ankles, or velvet, deep red, or white satin, her 'wedding dress'. She wore narrow black crêpe Ossie Clarke trousers tucked into long black Annello and Davide boots, with a very tight long black crêpe Ossie Clarke jacket that had forty tiny buttons down the side, an outfit she referred to as her 'sadist's costume'. Connie never wore a bra. At school she wore minidresses from Biba, with long tight sleeves, puffed at the shoulder, and pointy cuffs covering half the hand, almost Edwardian, ending seven inches above the knee. Outside school, Connie was in costume most of the time, and most of the time she was playing a part. In her long dress, that Sunday afternoon, she was very good at soulful wafting down the overgrown paths, trailing aimlessly through the graves, as if lost in solitary reverie.

Michael and Connie went to Highgate that day with a bunch of people; like so many adolescent encounters, there was a certain safety in numbers. Connie remembered Emma Thomson, a skinny little person who acted severely spooked almost as soon as they arrived, when Connie pointed out a gravestone bearing her name. Emma studied the text, which praised this long dead namesake, a mother of fourteen, with an anxious expression on her thin white face. This kind of coincidence was inviting to dwell on, as if it might mean something terribly profound, a symmetry, a mirroring of death and life. Connie went in for this kind of mystical stuff too, they'd all read *Der Steppenwolf*, but she thought Emma was over-doing it. She remembered Bella and Paul were there also, the one really solid couple in the gang, calmly connubial amidst the tempestuous heartbreak and longing that surrounded them, very nice, very kind, and a little dull.

That's what they called themselves, this group, 'the gang'. It was an amorphous entity of twenty or thirty kids, from the public schools of London, and the exemplary comprehensive, Holland Park; an indeterminate group which met at the weekends on the common ground of North Kensington and Notting Hill Gate. (Michael Stour came from outside, from boarding school: he wasn't part of the gang.) Most Saturdays, Connie would go and hang out at Notting Hill tube station, to meet the gang, exchange information on gatherings, where they were going for tea, whose house they'd be allowed to invade, which parties they were planning to gatecrash that night.

In retrospect Connie found it hard to believe that she'd spent hours standing around a dark underground station wearing a 1930s chiffon dress for fun, waiting for something to happen, hoping someone she knew would show up, some group would materialise. Occasionally they'd repair to the Caprini to drink coffee at formica tables, just like in the 1950s. Or they'd go to Kensington Gardens to play on the swings. Sitting at the dark little tables in the back of the Caprini, dealing was the topic that pervaded the boys' conversation, where, when, how: 'You should have been there, man, it was amazing . . .' Hashish and acid; Connie always found it terribly tedious, all that.

The leader of the party on this expedition to Highgate was Dominic Vogler. A wild man (of fifteen), and a poet, Dominic was totally obsessed by Tyrannosaurus Rex. T.Rex were his only study, his only joy. He invented a rhyme: 'Dom-in-ic/ Is mentally sick!', which he would chant while waiting for the underground, hoping to shock the other passengers. He had very long dark hair sticking out on all sides of his very pale, greeny-grey face, and huge bulging eyes which he stared and rolled to great effect. He was in the process of being expelled from school; hashish was his drug of choice.

Connie couldn't really see what was so great about T.Rex, she liked them all right but it wasn't like the best thing ever. She loved Hendrix though, and so did Dominic, so that was OK. Connie always leaned toward the Americans, Janis, Hendrix, Gracie Slick, as if to emphasise her exoticism. She remembered being round at Dominic's and sitting staring at the record player, listening to the single of 'White Rabbit', over and over again, amazed.

Dominic's dad was a writer, and his mother was a doctor; they had high liberal ideals of free choice and self-determination. Connie remembered Dominic's mother Susan saying, 'If I don't allow my son and his friends to smoke marijuana and listen to loud music here, he'll just go somewhere else and do it, he'll spend all his time at someone else's house, and I'll never get to see him.' They lived in a tall house in Highgate, where Dominic had a room at the top of the house which he'd painted entirely black. Explaining why he didn't bathe, Dominic said, 'It's too expensive.' Connie didn't understand. 'The hot water, I mean. It costs my father seven and six every time I have a bath. I mean, it's not worth it.' Your mother, more like, Connie thought, but said nothing.

Dominic was the only boy she knew who talked openly about sexual frustration, he would call her up and talk about it for hours. At parties in the country, the kind of parties Ruby went to much more than Connie did, posh ones, boarding school boys would complain bitterly of this thing, 'frustration', as a justification for putting their hands down your front. But Dominic talked about it as if it were an everyday thing, and would occasionally voice his hypotheses as to what sex itself, fucking, would be like. Connie remembered another public school boy from that era, Richard Beaton, saying that his ultimate fantasy was to do it strung up in a clear plastic hammock filled with olive oil. At the time Connie was struck by the emphasis on artifice, as if mere bodies weren't enough. Mere bodies were too much, needless to say; Richard, who doubtless had never fucked anybody, was focusing on plastic and oil as a substitute for the unknown body, just as Connie substituted romance, the traditional feminine veil for sex. She found all this slightly repulsive, a horrible side-effect of sexual segregation at boarding school. Connie wondered what became of Richard. He's probably running the BBC now, she thought.

Highgate: Connie remembered the way they wandered, separately and together, through the overgrown graveyard, she remembered looking up, seeing Emma in the distance, standing on a flat tomb, seeing Bella and Paul, hand in hand, walking through the alley of catacombs. She remembered how their six paths crossed, and re-crossed, arbitrarily, as if they were doing an elaborate dance, scattered across this strange decaying wilderness, coinciding and parting in ways that made some kind of pattern, possibly. She remembered the sun, and the long grass, and stepping delicately through the undergrowth to get nearer to a tomb, to read the inscription on a ruined monument. It wasn't spooky, this place; for Connie, it was perfect. The air smelled dusty and warm, it was heavenly.

Beneath this drift, which appeared inconsequential, ran a current of desire. Because they were fourteen, fifteen, they were sexually frustrated, romantically frustrated, and anything could happen. Connie was trying to be cool, but she was alert, one eye open, casting sidelong glances to see if Emma Thomson was following Mikey around. Connie emphatically displayed her independence, wandering off by herself, but she would have been furious if Emma had succeeded in this covert quest.

On the other hand, Michael was connected to Ruby, in ways Connie didn't want to think about. Michael was definitely off-limits, perhaps, because Ruby was Connie's best friend, Connie adored Ruby, and Michael was Ruby's cousin, her lover, her ideal object. Mikey was it. Mikey and Ruby spent every summer in Scotland together, their families had summer houses there, beside a little bay, and Mikey and Ruby spent the summers in Scotland, in each other's arms.

Ruby's parents also had a cottage in Suffolk; they dragged their unwilling daughters down to the country every other weekend, otherwise Ruby would have been there too, maybe, that Sunday afternoon, wandering around Highgate with Mikey's arm resting on her shoulder, his hand gently touching the back of her neck. Maybe.

It was more complicated than that, though, because these days Ruby was going out with Louis. So Mikey was her summer romance, surely, her cousin, or something, not her boyfriend. Maybe not. Connie carefully pushed thoughts of Ruby away; that afternoon at Highgate it was as if she didn't exist. Connie didn't know what she wanted with Michael, or Mikey as he was called by his cousin Ruby, and Dominic; she didn't know what she wanted with him, or what she could allow herself to want. She knew she didn't want to see him going off with that Emma Thomson.

That day Highgate was romantic backdrop, a ruined playground, as they traipsed languidly through the funereal confusion, teenagers in elaborate dresses and wide sailor's trousers, in layers of thin cotton and silk chiffon, weekend hippies, schoolkids. Connie remembered Dominic crouching down to perch on a gravestone, and carefully removing from his pocket the joint he'd brought to smoke in the cemetery; they leaned against the tombstones as they quietly passed it around. Then they wandered off again, scattering in all directions.

At one point, at the memorable point, the centre from which the memory of these various details radiate, at this point, Connie was standing still, alone, and Michael walked up to her and gently put his hand on her ribs, just above her waist. He was very tall and very skinny, and Connie reached up to place her right hand near his shoulder, turning her face up to be kissed. It was broad daylight, late afternoon, standing there in the sun with the fallen tombstones scattered at their feet, they stood facing each other, leaning forward slightly, to kiss. Connie staggered back momentarily, and felt his arm close around her waist. This was perfect, dreamy. Connie was both surprised and amazed. At the same time she was sure that Michael had intended this, she knew he'd watched her from a distance, and he'd followed her only when she appeared to be getting far enough away from the others. He'd followed her, disguising his movements in order to seem cool, or detached. Connie felt desirable, and desired; she felt triumphant.

Connie didn't know what she wanted with Michael. She

didn't know what he could possibly want with her. She wanted to call him Mikey, as Ruby did. He was very sweet and gentle, boyish, and at the same time very sexy, with his long arms and legs, his narrow eyes looking.

In his absence, Mikey had been described so many times, he'd attained a mythic splendour, as Ruby, and Hope, who went to stay with her, brought back tales from the summers in Scotland, tales to pore over through the gloomy winters as they huddled over the radiators at school. He'd been presented as an object of fascination, extraordinary, and thus he'd become a little star in their small world, a world where Connie felt like nobody, almost, Ruby's sidekick, that's who she was. For Mikey to choose Connie — it was beyond her dreams. Thus she put Ruby out of her mind, wilfully. Ruby wasn't there, that day; they were free, supposedly, and anyway Ruby had other boyfriends during the year, she was going out with Louis, it was pretty serious, Connie thought, and Mikey had other girlfriends too. It was really only in Scotland in the summer, where their family's summer houses made an isolated proximity, a romantic repetition, that Ruby and Mikey were inseparable. Maybe not.

Connie didn't really know what to think, she didn't know what was happening. She knew that kissing Mikey in Highgate Cemetery felt like heaven, it felt like falling in love.

In the church-yard of St Giles-in-the-Fields I have observed with horror a great square pit, with many rows of coffins piled one upon the other, all exposed to sight and smell. Some of the piles were incomplete, expecting the mortality of the night. I turned away disgusted at the view, and scandalized at the want of police, which so little regards the health of the

living as to permit so many putrid corpses, tacked between some slight boards, dispersing their effluvia over the capital.
Thomas Pennant, *Some Account of London*, 1793

Michael Stour was Ruby Powell's cousin, by marriage only, a step-cousin you could say. After Mikey's father died, his mother Cynthia married Tommy Osborne, who was related to Ruby's mother. Tommy, Mikey's step-father, drank too much, in the inimitable style of the English upper class; that is, he was an infinitely charming and amusing drunk. Mikey's mother, Cynthia, was more formidable, but she was also very beautiful, and very charming, when she chose to be. Tommy had no choice. He had no hesitation in telling Mikey and anyone else who was interested that he'd married Cynthia as much out of love for her dead husband as out of love for her. It was virtually the first thing he said to Connie, drink in hand, as if to explain, to clarify the situation. Tommy had been friends with Edward Stour at Cambridge, and it was clear that his emotional investment in Cynthia and her children (she'd been left with three kids, aged seven, six and three, when she herself was twenty-nine) was deeply connected to his attachment to his dead friend. Tommy's eyes would fill, crystal tears intensifying the blue, when he spoke of it; smiling, waving the eternal glass of whisky, he'd say, 'But of course I married her, those poor little orphans!' In his account, it wasn't altruism, more like a perverse displacement masked as chivalry, this marriage to Edward's lovely relict, this rescue mission to adopt Edward's kids.

Mikey had a photograph of his father, a black and white rectangle, which he was given after Edward's death; Connie remembered him showing it to her when she went to stay. It was a formal portrait, which conveyed his father's beauty, his youth, and also the other world he would never leave. England in the 1950s. His hair was dark, his face was pale, and well constructed, a good jaw and nose and brow. He looked out at you with a slightly empty stare. If anything, he seemed a bit too good looking, in this photograph, to be believable; he appeared almost like a paragon, or prototype of the promising young father circa 1959. Which is what he was, more or less, condemned to remain forever frozen in that role. That's part of what happens when people die, Connie thought; they get left behind, they remain stuck in a world that we can't really remember, that we distort with nostalgia, or mis-remembering, or repudiation.

Edward Stour was beautiful, more beautiful even than his orphaned children, but it was the knowledge of the fact of his death that made him seem, in this photograph, so archetypal, fixed, his good looks remaining, invulnerable somehow, outside the collisions of history or time. Even Tommy, safe in his rigid cocoon of alcohol and charm, had been forced to meet the 1960s, to fend off some blows and give in to others. Everyone's face bore the marks of these collisions, lines of wear and tear, as their sense of humour, of propriety, of possibility, or sexuality changed. Only Edward's photograph, his face pearl white, his dark hair short and elegant, remained impassive, opaque.

Meanwhile Tommy Osborne seemed to be about the least paternal person imaginable. He adored the company of young girls, thirteen or fourteen years old, he couldn't resist teaching them how to flirt. That's how he saw it. Usually their response was to bask in the attention he lavished, and in his obvious delight. He was constantly pressing glasses of whisky into their hands, anyone's hands, he loved the messy warmth, the quiet shrieks of everyone being slightly out of control. Typically Cynthia would be making lunch for nine people in the background, Sunday afternoon, an image of competence as she induced the children to help set the table, carry the dishes, while Tommy sat on the sofa, monopolising the attention of whatever young girl was around, listening to very emotional classical music on the record player, Italian opera, and talking about everything, being fascinating. Tommy was available to all comers (on the sofa, drink in hand), and in another sense he wasn't there at all.

When someone was in trouble, you never felt even a whiff of disapproval, only a sense of pained disappointment, a sense that something had gone wrong, the easy pleasure of daily life interrupted. Of course it was constantly being interrupted, with five children in the house, Edward's children, Charles and Michael and Judith, and then Tommy and Cynthia's two little girls. Yet it was always something that had somehow, inexplicably, gone wrong; no one had ever *done* something wrong. No one was responsible for this temporary break in the perpetual sequence of talk, drink, music, charm. Just as no one had been responsible for Edward's death. Terrible things happen. It was as if, in this world, there was no cause, only effect, and Tommy represented the ability to remain continually charming, to roll with the punches, to ignore the worst. He made constant jokes.

In everyday life, in public, out of sight of the family, Tommy Osborne was a molecular biologist, not at the absolute top of his field, but still a highly-respected research scientist and academic. He was involved in the project of deciphering the genetic code, working at one of the prestigious research institutes associated with Cambridge University. It was hard for Connie to imagine the transition from one thing to the other, it was hard to picture Tommy being effective in a public space. But his charm was only the surface manifestation of an uncommon intelligence; his long fingers stopped shaking when he spoke about his work, his blue eyes focused.

He loved the work and was loved by the people he worked with.

Anyone can be an alocholic, it requires only tremendous discipline and a certain defiance. It requires that you never take responsibility for the effect you have on those around you. It requires immense charm.

Edward Stour had been a mathematician. The usual clichés clustered around his memory: brilliant, a dazzling ability, meteoric, burned out, a tragic loss. It was never very clear, to Michael at least, whether his father had sidestepped the terrifying problem of burn-out by dying suddenly instead, or whether this unanticipated death had thankfully saved him from the humiliation of living powerless, the thrill of mathematical brilliance already fading.

In contrast, Michael was an artist from the start; he eschewed calculation. As a child, Mikey sat at the kitchen table, incessantly drawing. Later he told Connie that occasionally he had allowed himself to imagine what that kind of genius, or talent, or whatever you would like to call it, might feel like, what it would be like to be a brilliant mathematician, like Edward Stour, his father. Again the clichés flooded in: the icy cold clarity of infinite space and time, the fluid rush of numbers, the almost tactile sense of problem solving, or dissolving, problems shifting endlessly into new forms, new shapes to feel out. It was supposed to be like music, and Mikey knew something about playing music, but he couldn't picture what it would be like to move through an imaginary landscape of sound. Vision, possibly, was more apt, maybe mathematics was sculptural, tactile, with numbers palpable as shapes and colours. Possibly. Mikey could barely add and subtract. Ironically, it was Becca, Tommy's daughter, who seemed to be brilliant at numbers. Jude was pretty good too, but didn't care about it. Chas cared too much.

Michael knew mathematics was always either pure or

applied, and he thought his father's kind must have been absolutely pure, abstract. Tommy, on the other hand, had ended up shifting from mathematics to genetics, which Michael thought of as something like botany, or biology. He thought it was something to do with plants, or viruses, or something. He didn't really know much about it.

Later Michael imagined the pleasure of mathematical brilliance as not unlike taking speed: the clarity, sharp focus, utter lucidity, and of course the effortless quality, the sheer rush of ideas. It was a curiously passive image that he had, of someone like his father (he couldn't really remember him very clearly), someone like him stretched out on a sofa, or a chaise longue of some kind, head thrown back, in a state of seeming lassitude, while behind his half-closed eyes (the eroticism of this image began to make itself felt), behind these eyes (that he would never see) numerical shapes cohered, dissolved, taking form with amazing speed. As if his father's mind were a computer screen, with data whizzing past, too fast to follow. Michael's father died before the age of personal computers. He'd lived in another world.

Michael hardly remembered him, anyway. He remembered his voice, one phrase, saying, 'Mikey, come here, I want to show you . . .' — something. Or: 'this'. He couldn't remember what it was. He remembered his father saying. 'Mikey, come here . . .' He didn't know what else there was to remember.

Tommy said Edward walked up and down when he was working, he would pace the room. He joked about a worn track on the carpet in his rooms at Cambridge. Michael preferred to think of him reclining, on a sofa, an emblem of lassitude. He could remember his height (Edward was very tall, as were his sons, later), Michael could remember being little, and being close to this very tall thin man. He imagined standing next to him, his eyes at a level with his father's thigh. He imagined being a little boy. Yet he preferred to picture this paternal body elongated, prone on a sofa, day-dreaming (this was his work), mysterious mathematical forms flooding his mind. He lay his father down, in imagination, to protect himself from the pain of the little boy, too little to take possession of this tall man.

'Mikey, come here, I want to . . .'

Michael refused to picture him pacing, active, hard at work. Pure mathematics must mean effortless progress, flat on your back, no sweat or tears. This vision was as far removed as it could possibly be from Michael's own practice, his art work, which was always tangible, material, bodily. He was continually handling things, physically, transforming them by his touch. Michael was a child of minimalism, inevitably, but emphatically sensual, corporeal. He was always digging holes and filling them in, making moulds, leaving marks, handprints, signs of the body, insisting on the complex pleasures of sensation.

At fourteen, it was perfectly clear that the one thing he couldn't do was to follow in his father's (eminent) footsteps — or supposedly eminent, Michael was never really sure how much Edward's brilliance was a fiction cooked up by Tommy and, to a lesser extent, Cynthia: another component in the mythology of their marriage. Michael felt sorry for Chas, a year and three quarters older than him, condemned, it seemed, to try to take his father's place — just as Michael forbade himself to do. In a sense, they were both compelled, in opposite directions, by the fact of their father's death. At sixteen Chas was torn between attempting either mathematics or molecular science as an eventual course of study, unable to decide on Edward or Tommy as the model to be duplicated. He wasn't exceptionally promising in either field, but he was very tall, and very good looking, with dark hair and dark eyes (like Edward), and people liked him. Chas was easy to get along with, and from the right sort of background, and so they would let him in, to study, probably, wherever he applied, and so he continued to be perplexed. Mikey would go to the Slade.

Many do not realise that crêpe, symbol of the deepest mourning, cannot be worn with non-deep mourning materials. Thus, crêpe is inadmissible with velvet, satin, lace, bright or glacé silks, embroidery, fringe — excepting the special 'crêpe fringe' — or, indeed, with anything but mourning silk, paramatta, merino, cashmere, woollen barège or grenadine, or barathea . . . It should be borne in mind that, with crêpe, only jet ornaments are permissible; neither gold, silver, nor precious stones can be worn, nor can lace be worn with crêpe . . . Linen collars and cuffs cannot be worn with crêpe; crêpe lisse frills are de rigueur. Sable or any coloured fur must be left off; sealskin is admissible, but it never looks well in really deep mourning.

The Queen, 1880

In Connie's memory, it was a kind of slow ballet that took place that afternoon in the cemetery. Everyone circled around each other, vaguely, until finally the lines of tangents intersected, paths crossed, and the destined lovers coincided, in a gentle collision: the embrace. After that, she couldn't remember. What happened next?

Maybe they went back to Dominic's, to lie on the floor, Mikey's arm flung around her neck, to listen to records and kiss. Or they went back to Connie's house, to her mother's house which was always empty, her parents always out of town. Maybe she showed him where she lived. Or else Mikey had a train to catch, a lift; he had to get back, Sunday night, the weekend was over. He'd been thrown out of school, but everyone else had homework to do, so Mikey had to go home.

Connie invented a scene in which Mikey asked for her phone number, and said he'd call. She was in a state of suspension, too dazed to be able to measure her wishes or expectations. She was completely surprised by his phone call, which came at eleven-thirty that night.

Connie got out of bed to answer the phone. It was Mikey. He said how much he missed her already. He asked for her address, so that he could write. Connie was walking on air, a speedy anxiety flooding her body, the repeated rush of pleasure. Climbing back into bed, thoughts of Ruby became pressing. What would she think?

At school, in the art room, there was a clear hierarchy of excellence. Everyone exclaimed loudly how terrible they were, how they couldn't draw, except Ruby, and in second place, Nell. Ruby was top, unquestionably. And she really could draw, she was brilliant. Connie liked art, but sitting next to Ruby week after week, she gladly ceded supremacy in this to her friend. If anything, she saw herself basking in the reflected glory of Ruby's brilliance, especially when Ruby did drawings of her.

Ruby was always drawing, in the back of her rough book, on scraps of pink blotting paper, margins of file paper. Hundreds of pages were covered in regulation-blue ink drawings of imaginary women: elaborately made-up eyes, pouting Brigitte Bardot lips, long legs in high heels, princesses in medieval gowns. The visual vocabulary of femininity was reworked endlessly, page after page of lined paper scattered with these overlapping, fragmentary pictures of women's bodies. It was as if an ideal was being explored: dissected, reconstructed, and at the same time, simply repeated, in a continual offhand practice of drawing. Everyone loved to watch Ruby do it, to watch the pen move so easily and surely over the page, making the beautiful women appear, and then, scratching them out without warning, an eye disappearing beneath a scrawl of ink, not quite right, not good enough.

Ruby, and her older sister Viola, were the kind of people who imperceptibly and even inadvertently determined what was fashionable and what wasn't. They were aware of their power, and sometimes they would make jokes with their mother about so undeniably setting the style, with only the slightest note of contempt for the punters creeping in. It wasn't clear quite how these standards of fashion were established, how their influence filtered through the school, the process was a mystery Connie never resolved. She was convinced, simply; Connie believed that Ruby and Viola's taste was incontrovertible.

Viola was the first in a school of six hundred miniskirted girls to wear a dress that fell one and a half inches below the knee. The effect was revolutionary; at first they gaped in amazement, some even laughed openly, laughed at Viola (unthinkable), but within six months, everyone who aspired to any kind of chic wore such a skirt, at least occasionally. The teachers, until then concerned only with trying to keep miniskirts from vanishing altogether, suddenly found themselves policing hemlines from the floor up, as retro-style (Viola wore bobby socks too, another revelation) mingled with the hippy look, and gradually long skirts became ordinary, everyday.

Ruby's influence was less ostentatious, but equally rigorous. The rules were complicated, though, because mere slavish copying was contemptible. When Ruby found the perfect shoes, for example, it wasn't enough to simply go out and buy them in another colour. Thus Connie was pushed out of the nest, so to speak, and forced to choose something appropriately groovy for herself. Her parents' tendency to supply Connie with cold cash, on demand, allowed her to buy clothes that Ruby and Viola admired, but couldn't afford. While Connie knew this purchasing power was no substitute for real style, possibly it was the best she, as a benighted American, could hope for. There was no question that she mythologized the Powells as personifications of style, or taste, this thing she could aspire to, but never wholly possess. What part they played in this process of deification is harder to determine.

Between Connie and Ruby, the compulsive dynamic of identification and differentiation was incessant, though unacknowledged, just below the surface: a constant comparison of faces, bodies, skills, attributes. The things Ruby was good at, like art, were somehow unquestionably, decisively hip, like the clothes she wore, and concomitantly, it seemed completely uncool to be good at the things Ruby hated, like physics. Since she couldn't be as good as Ruby at the things Ruby was good at, Connie ended up feeling she wasn't good at anything very much. Nevertheless, Connie identified with Ruby; she wanted her to have these things, to be cool and groovy, and then she could be associated with these things through Ruby. In a way Connie sidestepped a whole set of problems by refusing to recognise her own virtues, her own power, by simply attributing it all to Ruby.

One time the usual art teacher (who generally speaking agreed with the students in praising Ruby's formidable talent) was away, and a substitute teacher appeared, a stranger. This woman gave them a project; after showing them a Paul Klee reproduction, she asked them to divide a piece of paper into a grid of squares and paint the squares different colours. It was an exercise in abstraction. They sat down to work. The room was filled with double easels, so Ruby and Connie faced each other, as always, occasionally getting up to go around the other side to see the other's painting. Connie made an almost scientific painting, in which red, green, blue and yellow started from the dark corners of the paper, and moved towards the middle, becoming brighter and paler until the centre was a blaze of white. Ruby made a painting that had no such rationale, in which the colours overflowed their squares, flooding their boundaries, with an effect reminiscent of light flowing through stained glass.

At the end of the class, the substitute teacher held up Connie's exact little exercise as the perfect example of what she had wanted the class to produce. Then, to everyone's horror, she held up Ruby's picture as the example of what not to do. Connie was mortified. Ruby looked slightly cross. As they were moving down the noisy corridor, after class, Connie said, 'It just shows how stupid that woman is — I think yours is beautiful, it reminds me of Gustave Moreau.' Ruby was gracious, and implicitly they agreed, that the substitute teacher was wrong. Again Connie felt herself to be someone who only received praise by mistake.

On the other hand, it was Ruby who praised Connie, suddenly, unexpectedly, the generosity of her gesture taking Connie's breath away. She remembered one occasion on the bus home from school, when Ruby suggested Connie might go to art school. Connie immediately protested that she wasn't good enough, surely it was Ruby who was the artist, not Connie. It was inconceivable to Connie to think of herself in those terms, an artist. She liked to think she would be like Jane Avril, famous as a model, inspiration for the brilliant artists around her. She secretly imagined herself going on television talk shows as an old woman, saying, yes, yes, I knew Ruby and Viola Powell, and Hope Lewis, and Michael Stour. I knew them all. But that time on the bus Ruby said, no, she said Connie was wrong, she said the drawings Connie did, doodling in the back of her notebook, were much more interesting than most people's. Connie remembered Ruby's use of the word interesting. Connie remembered being very pleased: there could be no higher praise.

It was in this context that Mikey presented himself. Mikey, the 'brilliant artist', the rebel, tall and skinny and sensitive; Mikey, connected to Ruby, and to Ruby's family, arty, tasteful, cultured, and connected to their heavily mythologised summer holidays in Scotland; Mikey, the object of Ruby's fascination — with these attributes, to Connie, Michael was virtually a sacred object. The effect intensified: his dead father, the great mathematician; his own (supposedly) 'bad heart'; it added up to a kind of adolescent apotheosis. Apparently he wasn't allowed to do games at school, because of his heart. It was Hope who told Connie about Michael, his brilliant art work, his dead father, his bad heart. He might die young, like his father did. Ruby was too cool to talk about it.

In the end it was a relatively simple equation: Connie adored Ruby; Ruby admired Michael. Possibly she adored him. Thus the whole elaborate psychic economy, deeply hierarchical, was blown sky high when Mikey turned around and decided to adore Connie. It was terrifying.

Ruby was very quiet about Mikey, about her relationship with him, but there was no doubt in Connie's mind that kissing Mikey in Highgate Cemetery was a tremendous act of lèse majesté. On the other hand, it was clear that Mikey felt perfectly free to kiss Connie, or to fall in love with her, if that was what he was doing. It was all terribly complicated. Connie didn't want in any sense to appear to be taking Mikey away from Ruby; at the same time she did undeniably thrill to this evidence of her value. It was a little like that Burne Jones painting, *King Cophetua and the Beggar Maid*, or something. Mikey had descended from Mount Parnassus, so to say, and he'd incomprehensibly found her worthy of his attention. His lordly eye had fallen on her, and found her desirable. It was bliss.

On the other hand, at the same time, deep down Connie knew Mikey must have made a mistake.

It was bliss and it was also misrecognition, on Connie's part, at least. Mikey was fifteen, he wasn't a god or a king or even a lord, he wasn't remotely like those things. He'd just been thrown out of boarding school, which was probably kind of a relief, but also a blow, and a family scandal that he could have done without. He didn't know what was going to happen next; it looked like his parents would send him to the classic coeducational liberal boarding school, Sedgemoor, next year, and meanwhile, he would go to Florence, to look at paintings. Mikey was fifteen, he had bad skin. He was much taller than most kids his age. He was ashamed of himself, confused, awkward, fucked up, and unsure of everything, except the escape route, which was art.

I suppose there are persons who admire those conventional forms of ugliness, with puffy faces of pink and white, black (often squinting) eyes, gilt hair and wings . . . certainly if tawdriness or colour can attract, these things look smart enough when they come out of the stonemason's yard — but let a few months pass, and what a change has taken place! The summer's sun has faded the red of the cheeks, and the damps of autumn have covered, perhaps, one half of the face with a mouldy green . . .

A Tract upon Tomb Stones by a Member of the Lichfield Society for the Encouragement of Ecclesiastical Architecture, 1843

What is it that is so seductive, that elicits the endless web of myth and fantasy, that invites these projections? Connie remembered a film that was directed by a woman whose beauty was notorious, that seemed to be all about that problem, the problem of being absurdly beautiful, being so beautiful that you become the empty centre, speechless, trapped, like a rabbit in the headlights, paralysed by the intensity of the expectations of others. She pictured it like a network of projections, as each person around this central figure inflicts his or her own myth of desire, freezing the beautiful woman in the relentless fierceness of their look. In the film, the beautiful woman was surrounded: a twin brother, an ex-lover, a daughter, each with their own fantasy of her power. She feels powerless, of course, and gives herself up to their wishful thinking. It's because she's too beautiful, she's too beautiful to be anything else.

Mikey was like that, trapped. But he wasn't beautiful, really, not like that. His brother Chas was much more conventionally good looking: Chas looked like a hero in an early-Victorian novel. Michael, in contrast, was extraordinary looking, and it was partly in comparison to Chas's symmetry that the flaws, the odd angles and intensities of his face, became apparent.

They were both very tall, and thin, though Mikey was always skinny and ill-looking, while Chas generally seemed to be in the best of health. They looked alike, with good bones, a narrow forehead, clear lines to the jaw. Mikey's nose was crooked, Chas's was straight. Mikey's eyes were small, and pale blue, and sharp; they moved quickly, like a small animal or monkey. Chas's look was slower, lazy, and his eyes were dark, like his hair.

There was something monkey-ish about Mikey; his large, long-fingered hands were always moving, always handling something, or waving and flashing in front of his face as he talked. Connie remembered those pale eyes, narrowed in amusement, or shooting over to one side, to make a joke. She remembered Mikey's eyes rolling suddenly, or cast down, thrown sideways, punctuating his words with a flirty charm. His hair was straight, a dirty blonde, that peculiarly English non-colour that looks almost greenish-grey in winter, and streaks gold in hot sun. For years Mikey rarely washed his hair, using the naturally occurring grease to hold it back off his face. You could see the tracks of his fingers like a coarse comb through the thick straight hair, falling straight back from his bony forehead, hitting the top of his shoulders in back. Everyone had long hair, then. Chas washed his every other day. Like all English people, Mikey's teeth were crooked, as were Chas's, but less dramatically. Mikey had bad skin, dead white like the belly of a fish.

Mikey always looked a little degenerate, except on the day that he went to the American Embassy in Grosvenor Square to get his tourist visa to go to New York. He borrowed a sand-coloured corduroy suit from Chas, he wore a yellow shirt and a deep orange tie, and he carried Chas's large Nikormat camera slung over his shoulder. Connie remembered being surprised at this worldly strategy, it reminded her of Iris festooning herself with gold chains on her way to Egypt, insisting that a little jewellery doesn't do you any harm on your way through customs. Connie remembered another occasion where she'd seen Mikey in Chas's clothes, it was at a party in a garden in London. It must have been the autumn of '72, when Mikey was about nineteen. It was their first year in London, Michael and Chas and later Jude, too, they were starting college, moving into the big house in Ladbroke Grove.

Hope's birthday fell near enough to Guy Fawkes to be an excuse for a firework party in their vast garden. She lived with her parents in an enormous house in the Boltons; it had an L-shaped garden with wide lawns and a towering pear tree with a swing. Hope's firework party was a yearly ritual, and for once both Chas and Mikey were present, along with Ruby and Connie and numerous others. At one point, on this occasion, Ruby was sitting on the lawn, on a rug, it was evening, darkness was just falling, and Mikey came up to her from behind, he put his arm around her (they were going out at this point), and there was a moment of complete confusion when suddenly Ruby realised it was Chas, not Mikey, it was Chas in Mikey's clothes. Meanwhile Mikey was pretending to be Chas, in his dark green jacket and baggy trousers, and the effect was uncanny. Everyone could see how much the differences between them, which were apparently to do with light or dark hair, light or dark eyes, were sustained in practice by their diametrically opposed dress, by Mikey's slouch and Charles's brisk walk, by the air around each of them. Dressed up, they looked interchangeable. And it was surprising, also, to note that both Mikey and Chas were adept at imitating the other's gestures, demeanour, and tone of voice, to the extent of momentarily taking in even an intimate like Ruby. 'It was Mikey's idea,' Chas explained, standing in Mikey's torn and dirty off-white trousers and his unravelling gigantic pullover. Meanwhile Mikey looked quite the young man about town, in his brother's velvet jacket. It was hilarious, and slightly shocking. Embarrassed suddenly, they quickly changed back again, reassuming their identities.

When Connie first met Mikey, when he was fifteen, he was shy and awkward, and his eyes didn't flash flirtation and make jokes. His eyes were sad, and tired, a little bitter, as if he were feeling slightly worn out by his own misdeeds and the institutional response to them. Years later Hope told Connie why Michael had been thown out of school. Toucester (pronounced Toaster, absurdly enough) was a classic British public school for boys, with, if anything, a leaning towards the military. You were supposed to become a Guard or an officer of some kind when you left. Connie wondered in amazement if Cynthia and Tommy thought sending Mikey there would make a man of him, or something. Maybe he couldn't get in anywhere else. She pictured Mikey aged twelve, skinny and shivering, the sensitive artistic type par excellence, thrown into the freezing shower rooms and crowded noisy corridors of Toucester. It was a ridiculous name for a school, were you called an old Touceterian? Michael wouldn't be, not if he'd been kicked out. Hope said he'd been expelled for dressing up in the headmaster's daughter's clothes, which he had stolen.

Connie was deeply shocked. This was evidence of a precocious perversity beyond her wildest expectations. In retrospect, however, it was impossible for Connie to measure the true lasciviousness of this crime. She allowed herself to hypothesise a certain innocence, or naiveté, which at the time she would have dismissed without hesitation. She imagined Mikey partly driven, partly innocently amused, some kind of lark, to prance about in a skirt. Or a bra. How serious was it, how severe this pleasure? Connie could almost imagine that it could have been a kind of naughty joke, the frisson of perverse sex going almost undetected, lost in the general excitement of such a crime. What if we're caught?

Boys were continually being caught. The door of the dormitory would open after lights out, some junior master looking in on the way back from the pub, and there would be a sudden violent flurry, a scuffle of boys jumping back into their own beds. Occasionally the master, in a particularly sadistic mood, would switch on the lights, and everyone would see who was flying through the air, leaping like frogs over the narrow beds to desperately shove his legs under the covers of his own. 'Braithewaite!!' 'Yes sir?' 'I'll see you in the morning after chapel.' 'Yes sir.' Quiet murmurs of sympathy would emanate from the narrow beds as soon as the lights were out again.

Asking William about it, about boarding school, years later, he gave as his considered opinion that the boys in each other's beds were unlikely to be necking, or doing sex, or whatever. Connie wondered if this was naïve on William's part. He reminded her that there were usually a minimum of about twenty beds in these dormitories, and most people, even schoolboys, prefer sexual privacy. He thought they would be more likely to be talking, whispering, so as not to disturb the ones who wanted to sleep. 'Shut up Porter!' '*You* shut up!' et cetera. Connie pictured little boys in flannel pyjamas, striped blue and grey, lying side by side in the narrow iron bed, one arm flung around the other's neck, staring at the dark ceiling, talking. What would they be talking about? Secrets.

The horrible truth was, that in all the years she'd known Michael, she had never dared ask him about being expelled from Toucester. So all that about the headmaster's daughter's clothes might be untrue. He might have made it up to shock Hope, Hope was so easy to shock. On the other hand he may have confided in her, she was also easy to confide in, too solemn to be scathing or scornful. Mikey never spoke of it to Connie, not even in jest, and whenever people raised the subject of British boarding schools, Mikey would take a capricious delight in insisting how wonderful they were. He praised his prep school, Pryor Lodge, which he'd attended from the age of seven to twelve, with only slightly ironic enthusiasm. 'It was like organised gang culture; the idea is simply to tire you out. You relinquish your identity completely, it's like a prison for eight-year-olds. Of course this kind of thing is less amusing when you're seventeen, or even when you're twelve.'

By the time Mikey was seventeen he'd long since abandoned

this rather vigorous regime, he'd left it far behind; by then he'd become the art star of the famous progressive school, Sedgemoor, where he didn't do anything at all except art. No more cricket, no more mathematics, no history, no literature, no science: Michael was in the art studios all day every day, and lying around on a mattress on the floor, his arm around a girl in a loose smock and a long patterned skirt, smoking cigarettes and listening to records, the rest of the time.

In accordance with the plan generally observed or adopted throughout London: this is, the opening, what is called a public grave, thirty feet deep, perhaps; the first corpse interred was succeeded by another, and up to sixteen or eighteen, and all the openings between the coffin boards were filled with smaller coffins of children. When this grave was crammed as full as it could be, so that the topmost coffin was within two feet of the surface, that was considered as occupied.

Report from the Select Committee on the Improvement of the Health of Towns — *Effects of Interment of Bodies in Towns*, June 1842

Cynthia and Edward Stour had always planned to send their boy children to the proper schools, and after Edward's death, boarding school seemed even more like the right thing. So when Charles was eight, and Mikey was seven, off they went, with the elaborate school uniforms packed into two regulation trunks, dark blue with their initials painted on them in white.

They went to the same prep school, Pryor Lodge, although they quickly learned that it was almost impossible to visit each other, so absolute were the divisions between the years. These divisions were maintained by threat of humiliation, as if it were somehow shameful in the bigger boy to want to see his younger brother. Chas told Mikey to stop coming and standing around outside his form room, he was tired of the other boys teasing him about his 'bro'. Mikey, or Stour Mi, as he was called here, to distinguish him from Stour Ma, Charles, felt exhausted all the time. Yet there were moments, like playing football, or running around wildly in the yard, when he lost himself in this world, a world complete unto itself, made up of incomprehensible rules and rewards, a world of terminal isolation in the midst of hundreds of screaming kids.

You had to survive the masters, and then you had to survive the regime of the kids, the elaborate system of shame and status that formed the fabric of every day. To avoid being teased, or tortured, in the dormitory, where you slept with twenty other seven-year-olds. To avoid the cane, the disapproving look, detention, lines. To avoid crying, or being seen to cry. You learned to eat very quickly here, since those who finished first, might get seconds. Since the other boys would grab your food off your plate, if it was still sitting there when they'd finished. Their forks would appear, to spear your sausage, your last lump of roast potato. You learned to eat whatever your favourite thing was first, not last.

You never saved anything for last, anything you liked, not sweets, not any kind of treasure, because someone might take it from you. You learned to wash in cold water very early in the morning; you learned what it's like to stand around in the yard, under the sloping roof, freezing rain falling and your hands white and blue with cold. You discovered chilblains. All winter long you were cold, except in bed in the morning, when you had to get up, to leave the warmth. Your skin felt tight, drained of colour, everyone looked pale and cold, except the red-faced ones who were fat and always running around, careening into things. Later Michael used to maintain that it really wasn't so bad, preparatory school. You just submit completely, like some kind of camp or army or prison, you submit, and then it's not so bad. You're only a little kid, after all. It's much worse later. And anyway, it was the transitions back to family life that were hard to take.

Every vacation Cynthia would meet the school train as it pulled into Paddington, and the boys poured out of it, to sit on their trunks and casually await the arrival of a parent or servant, to take them home. It was an extraordinary scene, with four hundred boys between the ages of seven and thirteen, each dressed identically in grey flannel shorts and blazers, dark blue raincoats, each with his dark blue trunk, his *Beano* and his sweets, acting blasé about being reunited with his family. Michael and Charles quickly learned that you didn't embrace on the platform, that if anything you had to look uncomfortable if your mother, over-emotional, insisted on kissing you. They'd pile into the big maroon car, and take the road to Cambridge, to Grantchester, and the house where they lived with Tommy, and the girls. It was a modern house, built by Cynthia and Tommy shortly after their marriage, the architect was a friend of the family. It spread out in various directions, all on one level, with plenty of room for the children on one side of the house, and the parents' area in a wing on the other side. It was unusual, it was most un-English, this house, much more like an American or even a Scandinavian idea of an appropriate kind of house. There was a paddock or field behind the house, and trees, an uneventful view that nevertheless conveyed a sense of English landscape.

Leaving Paddington in the car, Charles in the front seat, of course, and Mikey lolling about in the back, their reserve would crumble under Cynthia's charm. It was as if she had to win their hearts all over again, at the end of every term, but it wasn't so difficult. She would ask about everything, and their news would gradually come spilling out, with interruptions, and contradictions, as they tried to give an account of life at school. She'd tell them she'd made trifle for tea, she'd describe the treats in store for them.

That was the sort of thing that happened, Michael would explain later: you spend three months in the equivalent of a prison for kids, and then you come home for the holidays and your mother feeds you sweets and luxury items and buys you things, until the day when it's time for you to go back, back to prison. Sorry. That's it, time's up. No more trifle for you!

What a contrast there is between that picture of the noble Roman woman, surrounded by her maidens and friends, herself bearing her husband's ashes to the tomb, and the black array, the paid, half-besotted mutes, and the hideous box in which the remains of poor humanity are nailed up for a decay as needless as it is odious, to any one who has seen it or thought of it. What a gain it would be to get rid of much of the Monster Funereal, the most impudent of the ghouls that haunt the path of progress!

William Robinson, *God's Acre Beautiful, or the Cemeteries of the Future*, 1880

Connie imagined this conversation.

She imagined a time, when Michael was home from school, twelve or thirteen, a moment when Michael overcame the profound internal prohibition he felt about speaking his dead father's name, Edward, when he went to Cynthia, and asked, 'What was it like, being married to Edward?'

Cynthia was shocked by the naïve complexity of this question. She didn't know what to say. There was the simple, correct answer, the reductive myth of a marriage cut short by tragedy: we loved each other, we were happy, he died suddenly, I was devastated, it was terrible. Tommy saved me from this sorrow. But that simplified version didn't do justice to any of her feelings — her anger and resentment, her frustration, her sense of powerlessness, and her anxiety. Cynthia believed Edward's 'heart' was hereditary, she feared their children would also die in this way, suddenly. At some level, deep inside, the best way for her to deal with this fearful anticipation, this terror, was to write them off from the start. That's why Mikey wasn't allowed to play football, that's why Cynthia took them to the specialist in Harley Street every other year. If she expected Edward's children to die at the age of thirty, like he had, then it would be a pleasant surprise when or if they didn't. Die, that is.

'Oh I don't know, Mikey . . . You know, we loved each other, that's the most important thing. We were happy together. We were so young . . .'

'No, I know,' Michael said. 'What I meant was, what's it like being married to a mathematician? I mean, like father.'

Cynthia laughed. 'Why, are you planning to marry one?'

Michael blushed. 'No. I just wanted to know.'

Cynthia thought, again, sitting by the window in her bedroom, as Mikey awkwardly leaned against the back of a chair opposite, sun falling across the beige carpet; Cynthia turned her attention to this question, a question that she'd grown out of, so to speak, with the passage of time.

'It was wonderful, of course. And it was hell. I mean, in some ways. I expect it always is. Mathematics is like a private world — that no one else knows about, except other mathematicians. And not all of them, obviously. It's as if you've got the key to this world, and you go there all alone, you're the centre of it, it's yours. And no one knows about it. This is a world of numbers, and the numbers are like slaves, they have a life of their own, but they're slaves still — because you're the one who understands that life, you're the one who knows how they work, and therefore you control them. It gives you power over them. Within that world, you're all alone and you're all powerful. It's very private. And of course I was left out of that, I mean, I had you children and the house, of course, but I could see that what really gave Edward pleasure was being the emperor, the king of numbers, in another world that was as far away from me as it was possible to go.'

'So you minded that, being left behind?'

'No, I didn't. I mean, I didn't think I did. I minded when he would worry about losing it, about burn-out. You know about that, don't you?'

'Mm.'

'From what he said, from how he would behave, I had the sense that he thought living without this world, without this unlimited power, living without this would be unthinkable. He'd seen it happen (it almost always does happen) and there were times when I believed, or at least when he gave me the impression — he gave me reason to believe that he thought life wouldn't be worth living without it. Maybe I was imagining it. And then he died, and so I'll never know — I mean, what would have happened. To him.'

'It's such an obstacle, you know,' Mikey said. 'Every time I try to think about anything at all to do with all that, I come up against the fact that he died. That he's dead. I can't get past it — it's as if that's the most important thing, the only important thing.'

'What do you remember about him?'

'Some things. Not much. I remember having to be quiet.'

'Yes, that's right. Of course.'

'Tommy was a mathematician too, wasn't he?'

'Tommy's different. Anyway, there's a difference between the kind of mathematics your father did and the kind you do in genetics.'

'I know. Did you ever want to be anything like that?'

'No, not at all. I wanted to be married and have my babies. And that's exactly what I did.'

The greenhouse myrtle flourishes in the parterre dedicated to affection and love; the chaste forget-me-not blooms over the ashes of a faithful friend; the green laurel shades the cenotaph of the hero; and the drooping willow, planted by the hand of the orphan weeps over the grave of the parent. Everything is there tasteful, classical, poetical and eloquent.

J. C. Loudon, *On the Laying Out, Planting and Managing of Cemeteries and on the Improvement of Churchyards*, 1843

Photographs were taken that day, the day in the country, pictures of Connie and Michael on the lawn behind the house. Connie was wearing a long black Ossie Clarke skirt; it was lined black crêpe, well cut, with a clear waistband, and it fell to her shoes. She wore her Biba shirt, an Edwardian reference, khaki with maroon stripes, like pyjamas or mattress ticking, with puffed sleeves tightening to the long buttoned cuffs. It was fitted, with darts under the breasts, to show off her waist. She wore three and a half inch heels, what her mother's American friend Phyllis called 'Joan Crawford Fuck Me

Pumps', hidden under the skirt. Her hair was very long, with a thin black velvet ribbon tied carelessly to keep it back. She wore no makeup, other than a purplish lipstick, Mary Quant, 'Crushed Prune'; she was tall, and she lifted up her skirt to her knees when she ran across the grass, exposing long legs in black stockings, flashing high heels, and everyone found her very charming. They had no hesitation in repeating this, to her, to each other, how charming she was. Connie felt very self-conscious.

Mikey had written to her every day since the afternoon at Highgate, declaring his passion. Connie was overwhelmed. He telephoned also, and on Thursday he rang to ask her down to the country. This had never happened to her before. She'd never met someone's parents, sat at the family table, spent the night in somebody's house. She'd never spent the night under the same roof with some boy she was supposed to be in love with, or going out with, or kissing. She had no idea what would happen.

On Saturday morning Connie took the train down to Cambridge, carrying her grandmother's ancient carpet bag, with a careful selection of clothes to wear. All week she'd been going to school, sitting at her desk next to Ruby's, each morning increasingly anxious and unable to determine the seriousness of her crime. Ruby was very cool about it. On Monday Connie explained, hesitantly, that she'd gone to Highgate with Dominic, and Mikey, and they'd started seeing each other, or something. Ruby looked slightly irritated, as if someone must have plotted this, Dominic probably, but she evinced a kind of detached curiosity, as if all this had nothing to do with her. It was like, 'Oh. Really. How interesting . . . So is he coming up again this weekend?' And when Connie absurdly said, 'Do you mind?' Ruby sighed wearily, and said, 'Oh Con . . .' Connie felt ashamed, once again she'd said the wrong thing.

As far as Connie could tell, Ruby's romance with Mikey was more or less confined to summers in Scotland. Hope told Connie that Ruby was the first girl Mikey ever kissed, two summers before, when Ruby was thirteen and Mikey was just fourteen. Last summer they'd gone on, kissing, falling in love, and there was a sense in which their amorous attachment was bound up with being in this beautiful place, by the sea, surrounded by their families, on holiday.

Still there was a problem. Connie was used to an intimacy with Ruby that could no longer be taken for granted, clearly. For all Ruby's air of detachment, she managed to convey the fact that she had no desire to hear a blow by blow account of this budding romance. Connie couldn't tell if Ruby really minded or not; she must, she thought. In any case, if Connie couldn't talk about Michael, then all their other conversation would become self-conscious, as the line around the forbidden topic, the unspoken romance, defined the limits of their intercourse. This was painful to both of them, and the problem was evaded, this first week, by Ruby simply making herself unavailable, by going off with Nell. Connie saw them, arm in arm, heads together, talking and laughing, during break. She saw them in the distance, across the paved courtyard between the main school building and the Science Block, looking up, she saw them together, laughing, and it was excruciating. Connie turned back to her book.

The girls at St Peter's generally formed inseparable units: couples, or else equally intense groups of five or seven. Ruby and Connie were attached in this way, from the end of the first year, when they were eleven; in some ways the couple relationship protected them from the threat of a larger group, in which power games were even more dramatic. Occasionally, when some conflict resulted in a temporary split, there would be nothing to do in the free time, break, or lunch, one was condemned to solitude. Usually another friendly couple, arm in arm, would approach and offer their condolences, they'd rescue you from this misery, implicitly expecting to be rescued in turn when they were lonely or abandoned.

Connie remembered sitting on a bench, holding a book and staring at the tennis courts, and looking up to see Sylvia and Jane standing over her, Sylvia saying, 'Rift, rift?' To which Connie ritualistically replied, 'Rift, rift.' Wry smiles of understanding were exchanged; this was their invitation to walk with them, to pass this empty time together, break, the compulsory forty minutes out of doors, before the afternoon classes began. Connie was grateful.

At school there were some girls who floated, so to speak, outside these semi-permanent couples, like Dido, or Nell, who was always available to Ruby should she wish to get away from Connie. Nell was brilliant, and fat, and extremely funny. She had what's called a ribald wit. She could make up rhymes, and wrote long poems in couplets that set the table on a roar. One year Nell wrote an epitaph for Connie, when all she'd done for months was moon about the place, talking about various unattainable love objects. It went: 'Although in life her love was slighted/ We hope it's now by God requited.' Nell could play the piano, and sing, and draw; she was good at classics and French and English and history; she was on a scholarship, and she had three older brothers, one of whom wrote unpublishable novels. Connie remembered the time when Nell reported that her brother Arnold, speaking of women's breasts, declared that he preferred them 'no bigger than bee-stings'. The very idea of such a perverse preference was revolutionary.

When Connie told Ruby she was going down to the country to stay the weekend with Michael, Ruby's eyes widened, as if to say: sooner you than me, dear. What she actually said was, 'Good luck with Cynthia. She always *hated* me.'

On Saturday morning Michael met her at the station; he

was standing on the platform as she stepped down from the train, clutching her bag. Mikey was wearing dirty jeans and an enormous, baggy sweater, its cuffs unravelling around his bony wrists, his naked neck exposed. Connie was terribly nervous. Tommy drove the car, with Connie sitting in the front, and Mikey, looking rather strained, lounging diagonally across the back seat. Tommy was smoking, making jokes and pointing out sights, smiling and glancing sideways at Connie in her long black skirt, her tight black jacket, as she politely responded on cue. She was a nicely brought-up young girl, she knew how to be polite to grownups.

They arrived at the house in time for drinks before lunch; there was Cynthia, tall and strong-featured, with thick coarse blonde hair, like golden wheat, and greenish eyes. A formidable adversary, Connie thought; Cynthia looked tough, as she sized Connie up, smiling. Not someone you'd want as an enemy. Connie gathered that Charles and Jude were away at school; the two youngest, Rebecca and Prudence (or Becca and Pru, or Prune, as they were called) frolicked around seductively, demanding Connie's attention and providing a distraction from the embarrassment of encountering Mikey en famille. The girls were around six and eight, something like that; they were gorgeous, irresistible. Mikey was silent.

Standing on the carpet in the big living room, Tommy offered Connie a drink. 'What would you like?' he said with a smile. Connie hesitated. What was one supposed to want to drink? Whisky? 'A sherry, perhaps,' Cynthia suggested, forcefully, and Connie acquiesced. Mikey drank lager out of a can. The sun was out, pouring through big picture windows; Connie took in the wide stretch of bright grass outside, trees. There were guests for lunch, some forgotten couple, they made no impression, neighbours, maybe. Connie and Mikey sat silently together, staring. What was there to say? They sat side by side at the long table at lunch, eight people including the little girls, and Connie was asked about St Peter's ('a very good school, isn't it?'), whereupon she listed its inadequacies, inequalities, injustices, and generally held forth on what a dump it was, what a torture chamber. The adults were amused by her vehemence. Later she had to explain that her mother was American, and her father was English, but they'd lived in Chicago for years, they'd only moved back to England when she was eleven, in time to start secondary school, to go to St Peter's. Yes London was very different to Chicago. Yes she was against the war in Vietnam. No she didn't miss the States, not any more.

In retrospect Connie sensed a certain inevitability to the weekend that seemed to be at least partly class-determined. These people, the Osbornes, lived in the country, outside Cambridge, their children went to boarding school. Mikey may have been an adolescent art-star of sorts, but he was also undeniably a public school boy. Probably it was normal for him to have a friend for the weekend, a girlfriend, to contain the explosive power of adolescent romance within this easy-going, liberal family. It wasn't normal for Connie, she wasn't at all sure of the rules of this game. As an urban child of often absent parents, a certain anonymity was easy, it was expected. It seemed ordinary to Connie for her friends to pursue passionate (if virginal) love affairs for months without ever having to introduce the boy in question to their parents. The parents may never even suspect, unless every time they answered the phone, some strange young man asked for their daughter. Connie hadn't had any boyfriends, really, anyway. Mikey was the first one, and here he was, embedded in the family, and Connie didn't know how to continue to be cool, to be desirable, to go on liking him and at the same time be polite and acceptable to the Osborne ménage. She was consumed with anxiety.

After lunch Mikey showed her the artwork he'd made for

her; it was an enormous Calder-esque mobile, made of thick black metal wire and flat circular hanging panels, thin plywood circles of various sizes, painted different shades of blue and blue-grey. It was extremely impressive, and slightly terrifying to Connie: what was she supposed to do with it? She couldn't hang it in her bedroom in London, it was much too big, about five or six feet across. Michael pointed out the smallest oval, deep blue, where he'd written 'for Connie with my love Michael', and the date. This dedication seemed terribly romantic to Connie. She couldn't imagine how Mikey had made this thing; it was beyond the scale of any artwork anyone she knew would think of attempting. The mobile, hanging suspended and moving silently in the air, testified to Michael the artist, ambitious, 'brilliant', and to Michael's attachment to her. Connie felt out of her depth, as Mikey looked at her, inarticulate. He was crazy about her, so he wanted to give her a piece of work. It was that simple. She told him how much she liked it. She asked to see more of his work. She was embarrassed by this gift.

They sat down together, Mikey untying the cotton ribbons of an enormous portfolio, carefully turning over each drawing or print. He explained that he was leaving for Florence in a couple of weeks, he said, 'Maybe you could come out to Italy in the holidays, we could travel around. We could go to Siena, maybe.' 'Maybe,' Connie said, thinking her mother would never let her. She was surprised she'd let her come away for the weekend. When Connie explained that Michael was Ruby's cousin, that made it all right. Connie's mother didn't know Ruby's parents well, but Ruby went to the right kind of school, so her cousin must be all right. Looking through the pictures, Connie saw how very good Michael's work was: she was terribly impressed, again. Pru and Becca appeared, teasingly, and Mikey made them go away; they scattered across the lawn.

In this way time passed. Mikey and Connie sat together on the blue sofa in the children's end of the house, in the kids' room, large and square with a linoleum floor, a record player, a telly and lots of posters sellotaped to the walls, the portfolio open at their feet. They sat together there, silently making out for hours. Once in a while Connie would sit up, wipe the back of her hand across her sore lips, push her hair back off her face. Then she'd plunge again, turning her face to kiss him, closing her eyes. It was ecstatic, this combination of endless pleasure and simple fear. She was frightened of going too far, and wanting more and more all the time. Michael held her in his long arms, placing his hand over her left breast, fiercely kissing her neck. When they looked up, they saw the two little girls watching through the window, two round faces completely absorbed. Later Connie helped set the long table for dinner, in a daze as she tried to answer Cynthia's questions, while Cynthia moved efficiently around the kitchen, talking. Mikey was lying on his bed, in his narrow room, staring at the ceiling.

It was that weekend that Tommy told Connie about his passion for Edward Stour, Mikey's dead father. It was that weekend that Michael showed her the old black and white photograph of his father, and told her how he couldn't really remember him. Connie didn't know what to say. She stared at Edward Stour's pearl-white face, short dark hair, and the image seemed completely opaque. That weekend, Connie remembered being amazed by the diminutives: Tommy, Mikey, Chas, Jude, Becca, Prune. Only Cynthia kept her name. Connie hated her own name, Constance, she was glad to be called Connie, or Con, for short. Only Ruby called her Con, really, Ruby and her own family. Once a horrible boy called Jonathan, a boy she used to see at the bus stop, someone she and Ruby would chat to on the way home from school, this boy tormented her with an accusation of hypocrisy or deceit, he blurted out: 'Now I understand, Con is a con!' It was a terrible moment.

That night Connie lay in the narrow bed in the little oblong room that belonged to Jude. There were plastic model horses lined up on the windowsill, and a big poster of the Bee Gees over the bed. Connie lay sleepless, turning in the darkness, listening to the strange sounds of the country, and wondering what was going to happen. After dinner, Tommy had walked with them out to the split rail fence at the end of the broad lawn, and leaning there, smoking, he'd pointed out the sound of a nightingale. 'Can you hear it, Mikey? There, there it is!' The three of them stood there, listening, in the clear night. Now Connie lay on her back, in the darkness, waiting.

She thought Michael would creep quietly down the hall, and climb into bed with her. She thought that's what must happen when you went to stay the weekend with somebody. She'd never spent the night under the same roof with someone, someone who'd kissed her passionately all afternoon, someone who'd written her love letters every day for a week. Connie lay flat on her back, in the dark, waiting for Michael. She imagined he might be about to appear at any moment. She felt like Sleeping Beauty, with a difference: she was wide awake.

After a couple of hours Connie reluctantly forced herself to admit that Michael didn't seem to be coming. She began to imagine creeping down the hall and climbing into bed with him. Maybe that's what was supposed to happen. She tried to remember country house novels she'd read; surely it was the host who did the creeping? She wanted to be in bed with him, she wanted it very much. At the same time she was terrified, she was a virgin, fourteen years old, she didn't want to do it, to fuck him, or anything. She was frightened of seeing him naked, of touching him, or being touched. She was tense with anticipation, hours lying expecting the sound of Mikey at her door, she was furious that her fears hadn't been simply swept away by his dramatic action, his passion. She pictured Mikey sound sleep, as she crept in, she imagined Mikey surprised or amazed to see her in his room. She felt deeply embarrassed to have lain awake for so long, expecting him. He wasn't expecting her.

Connie got up to go to the bathroom. It was a last-ditch attempt to make the fantasy happen. She padded barefoot down the tiled hall, past Mikey's closed door, to the bathroom. Switching on the light, she pissed, briefly, as her tired eyes adjusted to the glare. She stood up, watching her face in the mirror. Connie looked exhausted and sad, she looked worn out, with dark rings under her eyes. She felt terrible. She opened the bathroom cabinet and took in the bottle of Clearasil lotion sitting there on the shelf. Connie unscrewed the cap, and smelled it. Then she read the label of instructions. Mikey must use this stuff on his spots, she thought.

Somehow she'd imagined, or she'd hoped that Michael would open his bedroom door as she passed, as she padded down the hall, that he'd see her there in her long white Victorian nightdress. Sleepless too, he'd take her hand, and pull her gently into his bed. Now, in the bright bathroom light, she knew it wasn't going to happen. Mikey was sound asleep, oblivious to the internal conflict she'd endured. She wished she hadn't come, she wished she hadn't seen him here. She put the Clearasil bottle back in the cabinet and closed the door.

Ruby

Every afternoon after school, Connie and Ruby travelled home together on the bus; they lived near each other, Ruby in Chelsea, Connie in South Kensington, and every afternoon, when they arrived at the bus stop, Ruby would say, in an offhand manner, 'Do you want to come to tea?' Connie would say, 'Yes.' This ritual took place day in, day out, for years.

Connie loved going to Ruby's house. She always associated the Powell's house with a specific smell, slightly sour, that evoked bodies, damp, a particular intimacy, perhaps. It was quite small, and completely different to Connie's family's house. Ruby always said with a certain disgust that Connie's house was deadly, it was so horribly clean. Connie's mother had acres of yellow ochre wall-to-wall carpets, tall brass lamps with silk shades, floor-to-ceiling chintz curtains.

Ruby's house had straw matting on the floor in the kitchen, and a Scandinavian lamp hanging over an oval table. The walls in the tiny living room were covered in rust-coloured hessian, with white plaster casts of Greek bas reliefs and shelves full of books. There were sheepskins thrown across the low sofas that lined the room; there were Japanese paper blinds in the windows. Everything was just so, each thing chosen for its specific combination of utility and beauty. Later Connie would describe it as a cross between 1960s Danish modern and Biedermeier. The paintings were eighteenth century, or early Victorian; the beds had duvets with striped covers; the panelled walls were painted white, like in a Carl Larsson drawing.

Connie's mother's house felt out of control, by contrast, despite being so relentlessly clean. Ruby's house was perfectly clean, that goes without saying, but it felt different: perhaps it was the proximity of the inhabitants, perhaps it was their bodily presence. Later Ruby said that when Connie moved out of her mother's house, her bodily smell changed. She stopped smelling so American.

Ruby's house smelled European, perhaps. Ruby's house was warm, and Ruby's mother Christine sat with them in the kitchen, getting up occasionally, preparing dinner or whatever, while Connie and Ruby consumed tea and toast indefinitely. The telly was on, showing children's programmes for Ruby's little sister, Rose. Viola would come in, telling stories of her day, the glamorous older sister. Connie was blissfully happy, she felt welcomed by Ruby's mother, and at the same time comfortably ignored.

Her own house was dark in the late afternoon; some of the time her parents were out of town, sometimes they were just out. Generally speaking she didn't see them when she got up in the morning to go to school; usually she didn't know if her father was there or not. He travelled a good deal, on business. The house was very big, six storeys, and when she was around, Connie's mother Helen was constantly yelling up or down the stairs, calling Connie to the phone, or to be lectured for some domestic misdeed. Everyone seemed very far away from each other, you had to yell to get their attention.

Recently Connie's parents had separated; they seemed to

be in the process of getting a divorce. During this period, her mother was often in the States, and Connie got used to the freedom these frequent absences allowed her. In any case, with her parents often absent and her older sister away at boarding school, a teatime scene of cosy domesticity in the kitchen was a rare event chez Connie. The cook lived in a flat in the basement; she didn't interfere with Connie, and Connie didn't interfere with her. Connie took it for granted there'd be lots of food, lots of leftovers, in the fridge. She didn't take anything else for granted, much.

Ruby's invitation was a daily reward, after the long exhausting day at school. It was like a test Connie had to pass, to be allowed into the inner sanctum. Ruby knew how much Connie wanted it, how much she needed it, and doubtless there were often afternoons when she'd much rather Connie didn't come to her house, when nevertheless she invited her, sensing Connie's need. Quite often Connie would be the one to ask, she would be driven to say, 'Can I come to tea?' And Ruby would reluctantly say, 'OK.'

It wasn't until many years later that Connie recognised, that Ruby let on, how problematic it was for Ruby, having to share her mother's attention with Connie. In this scenario, Christine Powell took Connie in, from the cold, so to speak. Poor Connie, from her awful American home, where no one was ever around to look after her. Ruby's mother took Connie in, and gave her a kind of uncritical, easygoing, friendly attention that may have seemed almost impossible with her own daughters. It was the typical family deadlock, and Connie sidestepped it, somehow. With Christine, or Mrs Powell, as Connie called her, there were no demands, no expectations: it was pure gift. It wasn't that Christine singled Connie out for attention, it was more as if she simply provided a reassuring uncritical presence, something that Connie craved. Perhaps this presence wasn't enough for Ruby, she wanted something else from her mother, recognition, or confrontation, even. Yet in a sense Ruby absorbed this maternal presence vicariously, even though it was her own mother, her house, as if by having Connie around, Ruby could have her mother too. At fourteen, Connie didn't think about rivalry, or envy; she only knew how much she wanted to go to Ruby's house, after school.

After the weekend in the country with Michael, Connie survived another two days at school. She went to tea with Ruby on Tuesday afternoon, and spent most of the time there watching the kids' programmes on telly.

Sometimes Connie worried about the amount of toast she ate, the amount of jam she consumed. She worried about how much these things cost, how she could never pay the Powells back for all the tea she'd consumed. Because Ruby never came to her house, hardly. She never sat around having tea. Ruby thought Connie's mother didn't like her. Connie didn't like to contemplate what her mother might think, about the Powells, or Ruby, about Connie going to their house virtually every day. Meanwhile, Mikey continued to write to her. He was coming up to London on Wednesday, bringing the mobile. Connie became more and more depressed as the days passed.

Looking back, Connie remembered the shock of pleasure she felt the first time she went to Ruby's house. They were in the same class in the first year at school, and one dark wet afternoon they ran into each other in the street outside the bookshop around the corner from South Kensington Station, both in their school coats and hats, standing on the crowded pavement as people going home from work rushed past. Their reaction was simultaneous, exact: 'What are *you* doing here?' It was an invasion of territory, a sense of possibility, to discover they lived nearby. Connie took the underground, then; Ruby took the bus. Connie had only just arrived from the

States, she didn't know about the bus. A few months later Ruby showed her the bus route, and then she invited her to tea. No one had done that before. Connie wasn't quite sure what tea amounted to, as a meal. Afterwards, Ruby took Connie upstairs to the attic room she shared with Viola. On the narrow staircase, they passed Ruby's parents' bedroom; Connie looked in. She saw a small square room, with white painted walls and fine matting on the floor, a little rug and a very low bed, about five foot wide, with a blanket of fox fur spread across it. She gasped, and exclaimed to Ruby, upstairs, 'Your parents' room is so sexy!' Ruby was surprised, she didn't see it that way. 'It's arty, the whole house is,' Connie insisted. 'Surely you know that.' Ruby took this in; it seemed she hadn't realised.

Connie's parents slept in a very big bed, high and hard and at least eight foot wide. It was made of two beds put side by side: it was enormous. Ruby found that almost as fascinating as Connie found the Powells' bed; Ruby found Americans exotic, and she was attracted to Connie partly because of this sense of difference. At eleven, Connie was sophisticated in ways Ruby hadn't come across before; she used words like sexy and arty without difficulty. Ruby liked Connie partly because she unhesitatingly drew attention to these differences, celebrating the Powells' way of doing things as clearly, undeniably superior. Ruby soaked it up, the attention, the appreciation, or praise. Connie was like an interpreter, describing Ruby's family, reflecting it back to Ruby herself.

It was clear that Connie wanted it, passionately, whatever it was, this odour, this sense of style, an almost tangible air of culture and gentility and proximity. At Connie's house, no one ever saw each other, it seemed. Her parents weren't happy together, they fought a lot, and they travelled a good deal. At Ruby's house, they sat together in the afternoon after school, five women between the ages of thirty-seven and five, Mrs Powell, Viola, Connie, Ruby, and Rose, drinking tea, eating toast.

Connie usually went home before Ruby's father David appeared back from work. Sometimes he'd come in the door as she left, and they'd coincide in the narrow hallway. Like Christine Powell, Ruby's father was shy, and an awkward kindness would blurt out of him in the dark hall as Connie went out the door. Her mother didn't like it if she wasn't home by seven, although a good part of the time she didn't notice when Connie came in. The house was big enough to allow people to come and go without anyone noticing.

After she made the decision, after she broke up with Michael, Connie destroyed the artwork he had made for her. It was an embarrassment, this ungainly, this excessive object; she had to get rid of it.

The mobile was huge, made of thick metal wire, inflexible, bent into long curves, with thin flat circular and oval panels or discs suspended on clear plastic thread, fishing tackle. Connie didn't know what to do with this thing. She'd been embarrassed when Michael gave it to her, embarrassed when he stood in her bedroom and handed it over, carefully wrapped up in tissue and brown paper. Connie was certain her mother would never give her permission to hang it in her room; she didn't want to discuss it with her mother anyway. It was too embarrassing, this evidence of love.

Michael stood there helplessly in Connie's bedroom, as Connie explained that she couldn't possibly hang the mobile, the room was too small. He suggested it would go over the end of her narrow bed, by the closet. She said she would hit it every time she opened the closet door. She was angry:

couldn't he see, couldn't he understand that she couldn't have this beautiful thing in her little room, that it was too much? Michael was disappointed, clearly, but he told her he would leave it with her there, even if she didn't hang it, because he'd made it for her. A chasm of disappointment and misunderstanding opened up between them, they felt miles apart, hurt, standing holding the carefully wrapped artwork in the little room.

Connie had reached the point where she couldn't take it any more. All her conflicted feelings accumulated, forming a monstrous tidal wave of confusion that threatened to knock her down, sweep her under. She wanted to stop it, to break it off, and she told Mikey so. She couldn't go on seeing him; it had to stop. She couldn't say why, though she knew it was something to do with how crazy he was about her, something to do with Ruby, and something to do with what happened to her when she went down to the country to stay with him that weekend.

That night in the country Connie slept badly, and on the Sunday morning, she was dazed and unhappy; she found herself being cold to Michael, she didn't know why; she found herself paying a lot of attention to the two little girls. Mikey looked confused, as if he couldn't remotely guess what had gone wrong. Connie didn't know herself; she knew she wanted to avoid any confrontation, she knew she didn't want to spend the day in Mikey's arms. That afternoon she took the train home, relieved it was all over. As the reality of Grantchester receded, as the train took her further and further away, Connie began to pore over her memories of the weekend; she began to enjoy it, finally.

It was like a series of beautiful images: Highgate, Mikey's letters on the mat in the morning, then the lawn behind the house at Grantchester, the shabby blue sofa and the big portfolio of pictures at their feet. It was all so romantic, in retrospect, and Mikey was beautiful, desirable, in fantasy, in ways he could never be in real life. It was as if Connie wished he could be madly in love with her, without ever having to see him, or his family, without it upsetting Ruby, without her mother and father having to know about it. Reality, in the form of her parents, or Ruby, distant and cross, or even Mikey himself, disrupted this dreamy scenario, like sharp edges knocking into her soft flesh. She couldn't take it.

What happened was, her humiliation turned to contempt. This transformation occurred imperceptibly; buried deep inside, the change took place. Connie's sleepless night in the country was the turning point; Michael, sound asleep, had rejected her sexually, without even knowing it. In the morning, it was as if she didn't like him any more, he didn't seem worth liking. She felt guilty, and confused; at the same time she knew he was still the infinitely desirable object, at least in Ruby's unspoken hierarchy. Yet Connie was embarrassed, she was somehow no longer unencumbered by doubts, she was no longer free and easy, or open to love. Connie closed herself off inside, seeing him powerless, the fifteen-year-old boy, gawky and awkward, enmeshed in the undeniable humiliation of family life. She felt contempt for him, deep down, and on the surface she felt guilty.

This sensation of contempt and humiliation diminished on the train back to London Sunday night; Connie was relieved. Indeed it was reduced to a shadow during the days that ensued before she saw him again, days in which Connie contended with the reality of Ruby, the appalling question of emotional survival at school. When she turned her mind to Mikey, in fantasy, her tense body melted, sexual desire overspilling into romantic emotion: he loved her. His letters arrived, describing this love. Nevertheless, each day Connie stood at the bus stop with Ruby, miserable and wishing things could be OK again between them. Connie felt somehow that despite everything, Ruby's attachment to Mikey was absolute. And Hope was besotted with him, obsessed. But Connie didn't love Mikey; she wasn't in love with him. After the weekend in the country, Connie wrote in her journal that she'd been in love with Mikey for about two hours. Now she was lost, she didn't know what to do.

When Mikey came up to London, bringing the mobile, a couple of days later, his look of longing was too much, just as the mobile was too much. Connie couldn't bear it. They stood in her bedroom, discussing the impossibility of hanging the mobile, and then they tried to break through the coldness and embarrassment that pervaded the room; they sat down on the bed and kissed. It was easy to kiss, to make out, easier than talking, or deciding what to do about all this unhappiness. At one point Mikey suggested that they drop into Ruby's house for tea; Connie was shocked, she realised he was completely oblivious to the whole thing. She didn't know what to say.

As darkness fell, Connie looked out of the window, sitting on the straight chair by her desk, as Mikey lay sideways on the bed. Mikey listened as she carefully explained that she couldn't go on seeing him. She couldn't go out with him any more. Mikey was devastated; he protested wildly, in whispers, insisting that he loved her, that anything was possible, they could make it good, asking what it was that he'd done wrong. Connie couldn't meet Michael's eyes; looking away, she explained that he'd done nothing wrong, there was no reason for it, it just wasn't working, it had to stop.

Connie remembered when Mikey left that evening, he stood in the street outside her house, she was standing just outside the front door, at the top of the steps that led from the pavement to the front door, she was looking down at him, as he stood on the pavement, empty handed. Connie remembered how Mikey threw his hands out open by his sides, crying out to her, 'We can work it out.' Connie remembered him saying that over and over, 'We can work it out.' It was a line from a Beatles song. Connie said nothing. He didn't realise about Ruby. He hadn't realised that Connie was nobody, Ruby's sidekick, she had nothing. He didn't realise that he'd made a terrible mistake.

Connie couldn't allow herself this prize, Michael's love, she had to shut it down. Connie lived with Ruby, day in, day out, and Ruby's approval and disapproval, her warmth and her icy coldness shaped Connie's days. Connie adored Ruby, but she also loved her, she loved making her laugh, hearing her secrets. She loved merely being in her presence, she loved the way Ruby moved. Later she would always think of Ruby when she heard that line, 'your magnetic movements still capture the minutes I'm in.' Connie loved walking arm in arm with her, sensing her soft body, her milky skin. She loved her smell, her clothes, her beautiful hands. Mikey had beautiful hands, like Ruby; Connie's hands were short and stubby, she didn't like them, even though Ruby said they were OK. 'You've got *nice* hands Con,' she would say. Connie couldn't take it, Mikey's love; she had to break it off. She was left with his mobile, wrapped in paper; she shoved it in the bottom of her closet. She was left with the mobile, and a terrible feeling of guilt. It was heartrending, the image of Mikey standing in the street, his last protest against her cruelty, his hands open, saying, 'We can work it out.' Connie felt terrible.

Connie and Ruby made up quite quickly; if it was a choice between Ruby and Michael, Connie chose Ruby, that was clear. They didn't talk about it much; it was as if they preferred to pretend it never happened. The day Connie split up with Mikey, Ruby spent the whole afternoon making a drawing of her. For Connie it was inevitable, the break-up, she felt she had no choice.

Years later, Connie couldn't help but suspect that Cynthia had also had a hand in the disaster, by so relentlessly insisting on including Connie in the family scene, by domesticating this adolescent passion, by turning it into a spectacle for the amusement of the grownups. If your son brings a girl home, Cynthia's strategy was simple: win her heart, find her charming, delightful, take photographs, make her yours. It was very effective, successfully diluting or undercutting the element of transgression in the love affair, making it into something childish, or sweet. That was the word she used, Connie recalled, Cynthia announcing how *sweet* Connie and Mikey were, kissing all afternoon. Lying on the blue sofa, listening to The Doors on the record player, pressing herself against Michael's body, it didn't feel sweet. It felt dangerous. In the end though, it seems it wasn't dangerous enough.

That night Connie wrote Mikey a letter, blaming herself hysterically, insisting it was all her fault. She described herself as a neurotic, cold, incapable of love, or of receiving love. At the same time she was very clear: it was over between them. He must accept it. She was sorry, she was no good, it couldn't go on.

A couple of weeks later Connie received a letter from Michael in Florence; it described his room at the pensione, the art classes he was taking. He sounded desolate, obviously very alone, but he didn't refer to the heartbreak, it was almost as if he was trying to be polite, to keep in touch. He did say that he thought of her often. Connie wrote back a similarly unemotional letter, redolent with suppressed guilt, and that was that.

Connie was left with the mobile in the bottom of her closet. One afternoon she saw it there and she decided to get rid of it.

Connie removed the seemingly enormous mobile from its loose nest of brown paper wrapping. Then she took a plastic carrier bag and she crammed the thing into it. She had to use all her strength to bend the curved metal wires, to fold them into lengths small enough to go in the bag. The complicated threads of fishing tackle were irretrievably tangled, the painted discs jumbled against each other in a mess. Michael's carefully created balance was irrevocably ruined.

In the process of jamming the mobile into the bag, Connie's eye fell on the blue disc that bore Mikey's dedication, 'For Connie with my love Michael 17 May 1969'. She found her scissors and snipped the line that attached it to the chaotic web of thread and wire and blue discs. This she would keep, some kind of relic. The rest she took downstairs, carrying the bulky bag gingerly in both hands, she slipped quickly down the four long flights of stairs, hoping she wouldn't be intercepted, she made it to the front door. Leaving the heavy door on the latch, Connie went around to the gate in the area railings, down the wooden stairs to the basement area where the rubbish bins were kept. Heart beating fast, Connie lifted the lid, and shoved the plastic bag down into it, this bulging bag with wires poking out in accusation, she was terrified that she would be caught in the act, terrified that someone would see it, catch her committing this crime.

Connie felt like she'd killed something; she'd killed off Mikey's love, she'd destroyed his gift. She felt like she was left with nothing, that only with nothing could she hope for Ruby's love.

Connie was painfully aware of what she'd done; the recollection of bending the metal wires out of shape, and cramming the miscellaneous pieces into that plastic bag, this memory would come to her involuntarily, years later, causing an irrepressible shudder of horror. Connie put the little blue disc with Michael's writing on it in a white shoebox containing other treasures, romantic mementoes: a scrap of embroidered velvet Hope once gave her, a half-smoked Black Russian cigarette, a translucent pair of dice. She never forgave herself for doing what she did, for destroying everything, and somehow, as the years passed, keeping the little blue disc, this last fragment, in the long white box, seemed to be the worst thing of all, sentimental, narcissistic, despicable. Connie rarely opened the box: it was labelled DEEP STORAGE: TREASURES, and kept inside a larger box containing old notebooks, drawings, an inlaid box with her long hair inside it (later, when she cut it off), and various containers of shells, beads, old postcards, an ancient tin car, a 1930s ceramic statue of an exotic woman, et cetera. Souvenirs: somehow Connie felt she shouldn't have reduced her relationship with Michael to the level of a souvenir. Neverthcless, she didn't throw it away.

Intransigent

In this way the hours passed. The two women disposed themselves across the long orange sofas, as the low glass table before them became crowded with empty bowls of coffee, the scattered remains of lunch, miscellaneous papers, bright ashtrays filling slowly, the detritus of an afternoon.

Iris had a friend, a young woman from Guatemala, who was an exile, a political activist, a refugee. Her name was Rita. She used to stay with Iris, sleeping in her living-room, when she was in New York. In fact she'd lived in Iris's flat for about six months, or more. Now she was in Mexico City, working with the Guatemalans in exile there.

Connie had met Rita once, a couple of years before. She remembered a shy young woman, small and almost demure in aspect. Earlier in the afternoon, before Connie phoned Michael, Iris had been telling her about how she'd spoken to Rita on the phone recently, and Rita had asked Iris to send her some winter clothes, as it was cold in Mexico City, much colder than she'd expected. Since Connie was going to Mexico City in a few days, maybe she could take the clothes.

Connie thought that sounded reasonable. She was going to

Mexico City with William the following week. And after all, Rita was a political activist; Connie would do whatever she could to help her, wouldn't she. She wondered what William would think; she was meeting him in California, and then they were travelling south to Mexico together. An extra suitcase wouldn't be a problem, would it. It wasn't clear whether the clothes Iris wanted to send were old clothes belonging to her, cast-offs, or clothes that Rita'd left in New York. In any case, Rita was cold in Mexico City; Connie could take some winter clothes to her without too much difficulty.

Connie said, 'Sure, OK, I'll take the clothes.'

Iris was pleased. Now, as the evening closed in, it seemed time to figure out what she was going to give Connie to take. Iris got up from the sofa and opened her hall closet, which was packed solid with boxes and empty suitcases and broken things. Iris looked at the contents of the closet, her brow furrowed with concentration. Slowly she began to extract from the closet various bags with broken zippers, small suitcases with snaps that wouldn't close, a couple of large black plastic rubbish bags full of old clothes. As Iris started looking through her collection of department-store carrier bags, testing them for toughness and resiliency, the whole project suddenly seemed impossible. Connie couldn't help imagining her own irritation at the airport the next day, as she gradually understood that Iris was intending to give her at least two bags of clothes.

Tentatively Connie said, 'I didn't realise you were planning to give me so much; I've already got a great deal to carry — one enormous bag and rather a lot of hand luggage.'

'I never imagined this would be *easy* for you,' Iris snapped.

Connie was silent. Iris seemed merely punitive, and again Connie quailed in the presence of such ferocity. She paused for a moment, then Connie said, 'It's just that it would be best if I could check it in . . . if that's feasible.'

'We'll see,' Iris muttered, as she pulled another bag out of the closet. She seemed to be wanting to find a bag she wouldn't mind parting with, which was likely to be a smaller bag, a broken but still useable bag, in which case it would require at least two of them, since winter clothes tend to be quite bulky. Connie stared at Iris balefully, wondering what was going to happen next.

When Iris had covered the floor next to the closet with a chaotic heap of small suitcases and bags, she stopped. Heaving a great sigh, Iris gave up, saying, 'I think the best thing is if I bring the clothes up to you tomorrow morning; I could pack them up late tonight and come up and meet you, early; we could have coffee before you go to the airport.'

To Connie this proposal seemed fraught with danger. She saw herself early Wednesday morning, desperately waiting for Iris, wondering when she would arrive, as the minutes ticked by. Connie was always very nervous on the way to the airport. Then she saw Iris in a panic, stuffing clothes into shopping bags and throwing herself onto the subway, to get uptown to meet Connie in time for her flight. It all seemed too dreadful for words.

Nevertheless, after a half-hearted protest, Connie acquiesced. Her tendency was to feel that Iris was immoveable, the plan was non-negotiable. She also sensed how Iris seemed driven to do everything in the most impossible way, as if the world were an intransigent enemy to be wrestled with, endlessly. Nothing could ever go smoothly, or work out. And of course, this plan, to meet Connie early in the morning, also meant Connie couldn't veto the bags, the amount of clothing, it meant Connie would have to submit to whatever Iris deemed was appropriate for her to carry, not just to San Francisco, but to Mexico City next week.

Iris flung herself onto the sofa and lit a cigarette. Then she said, 'Oh, I forgot to tell you, Rita isn't called Rita in Mexico

City. This is terribly important. She's called Sara. You *mustn't* call her Rita. Under any circumstances. You *must* remember to call her Sara.'

'OK,' Connie said. She felt terribly tired.

'I'll give you her number. She's actually very hard to reach. The best time to call her is at about midnight. That's usually when you can find her there. Midnight, or in any case after eleven.'

Connie said nothing.

'The important thing is to remember her name is Sara. And, well, anyway you'll just have to keep trying, if you don't get an answer. As I say, I think you'll probably be able to reach her if you call late, around twelve, or one, maybe.'

Connie imagined herself in the cheap hotel on the Alameda, where she and William stayed in Mexico City. She pictured herself trying to stay up late, to call Rita, who was called Sara in Mexico City. Mexico City was so enormous, she pictured herself trying to find Rita in the enormous city. She pictured herself with a couple of bags of old clothes, not being able to track Rita down, wondering what to do with the clothes. Connie sighed, deciding to put these thoughts out of her mind. She would do it, to please Iris; she was on automatic, anyway. She listened vaguely, as Iris went on talking about Rita and her other activist friends, the Guatemalans.

At about a quarter to five, Connie began to stir, rousing her strength for the ordeal ahead. It was then that Iris's sensibility, her delicacy, really, took Connie by surprise.

Iris said, 'It's nearly time for you to go to Michael's, no?'

'Yes,' Connie said, 'I guess it must be.' It was almost dark outside, now; agitated particles of snow were visible, hovering in the light from Iris's high window. Connie was overwhelmed with dread.

Iris said, 'I've decided I won't come with you; I expect you'd rather see Michael by yourself, and anyway I have something I ought to be doing uptown. I can phone Michael and fix another time to meet and get this drawing or whatever it is.'

This reprieve was completely unexpected. Then Iris said, 'And I've been thinking about the five hundred dollars. I think there might be a solution.'

Connie was amazed; Iris seemed to have temporarily, incomprehensibly, shifted out of monster mode, to once again become the sensitive friend. 'Tell me,' Connie said.

She told her. She told her about an organisation set up to help the families of Palestinians who are killed or wounded or interned in the Occupied Territories. She told her it provided support services, health care, and emergency funds, things like that. Iris spoke quietly. 'I've been meaning to give them some money, for a while now, for a long time, really, and I thought, if you don't want to write the cheque to me,' — at this point Iris turned away, getting up to look through the papers on her desk — 'perhaps you'd be willing to write it to them.' She continued searching, and then produced the organisation's leaflet for Connie to read. Iris seemed shy, suddenly, and vulnerable, and her physical fragility, a sense of her too breakable bones, her liquid skin, made Connie feel gargantuan, monstrous, that her anger had been excessive, somehow sharp edged and cruel. She felt terrible, filled with regret.

Connie spoke quickly, she said, 'That would be fine with me, of course, I'd be happy to do it that way, but you know it's Michael's money, I mean it's *his* painting, right, but if it's OK with him, then it's really fine with me.'

In retrospect Connie believed this decision was profoundly mistaken, that she'd been deeply compromised by agreeing to Iris's suggestion. At the time she thought, well, it's as *if* — what? As if Michael gave Connie the painting, and in exchange Connie gave him five hundred dollars, which he gave to Iris, who gave it to the Palestinians. It seemed like a solution, or a semblance of a solution, to write the cheque to someone else. The tight little triangle opened up, introducing a fourth term in this geometric equation, the Palestinians, and letting Connie off the hook. She no longer had to choose between giving five hundred dollars to either Michael or Iris, she could give it to someone else altogether.

However, it seemed later that Connie's agreement only confirmed Iris's belief that her refusal to write the cheque to Iris was founded in a simple wish to deny her the money. Iris thought Connie didn't want her to have the money, and though there was an element of this in her resolution (that seems undeniable), it was not her primary motive, Connie thought.

As Connie told Ruby later, 'Iris doesn't seem to me to *need* the money, not like Mikey needs it, or you or I might need it, although of course none of us are totally poverty-struck, we're not *destitute*. Still, it *means* something to us, and it seemed to me that it meant something completely different to her, something about power, about getting her own way, or something, at last. Pure punishment.'

Connie felt Iris's pursuit of the five hundred dollars, plus interest, was vindictive, it was punitive. Connie flattered herself that she didn't want to give Iris the money because she was displeased with what appeared to be a translation of the terms of the exchange, the terms of her amicable transaction with Michael. Connie associated buying the painting with her dream of the bunch of flowers, dug up, while Iris's ancient claims were like old fish hooks, long buried in scarred skin, being tugged to the surface. It was agonising, this recollection of dark days and nights. And, projecting all her own vulnerability onto him, Connie desperately wanted to protect Michael from this, to protect him from Iris.

To Connie, it seemed as if Michael's past misdeeds, too

numerous and variegated to name, were rearing their hideous heads in the cold light of day, too many years later, like ghastly demons resurrected and demanding payment, demanding blood money. And of course Connie had played a critical if inadvertent part in this resurrection, by phoning Michael from Iris's, by offering the exact sum on the phone. It was like that time, another time, when she brought them together, by accident. It was an unfortunate coincidence, so to speak, a horrible rhyming of past and present, and Connie felt it was all her fault.

So she was immediately very willing to accept Iris's suggestion, to give the money to the Palestinians, for it undid the dichotomy, the either/or, it provided another path. The drug money would go to a good cause, to the Palestinians. They could all agree on that. The Palestinians needed the money much more than any of them ever would. It wasn't really a solution, though, in the end; it was more like an excuse, a way to sidestep confrontation.

Iris told Connie she wanted the money given in her name. She gave her the leaflet, so Connie would know where to send it. And they agreed to meet uptown the following morning, at nine, so Iris could give her the clothes. They embraced, and Connie left, walking down the tiled stairs from the top floor flat. Connie was terribly relieved, and she was exhausted; she was relieved Iris wasn't coming to Michael's, relieved to get away from her poisonous presence. At the same time Connie was grateful to Iris for coming up with a solution of sorts. Connie opened the heavy front door, and stepped out into the freezing streets.

Pastoral

It was the Fourth of July weekend, 1983; it was too hot in the city and Connie decided to get out of town. She was living in a tiny sublet in New York for three months, for the summer, doing research and trying to write a book. She'd finished her thesis finally, and at last she could work on something else. Connie decided to spend a few days with her mother in the country, she took the long bus ride north to Maine. It was a relief to get out of the city.

Connie's mother Helen lived near mountains and lakes, not far from one of her oldest friends, Olivia. Olivia's twin sons, Bobby and Jack, were a year older than Connie, they were all hitting thirty. When they were seven and eight years old, Bobby and Jack and Connie went to dancing school together in Chicago; when she was seventeen, while he was in London one summer, Connie started sleeping with Jack. They never even remotely thought they might be in love; on the contrary, they seemed simply to be attracted to each other, and therefore easily fell into bed in an uncomplicated way whenever their paths happened to cross, which wasn't very often these days. At this time Connie was unattached; she'd been pursuing the same reluctant object for some months. When her mother told her Jack would also be coming to Maine for the weekend, to see Olivia, Connie thought, that would be nice.

Sitting on the bus on the way up to Maine, listening to Talking Heads on the walkman, 'Burning Down the House', Connie suddenly gasped: she realised she'd left her diaphragm behind in New York. She laughed, pulling the earphones off; she felt caught out. A little while after she arrived at her mother's, Connie explained the problem. Connie's mother was always very enthusiastic about her relationship with Jack; indeed Connie suspected Helen had more or less pushed Jack into Connie's arms the first time, when they were seventeen. Now, faced with the crisis of contraception, Helen said, 'No problem: we'll go see my friend Rick, the pharmacist. Do you remember what size diaphragm you use?'

This was the sort of scene Connie's mother really enjoyed: slightly wacky, slightly risqué, standing in the old style shopping-centre pharmacy, explaining that her daughter had come up to Maine for a dirty weekend, and had forgotten her diaphragm. Rick didn't mind. Connie found it all rather amusing, as well as somewhat embarrassing, this scene of feminine plotting, this preparation for Jack's impending arrival. Of course there was always the remote possibility that Jack would have something else in mind; maybe he'd turn her down, anything was possible. Helen loved to joke with Olivia about how wonderful it would be if Connie and Jack ended up getting married. Very occasionally, when Connie was both heartbroken and depressed, she would contemplate this alternative with something resembling enthusiasm. It was completely unrealistic, however; Jack and Connie had nothing to talk about, really. They just liked fucking each other, they were old pals, nothing more.

At this point, Iris rang from New York. She called in a state of total desperation, crying, panting with anxiety, terrified, suicidal. Iris was panicking on the telephone; she said she was desperate to get out of the city, everyone was leaving town for the weekend, she had to get out. She said, 'Can I come and stay with you?'

Connie didn't hesitate; she said, 'Come, it'll be fine, just get on the bus. Come here, I'm sure my mother will be happy to have you.' So Iris went to the Port Authority, and got the Greyhound bus to Maine.

Helen had known Iris's mother Elizabeth; as young women they'd moved in the same circles socially. And Iris knew Jack from college; they'd coincided at Princeton for a year or two, as undergraduates. When Iris got off the bus, she was smiling and cheerful, all the anguish of the night before evaporated in the yellow July light. Connie thought Iris was making an effort to be a pleasant houseguest, she was grateful. When Iris heard Jack and his brother Bobby were expected; she said, 'Let's go over there right away.' So Helen drove them to Olivia's, where there was no sign of the boys; they had a quick cup of tea, and went home.

Connie's cousin Ruth had also unexpectedly descended on Helen for the weekend; this meant Connie and Iris had to share a room. Iris seemed slightly surprised. There were hard, narrow twin beds in this room, with flowered bedspreads that matched the curtains. The door didn't close, and the tiny, screened windows didn't open more than an inch or two. It was hot and airless; Iris threw her suede carryall down on the floor, and stretched out on one of the narrow beds. She sighed, intensely, staring at the sloping ceiling. Suddenly Connie felt exhausted. The task of mediating between Iris and the rest of the world seemed almost beyond her.

That night, in the bedroom, Iris lay on the narrow bed tossing and turning, groaning aloud. Iris was half asleep, it seemed, her limbs jerking, moans and groans emerging from her body uncontrollably. Connie realised this was cold turkey, this was kicking. It didn't stop, this suffering, these constant low cries of grief and physical pain; it went on all night. Connie lay there trying to sleep. She was worried that everyone else in the house could hear it, she was worried what her mother would say.

At one point, she said, 'Iris, Iris, are you OK?' There was no reply. It was clear to the dullest eye that Iris wasn't OK.

Connie realised Iris had taken it for granted that she would have a bedroom to herself, she didn't expect to have to share a room with Connie. Connie knew Iris believed she was completely in control of her drug use, that she knew exactly what she was doing. Iris didn't want to be questioned, she had no intention of discussing this. Thus Connie was put in the position of being the reluctant witness to the spectacle of Iris kicking; she hardly slept at all. She was also mystified: either Iris was asleep (despite her groans and cries and sudden jerking movements), either Iris was sleeping (and maybe she'd taken something to knock herself out), or she was pretending to be asleep, unavailable, unapproachable. Connie felt caught between anxiety and embarrassment. Connie's loyalty to Iris was compromised by this scene; she hated Iris for doing this to her, to her mother. She wanted to protect Helen from telling anyone about it, she wished she wasn't stuck in this dark, airless room with this body in pain.

In the morning, Connie felt exceedingly tired. Iris seemed rather perky, considering. Helen looked exhausted, she drove off to the supermarket to get something to give everyone for lunch. Connie's cousin Ruth took Connie aside quietly, she said, 'Is Iris coming off drugs?' Connie said, 'Yes, I think so. I hope it didn't disturb you too much.' Ruth said, 'No, it's just unexpected. It's weird, the sounds you make are like nothing else.' 'Yes,' Connie said. She felt completely in the dark.

Drinking coffee in the kitchen, Jack and Bobby swept in,

unannounced; they'd come to find Iris and Connie, to whisk them away for a walk. Connie felt very self-conscious when she laid eyes on Jack; it was probably all that laughing with her mother about her diaphragm, she felt somewhat embarrassed. Bobby was sweet, friendly and unthreatening as always. Jack was a little shy, resorting to cascades of slang as cover. They jumped into Bobby's little car, and headed back to Olivia's house; there was talk of going swimming in the quarry, or hiking up the river; it was hot.

Standing on the patch of lawn beside their house, feeling slightly nervous, self-conscious, Jack suddenly took hold of Connie around her waist and turned her upside down. Connie shrieked; it was like they were kids again, she was blushing as he set her on her feet, staggering slightly. Jack was the only person in the world who would take such liberties with her, tease and torment her, manhandle her, turn her upside down. She was tall, but he was taller and much stronger than she was; he was like a big brother, or something. Connie felt absurdly feminine, tottering as she regained her balance, she felt like he was insisting she didn't take everything so seriously, forcing her to laugh at herself.

Meanwhile Iris was talking to Olivia about the garden flowers, apparently oblivious to this scene. Connie was covered in confusion, flummoxed, and wishing she hadn't told Iris about her designs on Jack. Connie had recounted the pharmacy story roaring with laughter, as if it were all a huge joke. Jack's unexpected physical assault left her momentarily breathless and confused, and he seemed slightly amazed at himself too, and then it was over, forgotten, as the three of them squeezed into the front of Jack's pickup truck, and headed for the river. Bobby would follow in his car a little later. Iris was laughing with Jack about Princeton; Connie watched the sunlight dappling the roadside as they drove.

Connie was wearing bright pink plastic sandals and a thin

cotton summer dress, which she tucked into her pants as she looked up at the stream. She felt tired, anticipating the walk, clambering from boulder to boulder, surrounded by falling water, icy cold river water pouring down the side of the mountain. Losing sleep always wiped her out completely. The little river was shaded by tall trees, the water fell splashing into small pools and crevices; they were going to climb up the rushing stream, in the green shade, ankles wet, a pleasant walk, a hike, as Jack called it, an adventure. Connie wasn't sure. She looked up to see Iris ahead, Iris was leaning towards Jack, laughing, with her arms out, propped on a boulder as she found her footing, bare legs splayed, the low boat neck of her dress falling forward, her beautiful long neck and small breasts exposed. Connie saw Jack looking at Iris, smiling. Iris was flirting with Jack.

Connie's heart sank. She looked up again, she saw Jack laughing, she saw them moving away from her, gradually getting further and further ahead. Stunned, Connie couldn't quite believe it.

The decision was immediate and involuntary: she wouldn't compete. Connie wouldn't try to catch up with them, she wouldn't laugh and tease, she wouldn't desperately try to out-flirt Iris. She went on slowly clambering up the river.

Then, after a while, Connie gave up. She sat down on a fallen tree beside the water, and dolefully contemplated the pastoral scene. Occasionally she heard Iris's voice in the distance, peals of laughter ringing out, against the rushing sound of falling water. Connie felt terrible. Eventually she spotted Bobby, and she asked him to give her a lift home. She'd had enough.

They were all supposed to be going to dinner at Olivia's that evening. Connie lay down on a grass mat on the lawn behind her mother's house, and read Trollope for the rest of the afternoon. Iris reappeared towards evening, seemingly in very good spirits. 'What happened to you?' she asked, and again Connie sidestepped the issue. 'I got Bobby to give me a lift home, I was terribly tired,' she said. Iris went upstairs to lie down. At about six-thirty, Connie went up to change her clothes to go out to dinner.

Iris was putting her soft contact lenses in, applying mascara. As Connie sat on the edge of the bed, pulling on her black tights, she started to cry. She couldn't stop. Iris ignored this. Connie felt stricken; she pictured the evening before her: Iris flirting with Jack as they all watched, an audience consisting of Helen, Bobby, Jack, Olivia, George (Olivia's husband), other guests Connie didn't know. Tears silently streaming, Connie suddenly decided not to go. Her cousin Ruth wasn't going (she didn't know them); Connie could just stay home. She said, 'I've decided not to go.' Iris looked annoyed. 'Why not?' she said. 'I just can't face it,' Connie muttered, still avoiding open confrontation.

Helen was upset when she heard; all their plans had gone awry. As far as she could see, Iris was making Connie unhappy, and she might be Connie's dear friend, and her mother might be dead, and her father out of the picture, but the last thing Helen wanted to do was drive off to a dinner party at Olivia's alone with Iris. There was a moment of confusion, indecision, and then abruptly they left, Connie's mother powdered and pearled, Iris expressionless, and Connie suddenly terribly relieved to have escaped her fate. She sat quietly with Ruth, talking about their respective families, for most of the evening. She felt exhausted, partly lack of sleep, partly that terrible drained feeling after so much ridiculous crying.

At about nine-thirty, Helen stormed in. She was furious, almost incoherent with rage and disgust. 'That girl, she's unstoppable, making eyes at Jack, making eyes at George, it was awful. It's just as well you didn't come.'

'Yes, I'm rather glad I didn't, I must say,' Connie replied. Ruth was smiling, as Helen sat down on the sofa and tore off her high heels, throwing them on the floor. Then her mother looked at Connie with an expression of horror.

'Connie — she doesn't wear any underwear!' At this Connie laughed, she really laughed, because it was true, Iris didn't, and Helen's horror was palpable.

'No, Mummy, she never does.'

Helen said, 'She was sitting on the sofa, with her leg under her, you know, tucked under, in that dress, and she was talking to Richard Bernstein, he was sitting across from her, and — she had nothing on. I mean, she was showing off her snatch — to Richard, who's a ninety-year-old man!'

Connie laughed and laughed. Helen said she didn't think it was funny, she said, 'I've never been so embarrassed; I was appalled, appalled!' She went on, her voice rising higher as she gave in to hyberbole, unable to resist: 'You should have seen her with George!' Ruth and Connie laughed wildly. Helen continued: 'Olivia was horrified, of course. I couldn't stand another minute of it!'

'So Iris is still there?'

'Yes, I left her there. I didn't know what else to do!'

Connie was amused at this scene, imagining Helen and Olivia's expressions of disapproval, picturing the various men at the table responding to Iris's irresistible attractions. Iris had infinite charm, she could turn it on like a faucet, her big blue eyes would focus, draw you close. Connie was glad she'd abdicated, she'd given up, she felt extremely relieved, and tried to persuade herself that she didn't care about Jack anyway. Needless to say this fiction would have been easier to maintain had she remembered her diaphragm, had the ridiculous pharmacy scene not been etched so clearly on her memory.

Connie slept, and barely noticed when Iris came in very

late, after two a.m. There was more tossing and turning, more groans and cries, but for an hour or so, Connie slept through it, then she woke up. Connie lay still in the darkness, listening to Iris's muffled agonies. At about four a.m. she got up and went downstairs, to sleep in the empty half of her mother's enormous double bed. In the morning Connie got up extremely early. Over her solitary breakfast, she decided to leave.

When Connie told her mother she was going, Helen seemed to understand why. 'It is heroin she's taking, isn't it?' she said.

'Not at this moment, actually, not right now,' Connie said. 'I mean, she's stopped.'

'Yes, I know.'

'She's not addicted, Mummy.'

'No.'

'How did you guess, I mean, how did you know?'

'Good God, what do you think I am? You think that just because I'm your mother I've never known any junkies? That's awfully naïve of you!'

'No I didn't think that . . .' Connie said quietly. Helen was irritated. Connie realised Iris was acting out, confronting everyone, forcing them to engage with her, to take part in her struggle, or not. She was showing off her snatch, as her mother put it. Connie tried to imagine Jack and Iris fucking in his pickup truck on the way back from Olivia's dinner party; she wondered where they'd done it, in the truck, on the sofa, in Jack's bed?

When Iris got up at about twelve, Connie calmly said, 'I'm going back to New York this afternoon.'

Iris was surprised. 'What?' she said. She looked at Connie hard, as if her tough expression could make Connie come clean. 'Why?' Iris asked, and Connie said, 'I've had enough, I want to get back.'

'I'll come with you.'

'No, I think not.'

'Why not?'

'I don't think I could sit next to you on the bus for ten and a half hours,' Connie said, expressionless.

At this Iris burst into tears. Connie said 'I'm sorry,' in a voice devoid of expression.

Iris said, 'Well obviously I can't stay here.'

'I'm sure you can if you'd like to,' said Connie, gently sadistic.

'Don't be absurd. I can't possibly stay.'

Connie reminded Iris of a plan she'd mentioned earlier, to go see Harry, an old friend, who also lived in Maine. Connie said, 'You could get one of the boys to drive you, at least half-way.'

Iris appeared slightly stunned by Connie's coldness, her absolutely righteous withdrawal of affection. Meanwhile Connie imagined herself to be behaving impeccably. Iris said, 'Well, if that's what you want.'

'It's not what I want, Iris. Do whatever it is that you want to do, please; I'm just getting out of here.'

Helen was distraught, and scrupulously, icily polite. Everything had gone wrong and it was all Iris's fault. Connie was surprised, and pleased that her mother cared so much. Iris sat in the garden, waiting for her ride, reading a book. Connie stared at her with a piercing anger; she felt Helen had been burdened with secrets she shouldn't have to keep; she felt exploited, emotionally, when she remembered Iris's tears on the phone. There was a union, a solidarity between Connie and Helen that wasn't merely unusual, it was unique. They could wholeheartedly agree, for once, lined up against Iris, the bad girl.

Neither Connie nor Helen blamed Jack, of course. It was as if they thought that men aren't responsible for themselves, not the same way as women are. Later this seemed to Connie to be one of the most significant aspects of the whole incident, the way she'd let Jack off the hook, as if his part in it were insignificant, meaningless. It was a drama between her and Iris, with her mother Helen playing a crucial role, and Iris's mother Elizabeth off-stage somewhere, hovering as a ghost in the wings.

That day her mother drove Connie to the bus stop, refraining from putting pressure on her to stay. Connie got back to the steamy city Sunday night, relieved to be far away from all of them. Unpacking her soft bag, she found the new diaphragm, pristine, untouched, odourless. Now she had two diaphragms — and no one to sleep with.

A few days later, Iris returned. Connie had seen no one, she'd gone into some kind of retreat. It was quite a setback, really; she felt like she'd walked blindly into a brick wall; she felt she'd been an idiot, to imagine she could be kind to Iris, Iris in tears on the phone, and at the same time pursue Jack. Her relationship with the current reluctant object, as she termed him, was almost purely adversarial; it was as if her task was to persuade him she was worth falling in love with, as if she could knock this idea into him, get it through his thick head. She felt, absurdly, that he was choosing to withhold his affections, his passion, his attachment, he was choosing to refuse her love, out of sheer perversity, or sadism. It was Jack's easygoing kindness she'd craved, and lost. She'd just wanted a break from all this. She felt she'd been a fool; she went into some kind of reverse, retreat. She didn't ring anyone, she didn't go out.

Then Iris came back, and called her. Connie was surprised. Iris seemed to be wanting to make up, or at least to talk about it. Connie decided that if Iris wanted to talk, she wouldn't refuse. Connie went over to Iris's place, to her flat in Little Italy, ready to tell the truth.

'What did you think I'd think?' she said.

Iris paused before she spoke. 'I didn't — frankly, I thought nothing was going to happen with you and Jack, so I thought, well, why not.'

'That's it?'

'Yes — I thought Jack wasn't going to — he wasn't interested in you, and I thought, you know, if that's the case, why should I hold back?'

'Wow.'

'What do you mean, wow? You know I haven't had sex in ages . . .'

'Neither have I.'

'Then why didn't you try harder, why did you just give in?' Iris looked genuinely perplexed.

Connie was silent.

Iris went on, 'If you wanted it so much.'

Connie breathed. Her voice was very quiet. She said, 'I didn't want to compete with you for Jack. That was something I didn't want.'

Iris sighed, saying, 'Jesus, Connie, give me a break.'

Connie was silent. This was impasse, purely; neither one could understand the other.

Connie was almost shocked at Iris's insistence, her suggestion that Connie could have fought for him. Maybe that's what Iris wanted, to fight. Yet it seemed to Connie that it was all some kind of displacement, that the true battle between her and Iris was over junk. She decided to tell Iris this, to tell her what she thought about junk. She held forth for a while.

Iris was predictably dismissive; the moaning, the uncontrollable jerking and turning, kicking, that was nothing. 'Nothing!' Iris pulled condescension whenever Connie appeared to be coming on with some kind of moral superiority. Iris repeated, over and over again, that Connie really didn't know what she was talking about. And Connie had to admit, so OK she didn't do junk, so she never had, but, but, she loved Iris, she'd known Iris for years and years, and that gave her the right to say these things. Connie somewhat self-consciously tried to put her tendency to self-righteous disapproval to one side, to leave Iris's 'bad behaviour' (fucking Jack) out of it, to address what she felt was the much more pressing question of Iris's life.

This was their epic confrontation, when Connie said, 'I can't be friends with you on junk,' and Iris said, 'It's nothing.'

Iris said, 'You know nothing about doing drugs.'

Iris said, 'You know nothing about heroin.'

Iris said, 'I'm not addicted.'

Iris said, 'Give me a break!'

Iris said, 'It brings out the best in me.'

Iris said, 'Maybe I just need it.'

Iris said, 'Smoking heroin isn't addictive the way shooting up is.'

Iris said, 'Maybe the addictive agents go up in smoke, maybe the element that's addictive disperses in the smoke, who knows?'

Iris said, 'All my friends who smoke aren't addicted.'

Iris said, 'No I've never used a needle, though I'd like to.'

Iris said, 'The only time I ever had a chance to, it was in some scuzzy shooting gallery uptown and I was scared of getting, you know, hepatitis.' (It was July 1983.)

Iris said, 'How can you refuse any experience?'

Iris said, 'You don't know what you're talking about.'

And Connie said, 'I can't be friends with you as long as you're doing heroin.' And Iris went on with her justifications, explanations, pseudo-scientific hypotheses, and claims to an autonomy, the freedom to dispose of her mind and body as she chose.

Connie agreed, vehemently. She didn't want to force

anything on Iris; she wanted to persuade her, she wanted Iris to see how lousy it was, how she was choosing to give up, precisely, the autonomy she claimed to value. Connie kept arguing, repeating herself, talking about automata, machines, control, the fallacy of control.

Iris's last analyst had put her on various different antidepressants. He'd even suggested she take some drug that was unavailable in the United States, a drug that supposedly made you remember, something like sodium pentothal, some kind of dubious truth drug like in a war movie scenario. At one point Iris called her aunt, her mother's sister, in Paris to ask her to get it for her in Europe, because her analysis was progressing so badly. She'd lie on the couch and her mind would simply shut down. She would refuse to open her mouth. Apparently the analyst, or psychiatrist, thought this truth drug would speed things up, make Iris talk, make her remember. Anyway her aunt refused to try to get this drug for her; in the larger scheme of things, it was yet another example of her useless family letting Iris down. The shrink prescribed various other drugs; Connie argued that in so doing he'd given Iris license to seek her own relief, her own cocktail, her own mix. Indeed, as time passed, heroin became the drug of choice; it was so much more effective than those fucking antidepressants they kept giving her. Heroin enabled Iris to leave the analyst, to get up from the couch and walk.

Connie went on repeating her arguments, appealing to the side of Iris that hadn't been written off, the Iris she recognised as being like her. Connie invoked this Iris, the Iris who resembled Connie, as was her right, after knowing her all these years. She pushed this version of Iris under her nose, insisting that she wasn't being given a chance. Iris laughed, beginning to give in.

Connie kept saying, 'Iris I love you, I love you, that's why I can't stand seeing you like this.' And Iris would say, 'Like what? I'm not any different.' And Connie would say, 'Yes you are.'

Iris said she thought Connie got so upset about Jack because she'd wanted to have a crisis with her mother, with Helen, she wanted to weep and wail and have Helen be kind to her, have Helen agree for once, have Helen on her side. Iris insisted that Connie'd wanted a little mother-daughter melodrama, and Iris's flirting, amazingly enough, provided her with the opportunity. Connie'd never thought of that. At length she acknowledged that there might have been an element of this, a wish to make emotional contact, so to speak, with Helen. She didn't really know why she'd got so upset; all those tears seemed excessive, now.

Eventually they stopped, Iris had someone to meet uptown. Connie went back to her place, exhausted. The city was hot and grimy; homeless men, their skin shiny with dirt, lay sleeping on the sidewalk in the heat. Their swollen bodies lay in shallow, black puddles, on the sidewalk, as if to cool off. Connie ate something and then she read Trollope until she fell asleep. She'd arranged to meet Iris at Film Forum the next night, to see an Ozu film. Ozu and Trollope: during that summer in New York her consumption of Ozu and Trollope kept Connie sane. Connie was determined to go on seeing Iris; if she went on treating her like a friend, like an ordinary person, maybe she'd pack it in, give it up for good.

Connie knew too well the dynamic of kicking and returning, the rhythm of repudiation, then giving in again — she knew this dynamic was built in, it was what being on junk was all about. Still, she thought if she invoked the other Iris, the one she'd known since she was seven, together they could vanquish the Iris on junk, the one whose life was worthless, who couldn't make it without, who had to have it — that chemical shift, that little psychic adjustment, that supplement of junk.

Interest

It was Christmas, 1982, and Connie hadn't set foot in New York for seven years, amazingly, not since that time she stayed with Michael downtown, the time she slept with Nick and went away with the epithet 'bourgeois' ringing in her ears. She'd been living in London, studying at the Courtauld, and doing a thesis on Angelica Kauffmann. You couldn't get much more bourgeois than that. Now she'd decided to come to New York, for a break, for ten days, suddenly, encouraged by Iris who'd phoned, saying, come see me, come stay with me in New York.

Connie hadn't seen Iris for about a year and a half, and as she dumped her bags, and collapsed on a sofa, she was struck by how beautiful Iris looked, thin as a rake, with her olive skin, and her golden hair falling across her face. Iris was in high spirits, full of manic energy, talking and laughing non-stop. Initially Connie took this to be a reaction to busting up with her latest boyfriend, Wolfgang, who was German, and very good-looking. The summer before last, the two of them had shown up at Connie's house in London, just for an evening, on their way to Greece. It was the only time Connie met Wolfgang; they didn't like each other much. She happened to be cooking an extremely elaborate meal, for a dinner party, when Iris phoned from the airport: we're here! It was totally unexpected, and Connie was pleased to see them, though the dinner party was completely disrupted, and the cooking allowed to slide. She gave up all attempt at control; drinking Russian vodka, she let it go, and everyone was left to make what they could of the evening, with Iris and Wolfgang taking centre stage.

One outcome of Connie's abandon was the main dish was overdone, and she kept apologising for this, a little drunkenly, until at the end of the evening, as they were leaving, standing at the door, Wolfgang solemnly told her, 'The meal was really very good. The only trouble was you kept saying how terrible it was. You have no self-confidence; you really shouldn't apologise so much.' Connie knew this was true, but she was offended by his ridiculous air of authority: it seemed uncalled-for, pronouncing judgement on her cooking, on her low self-esteem.

Later Connie felt this moment was symptomatic of something disturbing about Iris's relationship with Wolfgang. On some level Connie felt they were colluding in a ghastly masquerade: it was like he would be masculine, so she could be fem. He passed judgement, without hesitation, and she seemed obscurely impressed, as if this were properly manly behaviour. Connie found this spectacle relatively troubling, then later she remembered how Iris's previous boyfriend, Edmund, had chosen Iris's lipstick for her, an unusual pale orange that set off her olive skin. She remembered Iris telling her how Edmund would complain about the scars on her legs. It must be something Iris enjoyed, something she took pleasure in, this kind of masculine appropriation and evaluation.

It was like naming: Wolfgang, and Edmund before him,

knew what was what, they knew right from wrong. They knew how Iris should look, what she should wear, they knew her good points, and her weaknesses, and this certainty, this conviction appeared to be something Iris wanted. To Connie it seemed more like a covert capitulation, as if Iris had given something up, in order to be with these men. On the other hand, perhaps there was something lacking in Connie, that she couldn't imagine a relationship on those terms, she literally couldn't imagine giving any man those kind of rights over her body, her appearance. It felt like it would be handing it over to his jurisdiction, almost, as if her body would no longer belong to her.

That time in London, that summer night, the night Iris and Wolfgang showed up, Connie was a little shocked to see Iris so strung out, a huge glass of vodka in one hand, as she spoke of her summer in New York, life without analysis (she'd sacked the shrink), and their plans for travelling in Turkey and Greece. At one point, Iris mentioned heroin, she was very offhand, very casual about it. It was the first time Connie realised heroin was among the drugs Iris used. They were in the kitchen, Connie was still cooking, and Iris was standing beside her, watching as she cut things up.

Iris was talking about getting through customs, how one manages to travel, to get through customs, without incident. Connie wasn't paying much attention to this. Then Iris said she was feeling awful because she'd been doing some really lousy heroin the night before.

Connie expressed a certain amazement. 'Heroin? Really?'

'You're not *surprised*?' Iris said, disbelieving.

Knife in hand, looking up, Connie said, 'I guess. I don't really know anyone here who . . .' She stopped herself, thinking, of course she did, she knew lots of people. The difference was that they weren't her intimate friends. Then she silently admitted that wasn't quite the case, either: some of them were. Or they were the intimate friends, the boyfriend, or the girlfriend, of her intimate friends. Still, none of them were Iris.

Connie tried a different tack. 'Isn't it dangerous, I mean, isn't the risk of possession much worse than with other things?'

Iris said, 'Risk? I don't know. There's a shoebox of the stuff in my closet in New York. I don't think there's much risk.'

'A shoebox?' Connie asked, squeamishly.

'It's horrible stuff, actually, makes you really sick. As I said, that's why I'm feeling shitty now. And the flight was like hell on wheels, I didn't sleep, I'm totally lagged.'

Connie was shocked. She went on chopping garlic. Why take lousy heroin, why have a shoebox of the stuff? Surely if you're going to do it, it should be nothing but the best! And why do it, anyway, why fuck up like this? She was flummoxed, and internally she froze, it was like her feelings were paralysed, temporarily, while she processed this information, made up her mind what she thought about it.

But the next day Iris vanished, off to Greece, so Connie didn't have to deal with it. Now, she thought, in New York, with Wolfgang out of the picture, the shoebox would be gone too. It was never very serious, she thought, Iris isn't stupid enough to do that. Not like Michael.

Connie hadn't seen Michael since the time in '78, when he'd stayed with her in London for a while, but she'd heard that he was a proper junky, now. The genuine article, with all the trimmings, including a very beautiful, self-destructive young wife. Comparing notes, Connie'd told Ruby about Iris's shoebox, she'd said, 'Can you imagine, apparently she's got a shoebox full of heroin in her closet!'

Ruby smiled. 'But Connie, I suspect this is marriage à la mode, New York-style, marriage à la mode, circa 1981. As far as I can tell, that's exactly what Michael's doing with Annie, they're holed up in some loft somewhere, doing drugs. It's the way of the world, there, it's the thing to do!'

'Maybe,' Connie said, 'Still . . .'

In New York over a year later, Connie quickly understood that although Wolfgang was gone, out the door, Iris was still at it, spending her days on the phone, getting Beth to come over, or her friend Ingrid, to sit around, to stretch out on the long orange sofas, and smoke junk. Connie spent her days rushing around town, seeing friends. and exhibitions; she would come in at midnight to find Iris asleep on the sofa, her head propped at a terrible angle, the ashtray overflowing before her. Cultivating detachment, Connie didn't comment. It was none of her business.

After she'd been in New York a day or two, she tracked down Michael's phone number, and called him, He'd split up with Annie, he was living temporarily in his studio on 38th Street, apparently working hard. They arranged to meet for a drink at One University Place, at six that evening, Iris knew Michael, of course; she'd stayed in the house in Ladbroke Grove on various occasions, and later their paths crossed in New York, inevitably. When Iris asked what she was doing that evening, Connie told her she was meeting Michael, before going out to dinner with her current impossible object, Andrew Fell. It was a heavy date, the date with Andrew; they turned their attention to that, what to wear, or think, and later Connie walked over to the bar, nervous about the evening ahead.

Both Michael and Connie were shy with each other, but Michael looked the same as ever, washed out and unhealthy, his eyes sharp and bright, moving quickly as he spoke. They sat together at a table in the back of the bar, smoking cigarettes, drinking Johnnie Walker Black, as Michael held forth on the dangers of heroin. Connie sat silent, nodding solemnly, as he told her how close he'd come to losing it altogether, as he outlined the depths to which he had sunk. Connie felt numb; her mind felt swollen, stupid, listening to this quiet rant. But she believed it, she bought his line on junk, his vehement renunciation, his impassioned advice.

Michael said, 'Just don't try it, Connie. Don't mess with it. Heroin is so fantastic,' — here he paused for effect, 'it's really the best, better than anything. It's impossible to resist. So don't ever try it, it's just too dangerous.'

'No, I won't, I wouldn't,' Connie said quietly.

Connie told Michael about Iris, she told him about the summer before last, about the shoebox in the closet (which by now had taken on something of a mythic status), the lousy stuff that made Iris so sick. She told him this was still going on, apparently. 'It's constant, I guess,' Connie said. 'I mean, it's what she's doing now. I don't know what to do.'

'I'm never going to touch the stuff again,' Michael told her. 'I'm terrified of it, I'm never going near it again.'

Connie still had too much respect for Michael to dismiss his words as classic junky talk. She thought, wow, he's been through so much, he's really been through it. Her heart went out to him, all alone in this city, surrounded by demons of temptation. She bought him another drink.

At this point Iris stalked into the bar, the spectral figure of Beth visible behind her. Connie was surprised to see them, even more surprised when they sat down. Both Iris and Beth looked worn out; they ordered drinks and Iris talked, asking Michael about things, while Beth sat staring, slightly, as if she had very little to say. She didn't take off her coat. Connie didn't know what to do. It seemed Iris had come out solely in order to join them, and Connie couldn't think why. Beth seemed shy, and out of it, drinking her coca-cola, but Iris persisted, chattering away in a desultory fashion, as if they were all good friends, as if it were a perfectly ordinary situation. Which in a sense it was. Sitting there in the bar, Connie found it hard to concentrate, hard to follow the conversation, she felt preoccupied, as if she were thinking about something else.

Then suddenly Connie had to go, it was time for her to go, she had to meet Andrew at a restaurant, and she was late already. It was then that she realised she didn't want to leave Michael with Iris, she didn't want to leave him in her clutches. Her numbness had obscured what was really at stake here, which was junk.

Connie turned to Michael, saying, 'I've got to go, do you want to walk with me?'

Connie stared at him, but Michael looked blank, as if he didn't see the point, as if he had no idea what she was talking about. Connie started to panic. Then Iris said to Michael, 'Why don't you come back to my place? We were going to eat something, later. Come, it would be nice.'

Michael said, 'Maybe. Maybe, just for a while.' Connie didn't know what to say; she opened her mouth to speak but there were no words. She stared at Michael, he was looking across the big room, as if distracted.

Looking around, Iris said, 'I don't want to stay here; let's go, let's go back to the flat. What do you think, Beth, my dear?'

Beth acquiesced, easily, and that was it; Connie had failed. She tried one last time, turning to Michael, she said, 'Are you sure you don't want to come with me?'

Michael looked up at her, as she was getting up to go. He said, 'No, I think I'll just go over to Iris's for a while. Just for a short time.' Connie stood up to leave, then, tying her big black overcoat around her, powerless to undo the damage. 'See you later,' Iris said.

As Connie pushed open the heavy glass door, the cold night air hit her body like a blow. She reached out to flag a cab, and climbed in, to perch on the narrow back seat, rigid with anxiety. When Connie arrived at the restaurant, she sat down for a few minutes with Andrew, and then found a phone. She called Iris's number, she said, 'Hi. Can I speak to Michael?' They must have taken a cab too. Iris recognised her voice immediately; with only the tiniest hint of a question mark, Iris said, 'Sure.'

Michael on the line, Connie said, 'Mikey, what the fuck are you doing? Get out of there!'

Michael said, 'It's OK, really Connie, it's fine.'

'What do you mean?' Connie asked. 'What are you talking about?' Connie was beginning to feel terribly angry.

'Don't worry about it, Connie, really, I'm fine,' Michael said soothingly, as if she'd gone mad, as if she might take it into her head to come over and physically drag him out of there. 'Everything's fine,' Michael repeated.

Connie hesitated. As always with Michael, she was unsure of the appropriate limits, unsure how far to intervene. 'I don't believe it for a minute,' she said vehemently, with a certain edge of despair. 'You shouldn't be there,' she said, 'just leave, just go!'

'Don't worry,' Michael said. 'There's absolutely nothing to worry about.'

Connie was aware of Iris's presence in the background, aware of Iris and Beth, the two long sofas, the glass coffee table between them. She could visualise the little flat exactly, she'd stayed there so often.

Standing silent on the phone, powerless, Connie saw Michael in this room, sitting on the orange sofa, the gear spread out on the low table before him, as Iris brought the silver foil from the kitchen, found her lighter, as the ritual progressed. She couldn't stop this happening, there was nothing she could do. Reaching this point, Connie gave up. 'Oh OK, Michael,' she said. 'I'll call you. Take care.'

'Take care, Connie,' Michael said. 'See you soon, I hope.'

A couple of days later, it happened again. It was one of those classic scenes, one of those scenes that should never happen. It was the scene where two friends both want the same dress on sale. There was only one dress: Connie found the dress — reduced to $80 — in a posh dress shop on West Broadway. Iris had to have it.

The dress was a sludgy olive beige, made of thin knitted wool; the concept was simple: an extended cardigan, with a low V-neck, buttons down the front, wide raglan sleeves, the fabric loose around the hips and then coming in to a narrow band of ribbing at the knees. It was very comfortable, very ordinary and even subdued, and yet terribly sexy. It was perfect.

Connie was particularly thrilled with it because it resembled a dress she already owned, a dress she'd worn so much it was literally worn through. This would be the replacement. (She had a tendency to duplicate things she liked; she saw this as a sign of anxiety, wanting always to find and possess the replacement before she finally had to give up the original object.)

Iris was pleased with the dress because it was so cheap, because she never bought clothes, she hated shopping, because it was so perfect. The dress looked fantastic with her blonde hair, her olive skin. Connie envied Iris her small, pointy breasts, nippling through the thin fabric. The dress was like a conceptual joke: outrageously sexy, while pretending (so to speak) to be merely an ordinary, everyday cardigan. Yet the line of the deep V-neck, the places where the soft wool touched the body, at the breasts, the hips, these elements conspired (together with the casual disavowal of explicit sexiness, a disavowal embodied in the claim to be an ordinary, everyday cardigan), these elements subtly conspired to make the dress truly seductive.

Iris was reluctant to come into the shop; Connie said, 'Only for a minute.' Almost immediately Connie found the dress on its hanger, jumbled with a bunch of other things on the rail. Iris said, 'Wow, what a great dress.' Connie tried it on, then Iris took it from her. Iris took it out of Connie's hands; Connie heard herself say, as Iris vanished into the changing-room, 'I want that dress.' Her heart sinking, Connie went to see if there was another one. Iris emerged from the cubicle, and after a glance in the mirror, she announced that she had to have it. There was only one.

Connie felt miserable. She didn't want to fight with Iris over a dress. Iris was formidable, plus Connie was staying with her, sleeping on one of the sofas; Connie couldn't face a row. Yet she found it hard to believe that Iris could be so demanding, so ungracious. Iris didn't give an inch, she never said, 'Of course you found it, you tried it on first, I hope you don't mind . . .' She never said, 'Oh you have it . . .' Connie decided she didn't want the dress if she had to stand in this shop and fight over it. She let Iris buy the dress.

That night, lounging on the two long sofas in Iris's flat, listening to Om Kalsoum, loud, Iris wearing the new dress, Iris full of heroin, an unfiltered Camel cigarette between her fingers, Iris dropped off, momentarily, and burned a hole in the front of the dress. It was ruined.

Later Connie realised this must happen quite often; Iris's fingers were covered in burns.

Hyperbole

Connie walked quickly through the dark streets, turning her face away from the falling snow. When she got to Michael's block, again Connie phoned from the corner, and he came down to let her in. They talked furiously all the way up his endless staircase, panting and talking, recounting their different versions of what had taken place.

At the top, out of breath, Michael said, 'To tell you the truth, I think Iris is being a real bitch.'

'That's an understatement!' Connie shrieked, gasping for air. They'd both been taken by surprise; they were both shocked, and hurt, and amazed, in different ways. The words spilled out of them, and later Connie remembered how she'd tried to speak about the past, about how it impinges on the present, how it grabs your sleeve, forcing you to pay attention, Ancient Mariner-style.

Launching into hyperbole, she said, 'It's like a rotting hand reaching out of a tomb, clutching at you as you go by, it's like ghosts or something, *Night of the Living Dead*, ghoulish figures clanking their chains and leaving a gory trail as they drag across the floor, it's like: *you think you got away with it?* You think you left all that behind you? *Ha!* Have you forgotten? You owe Iris — five hundred dollars! You owe her five hundred dollars, and she wants *interest*.'

Connie was delirious, she was distraught, and so anxious to protect Michael, to be forgiven, she wanted to make him shriek with laughter, she was *so* sorry to have brought all this to the surface. Amazingly, he understood this, he saw her terror, and her wish to make it all go away, and he rather wonderfully addressed that mad wish, shifting the responsibility, getting it straight.

He said, 'You know though Connie I did a lot of *bad things*.' Michael's eyes flew around the ceiling, as an appalled smile lit up his face, at the thought of the things he'd done.

'A lot of *bad things*,' he repeated, more solemnly now, as if to convey the seriousness of these crimes. They were standing beside his tall table, and as he spoke Connie remembered his description of living with Annie in the loft full of rats, the abject abandon of those years. Connie believed him.

'And every once in a while,' Michael said, 'I get given a chance to put something right, you know, to make up for some of the things I did. And that's good, that's the right thing to do, and this was — this was undeniable, you know. I mean, I owe Iris the money. And there you were at Iris's place, Iris was sitting right there, and it was five hundred dollars, *exact*. It was like, somebody up there is — it's like a gift, you know? An occasion for doing something right. So it's really not about Iris, and this particular five hundred bucks. I mean, whether she deserves it, or doesn't, or whatever. That's really not the point. It's about me, how I deal with this stuff, stuff that keeps coming back, that doesn't go away.'

'Yes, I guess that's so,' Connie said.

Michael turned away from her, and as he walked across the big room to find something, he was saying, 'What I think is, everybody wants the cure. And the cure means — the definition of a cure is, you can walk away, you can fuck off out of it, you can pretend that stuff never happened. But it did happen, and it doesn't vanish just because you're not doing it any more.' He turned around, to look at her. 'There's no cure, there's just every day,' he said.

'Yes,' Connie said. She agreed with this point of view, generally speaking; she took real comfort in the idea that there's no cure, for anything, ever.

'So there's just these specific instances when the ghosts appear, right?' Connie said. 'The ghouls, so to say, dragging their chains, and you have to *do something* with them, talk to them, or give them some money. You've got no choice, really. Give them five hundred dollars!'

Michael laughed. 'It's a bit like that, I guess. Anyway, Iris was crazy not to come with you, because I picked out this really good print for her, and now she'll never get it. I'll show you.'

Connie felt anxious again, now it was Iris who would get nothing. This was a nightmare that didn't end. The print was beautiful, Connie didn't know what to say.

A little later Michael set about making a box for the painting, while Connie sat on the cold windowsill and watched. He put some waxed paper over the face of the painting, then he wrapped it in bubblewrap. Then Michael went into the back room and brought back a large cardboard box, and taking his Stanley knife, he cut it into a suitable shape, constructing a rectangle of interlocking flaps to enclose the painting. Each broad gesture was clear and exact, as he scored the brown cardboard with the razor, gradually folding it into shape.

'You know that mobile you made?' Connie said, awkwardly.

'Which one?' Michael said, concentrating on his box.

'That blue one, the one you gave me,' Connie said.

'I don't think so,' Michael said, not paying much attention.

'You don't remember it?' Connie was taken aback.

'Blue?' he said, looking up.

'Yes. You made it, when we were kids, that time, you remember, when we were going out.'

Michael's pale blue eyes were empty. Connie struggled on. 'It was pretty big, and vaguely Calder-esque, with flat blue discs hanging —'

'I remember,' Michael interjected. 'Of course, the mobile. Yes — what became of it?'

Connie paused for a split-second before she spoke. 'I destroyed it,' she said solemnly.

Michael laughed out loud, apparently amused by her doleful expression.

'*Really?*' he said. 'How?'

'Oh, I just chucked it out, you know, into the bin. I mean, it was ages ago; it was around then, in fact.'

Michael looked sad, suddenly. 'Why'd you do that?' he said.

'I didn't hang on to it for ages and *then* throw it out. I did it *then*, shortly after we split up, or whatever you want to call it. I've always felt terrible about it.'

Michael turned back to his task, taping the edges of the box with orange ochre gaffer's tape, fixing it so the box could be reopened, reused.

'Well there's no need to feel *terrible*,' he said gently.

'I think I felt ashamed, I feel ashamed — but I could never tell if the problem was that it was wrong to destroy an artwork, you know, or if it was worse to refuse —' Connie hesitated. 'To refuse your love.'

'Juvenilia.' Michael said. 'It's always interesting, although I can't imagine liking that work now.' He paused, looking up. 'I still can't quite imagine why you had to *destroy* it, though.'

'No, neither can I,' Connie said mournfully. 'I think I just couldn't bear to have it in my possession.'

Standing up, Michael handed her the box, saying, 'See, I've made it so you can undo it to show it to Catherine, tonight, if you want to, and then do it up again.'

'It's beautiful,' Connie said. 'Perfect. Thanks.'

They said goodbye, and Connie left, taking careful steps as she walked down the endless staircase, encumbered by her multiple overcoats, the painting in its thick cardboard box tucked under her arm, then once again stepping out into the darkness cold as ice.

The next morning after her gig, Connie woke extremely early, her body rigid with anxiety. She found it hard to breathe. Lying in bed, she pictured Iris packing the bags of warm clothes for Rita in Mexico City. She thought about how Rita wasn't called Rita in Mexico City. Connie exhaled, filled with horror at a sudden thought: Iris could place something in these bags, something illegal, something dangerous, or secret.

Connie dismissed this idea immediately. It wasn't possible, or plausible. It wasn't serious.

Nevertheless, lying naked, flat on her back, Connie was forced to recognize that she didn't trust Iris. She didn't trust her. Connie felt terribly sad, realising this.

She got up, out of bed, feeling like a coward. She splashed some water on her face. 'She thinks I'm a fucking mule,' Connie said out loud. As Connie made tea, obsessing, going over and over the same ground, she came to a decision. At eight o'clock, Connie put on her coats and walked down to the payphone on the corner, to call Iris. It was very sunny out, harsh pale light filled the empty street.

'Hi,' Iris said, cheerfully.

'Listen, Iris,' Connie said. 'I'm calling to say don't come. I mean, don't bring the bags for Rita, because I've decided I can't take them.'

'*What*?' Iris said, disbelief in her voice. 'Why not?'

'I just think it's an impossible situation,' Connie said, her heart beating sharply. She was scared to death. 'I think it's the wrong thing for me to do, because I feel — resentful, you know, I feel —'

'What?' Iris said coldly, angry now. 'What do you feel, Connie?'

'I feel really just so furious with you for what happened yesterday —'

'*What* happened yesterday?' Iris interjected.

'All that *shit* with Michael.' Connie was angry now. 'It drove me up the fucking wall, if you want to know the truth,' she said. 'And now you want me to do this for you and I say, OK, fine, anything, taking the line of least resistance, and then it's not OK. I don't feel OK about it. I really don't think I should do this for you,' Connie concluded, her voice flat.

'But it's not for me, it's for poor Rita, who's freezing in Mexico City!'

'I don't want to do this, I don't want to talk about it,' Connie said. 'I don't know when I'll want to see you again.'

Iris's anger appeared to vanish. 'Why are you doing this?' she said slowly.

'It would be the end of everything, if I took those clothes, because we'd be quits, you know? If I do this for you when I'm so furious with you, then that would be it, it would be all over, finished.' Connie was crying now, bright clear tears flooding her eyes, pouring down her face, as she stood in the brilliantly sunny street.

'Don't do this,' Iris said, very quietly.

Connie was silent, crying like a river.

'I'm going to hang up now,' she said. 'I've got to go, Iris.'

Iris said nothing. Connie sensed the landscape of utter devastation stretching between them.

'Goodbye,' she said.

'Bye,' said Iris, a slight tinge of bitter humour in her voice.

Connie hung up the payphone, and wiped her face. The sunlight was too bright. Then she went back to the flat to get her bags and leave New York.

Junk

When she got back to London, Connie had time to talk with Ruby at some length about what happened. They borrowed the Powells' cottage in the country for a couple of days, for Connie to recuperate from her rather gruelling trip. It was early spring, gusty and grey, with sudden blasts of rain soaking the bright green grass, making the sea livid, the colour of pewter.

They made supper together the last evening, and afterwards, sitting at the oval table, in the fading yellow light, finishing a bottle of wine, Ruby asked Connie for the rest.

Connie was peeling a pear with a sharp knife. Wiping her fingers, she gave Ruby a quizzical look, whereupon Ruby said, 'Well, go on.'

Connie hesitated, momentarily, before plunging back in. Taking a gulp of red wine, she continued her account of the trip to New York. She explained again how Michael had quickly agreed to the proposal ('it was like, *anything! anything!* at this point,' she said), and that she'd actually sent the money, a little while later, to the Palestinians, in the name of Iris Gowing. Thus the final agreement left Iris, the orphan, empty-handed, and in control, dictating the terms of an exchange that excluded her.

Some time later, when she'd ground to a halt, Ruby said, 'What's so striking about this story is the way in which the phone call, the whole scene with the phone call, is just like classic junky business.'

Connie looked doubtful. 'Business?' she asked.

'It's exactly like every phone call, every drug negotiation,' Ruby said. 'I mean, I've hung out in basement flats in Paddington with junkies, a hundred years ago — remember Louis? I've overheard these interminable phone calls, with the phone being passed back and forth . . . It's always the same, junkies. They're always arranging elaborate rendezvous and deals. They spend all their time on the phone, doing this. And then they steal your favourite book, as you hesitate — an old friend, — as you delay getting them out of the house. They're paranoid, and go off acting weird for a little while, as if they didn't know that you know that they know you know they're a junky. They carry around a little bag full of what they regard as their stuff. They like to play with wind-up toys, and they spend time watching TV. They like to have other people around, without having to really *talk* to them, to engage. They especially like having other junkies around, and if there aren't enough junkies they try and get you to be one. They kick — which usually means finding another addiction. They're control freaks, so they drink, heavily, but it's like a regime: six o'clock! time for my double brandy! They don't have sex, and they eat sugar, junk food, chocolate, coca-cola. Junkies. And then they die.'

Connie said nothing, slightly stunned.

'Except Mikey didn't — die, I mean.' Ruby laughed, as Connie looked up at her, trying to make out what she really thought about this stuff.

'Anyway,' Ruby continued, 'it was perfect, you were all

playing your roles. I mean, Iris is the dealer, right? And Michael's the junky, Michael's in trouble: you don't try to rip off the dealer, right? He owes her money, man, and there's no way out of that.'

'Yes, you're right — how extraordinary, I never thought of it that way,' Connie said.

Ruby went on. 'I think that's partly why you were so distressed by it all. I mean, it's not just about being angry with Iris for being — ungenerous, shall we say. It's the whole structure, the whole scenario that's so upsetting.'

'Yes, as I kept saying, it was like everything was being translated into another vocabulary, but I never really recognised that the other vocabulary was so precisely the language of junk.' Connie paused. 'It was like suddenly being pulled back, into another movie —'

'Yes,' Ruby said, 'as if this *other* story, the junky story, was running parallel, waiting in the wings, so to speak, and with a flick of her wrist, Iris pulled it in, she invoked it, she called it up like a genie . . .'

'To constitute a set of relations that placed *her*, significantly enough, in a position of power, like the dealer, the one who turns it on and off.' Connie poured more wine.

'It is — it is all about control, isn't it?' she asked. 'I mean, that's not just my obsession, is it?'

'It's pretty impressive, I must say.' Ruby stared out the window, at the blowing trees.

'I think what was so painful was watching Iris and Michael revert to type; they knew their lines so well, you know?' Connie said. 'As if this junk business was second nature, as if it was the easiest, the most familiar relationship in the world.'

Ruby said, 'Even though —'

Connie interrupted, 'Even though they don't do heroin any more. They haven't for years, now.'

'No cure,' Ruby said.

'Certainly no cure if all this shit is just under the surface, waiting to leap out,' Connie said.

'Still, it's not all shit,' Ruby said. 'I mean, Iris may have been taking up the position of the dealer, but she wasn't selling drugs, not actually.'

'Yes. And Michael wasn't buying them. And my place — I don't know *what* my place was. I was the fucking enabling device, the *sine qua non*. Without me, none of this would have happened.'

'Don't be too sure,' Ruby said. They were silent for a couple of minutes, thinking.

Then Connie said, 'You see the worst part for me is acknowledging how much I'm the one who sets this stuff up. Let's face it, the act of buying the painting was a transaction that excluded Iris. It was a transaction that took place before her, right in front of her, and which excluded her. So I'm the one that's triangulating here. And the implication of that exclusion was to position her as Ms Drug, Mademoiselle Junk, you know — unlike me, unlike Michael, who's Mr Clean, now, all cleaned up — it was me, however inadvertently, fixing her there at the centre of something, some ghastly drug scene — that I didn't want to have anything to do with!'

Ruby agreed: 'Yes, and once you'd put her there, she really shoved it down your throat.'

Connie said, 'But what I can't fathom fully is why I do this stuff. What's my investment in triangulation situations that repudiate, or exclude . . . You know what I'm saying, is this just some crass vestige of an oedipal drama, or is it something a little more complicated, not to say sophisticated, than that?'

'You mean, because she's left out, always.' Ruby paused.

'Yes, finally, she's out in the cold,' Connie said, 'and yet she's in control, too, determining the eventual destination of that five hundred dollars.'

Connie made the voice of a baby doll emitting a sound between whining and crying: 'Mama!'

Ruby said, 'But that was such a scream, you know, you saying, who needs it most. I mean, it's more junk talk, you know? Like, I need it, I really need it!'

Connie frowned. 'I have absolutely no doubt that Iris's political commitment to the Palestinians, *and* the Guatemalans, for that matter, is serious and real. And I wouldn't have given the organisation the money if I didn't approve of what they're doing totally.'

'I know, I know,' Ruby said. 'It's just — I don't know.'

'I know,' Connie said. 'It's that the whole conversation was this massive displacement, from a transaction about buying art, or friendship, or something, to a classic exchange between a dealer and a junky. And to invoke need, however implicitly, only reinforces this. Maybe.'

Connie paused. Then she said, 'Though I'm really not sure. You're right, in the sense that the whole discourse of junk simply took over, and everyone had to take up their positions, step back into their roles, into this other movie, the one that doesn't go away. As if you're still a junky, like it or not.'

'Yes,' Ruby said. 'Something like that.'

'I remember years ago being so angry with Michael,' Connie said. 'He was talking about Candy, and he said, once a whore, always a whore, and I just thought, once a junky, always a junky, fuck you.'

'Still, he said it, right?' Ruby insisted. 'He's the one who said it, he said, there's no such thing as a cure.'

The next morning they were eating breakfast, before going back to London. Ruby was eating toast, and she was glancing at yesterday's paper on the table as she spoke.

'I had a horrible thought about poor Iris when I woke up this morning,' Ruby said slowly, in a noncommittal tone.

'You thought, Iris really isn't such an awful person, you thought, poor Iris, this isn't *her* version. You thought, we're the ones who are narrating this story, and interpreting everything she does from this malevolent, twisted point of view . . .'

'No,' Ruby said. 'How fascinating, is that what you think?'

'Sometimes, yes. I think, I don't really know what happened. I still don't really understand what happened.' For a moment, Connie looked guilty and sad.

'Well, my thought was much worse than that,' Ruby said, laughing. 'What I thought was, I don't know, it's hard to explain, but let's put it this way. You set things up, right? So that you and Michael were over here,' Ruby gestured towards the jar of marmalade, 'Michael all cleaned up, and everybody terribly productive and healthy and successful, everybody doing fine. Full of good wishes and deep affection, and all that. And that placed Iris over here, somehow,' Ruby placed her hands around the cooling teapot, 'stuck in her flat with her scrips and her analyst and her misery.'

'Mmm,' Connie said.

'And what I thought was, her insistence on getting the money, plus interest, Iris's insistence, was like saying — implicitly, by implication only, saying: Well, if Michael were dying, I mean, if he's in the process of killing himself, destroying his life, then I don't mind. I'll kiss the money goodbye. But shit, if he's going to live, if he's going to survive, and be happy, be a successful artist, then *give me back my five hundred dollars*!'

'That *is* a horrible thought,' Connie said.

'Yes,' Ruby said.

'Well,' Connie said, leaning back in her chair, 'I can't help thinking that if there was any element of that, it really was all my fault — probably. Because I'm the one who sees them in these terms. My transaction with Michael, as you say, drew a line between him and Iris, leaving Iris outside, out in the cold, still mired in despair, intellectually paralysed, stuck in a dynamic of control (and uncontrol) that revolves to a great extent around drugs.'

'And food,' Ruby said, biting into her toast.

'Yes, and food. So I'm the one who put her there, and then, from that very position, she wreaks her terrible revenge.'

Ruby was silent, staring into space.

Connie continued. 'What seems doubly ironic is how this reversal, this triangulation triangulated, when Iris turned the tables, served only to bring me and Michael closer together — because we were both so angry, we were so furious with her. We were both so fucking *hurt*.'

'Yes.'

'Iris may have determined who the cheque was written to,' Connie said. 'I mean, if she thought my motivation was to prevent the five hundred dollars going to her, I have no doubt that her motivation was at least in part to prevent that money from going to Michael.'

'Mmm.'

'So Iris may have won control of the terms of the transaction, but in the end, Michael and I became more intimate,' Connie said, 'more fond of each other, having undergone this extraordinary ordeal together.' Connie paused. 'But I guess what's undeniable, I mean, what's absolutely clear, is the way Iris stands in for Michael, in so many senses. I mean, I never sat Mikey down and said, don't be a junky. I never confronted *him*.'

Ruby agreed. 'Yes, it's as if you've managed to attribute to Iris all the horror and nastiness of that whole scene, almost in order to keep Michael good and safe, the good object, white knight, positively glowing with kindness and generosity and well-being. You've made *her* into a wicked witch of the west. In your imagination only, of course.'

'It's true,' Connie said bitterly. 'I can't recall my love for her. I can't remember her smile, or her wit. It's lost, I mean, I've lost it, that possibility of love, or affection.'

Ruby said nothing.

'You see,' Connie said, 'though I'd like to think she killed my love for her, I can't believe that's really so. I think I did it. I killed it off, the pleasure I once took in her company. Now I can't even imagine it, she scares me so much.'

'What, because she's angry?'

'Yes — it scares me to death.'

'You can't remember anything?' Ruby asked.

'I remember once when we were in Paris together, it was my first year at university, ages ago, and Iris was in Paris, and she called me, and said, come for the weekend, and I'd never been, so I went. And one night we were walking near those cafés on the Boulevard St Michel, you know, the Flore, and the other one, the Deux Magots, and these two seedy looking Algerian men spoke to us, in the street, you know, it was one of those things where a properly brought-up anxious English girl would stick her nose in the air and walk quickly on. And I remember Iris was so amazing, she stopped, and she turned to them, and she spoke Arabic to them, smiling, and their whole demeanour changed. Of course, they were knocked out, needless to say. How completely unexpected, to approach a blonde American girl in the street and receive a reply in Arabic, but they were somehow transformed by it, in my eyes at least, they acquired a dignity and a presence, it was like this scene of mutual respect. Iris spent time in Egypt, she lived in Cairo, for a while, you know, but she always learned the language of wherever she went, and she could always talk to anyone, anyone, it was amazing. It's a real talent, her mother Elizabeth was the same, and I always admired it, I envied it, because I'm not like that, am I? Not at all.'

Wind was blowing through the trees, as Ruby began to pile up the plates. Connie stopped for a minute or two, then she continued, her voice rising sharply, as if struck by some final, terrible thought.

'But I think perhaps the *most* perverse thing of all in this grim scenario is the whole idea of symbolising or celebrating a newly rediscovered friendship by buying a fucking painting. I mean, what is all this about? Giving Michael money, as a way of saying, I really feel for you, I really care, I value the time we spent together, I haven't forgotten the years we knew each other, I'm glad you're alive. Or what. All of that.'

Except Michael didn't get the money.'

'No,' Connie said.

Ruby looked up. 'Isn't this a little extreme? I expect it's a very good painting, and I expect you're very glad to own it, quite apart from its symbolic value. It was certainly a bargain, there's no question of that!'

Connie looked slightly ashamed.

'Anyway, I like it,' Ruby said, smiling.

'Yes, I do too,' Connie ruefully admitted.

'I'd like to walk down to the river once more before we go,' Ruby said. 'Want to come?'

'Yes,' said Connie. The two women pulled on their coats and boots and slowly walked out across the wet green fields. Then they packed the car and drove back up to London.

Stetson!

Shortly thereafter, Connie and William went to live in Los Angeles.

'If I died here, would you bury me in Forest Lawn?' Connie asked one day.

'I thought I was supposed to throw you off the Vincent Thomas Bridge,' William said.

'The Bridge to Terminal Island. Yes.' Connie paused. 'I expect it's illegal, though. I mean, I *know* it's illegal to dump people's ashes wherever. You're not allowed, in law, to sprinkle your husband around the garden, or whatever.'

William looked up for a moment.

'But quite apart from that, I expect it's illegal simply to stop your car on the bridge,' Connie said.

'I'd just roll down the window and stick out my arm and,' – William made a gesture, like shaking out a handkerchief, or a plastic bag.

'If you stopped you might get vertigo,' Connie suggested.

'I don't suffer from vertigo. You do,' William said.

'That's a point,' Connie said. 'Do I want my ashes scattered where I myself would feel sick?'

William went on reading the paper.

'I think if *you* died, I'd buy a beautiful jar and keep you,' Connie said, smiling.

'Hmm,' William said. He claimed to have no interest in his own death, or in the vicissitudes of his corpse.

'I once read a story about a woman whose husband's ashes were in a cardboard box in the bottom of her closet. You know, with the shoes. It was meant to signify her inability to organise her life.'

'I don't care what you do with me,' William said quietly.

'I've got this idea, I think,' Connie said, 'about burial. About digging it up again.'

'Beware the dog,' William said.

'What?'

'You know. *Stetson!* That corpse you planted, has it sprouted yet?'

'Yes — beware the dog, or with his nails, he'll dig it up again.'

'Something like that,' William muttered.

'I think, I think what's buried in the earth will always, eventually, rise to the surface. Putrefying, but somehow preserved, and *returning*. Maybe water dissolves you, the dissolution of the body — that's what I like. Better than cremation.'

'What, you don't want to drift about in the wind, dust to dust and all that?'

'No. I don't really like it. I don't like the coffin part, the idea of one's bodily ashes being all mixed up with the ashes of this mahogany coffin, or whatever, lined with, you know, nylon satin or something. White nylon satin.'

'Like Van Der Zee,' William said.

'Mmm. But I don't think I'd mind so much, cremation, or burial, even, if you could be wrapped in a lovely shroud, instead of stuck in this elaborate wooden box, the coffin.'

William said nothing, looking at the paper.

'Perhaps one could organise a death at sea,' Connie went on. 'I've always liked those burials at sea in the old movies, where there's a sort of plank, and the body is wrapped in a shroud of white muslin, and they gently tip the body into the ocean. It slides down the plank, and then there's this gloomy thud and splash, and all the sailors stand around on the deck looking spooked.'

'I don't think they do that any more,' William said, turning the page. 'Unless you're on some very picturesque ship.'

'Yes. A death ship,' Connie said, meditatively.

'I like the idea of all the little fishes nibbling at you, through the thin muslin shroud,' Connie ventured.

'You could jump, I suppose,' William said.

'What, into the ocean?'

'Mmm.'

'William, darling, we were talking about methods of corpse disposal, not suicide.'

'*Some* methods of suicide *also* dispose of the corpse.'

'That goes without saying . . .' Connie paused. 'I really do hate the idea of coffins, though, buried in the earth. Rossetti dug Lizzie Siddal up again, you know, because he'd buried his best poems in a little book with her in her coffin. In Highgate Cemetery. After a couple of years, he wanted the poems, and so they dug her up. The coffin was full of her long red hair.'

'Well I won't dig you up, darling,' William said. 'Not even for my accounts stubs. Promise.'

'And I won't bury *you* at all!' Connie laughed.

CITY LIGHTS PUBLICATIONS

Acosta, Juvenal, ed. LIGHT FROM A NEARBY WINDOW: Poems of Contemporary Mexico
Allen, Roberta. AMAZON DREAM
Angulo de, Jaime. INDIANS IN OVERALLS
Angulo de, G. & J. JAIME IN TAOS
Artaud, Antonin. ARTAUD ANTHOLOGY
Bataille, Georges. EROTISM: Death and Sensuality
Bataille, Georges. THE IMPOSSIBLE
Bataille, Georges. STORY OF THE EYE
Bataille, Georges. THE TEARS OF EROS
Baudelaire, Charles. INTIMATE JOURNALS
Baudelaire, Charles. TWENTY PROSE POEMS
Bowles, Paul. A HUNDRED CAMELS IN THE COURTYARD
Broughton, James. COMING UNBUTTONED
Broughton, James. MAKING LIGHT OF IT
Brown, Rebecca. ANNIE OAKLEY'S GIRL
Brown, Rebecca. THE TERRIBLE GIRLS
Bukowski, Charles. THE MOST BEAUTIFUL WOMAN IN TOWN
Bukowski, Charles. NOTES OF A DIRTY OLD MAN
Bukowski, Charles. TALES OF ORDINARY MADNESS
Burroughs, William S. THE BURROUGHS FILE
Burroughs, William S. THE YAGE LETTERS
Cassady, Neal. THE FIRST THIRD
Choukri, Mohamed. FOR BREAD ALONE
CITY LIGHTS REVIEW #2: AIDS & the Arts
CITY LIGHTS REVIEW #3: Media and Propaganda
CITY LIGHTS REVIEW #4: Literature / Politics / Ecology
Cocteau, Jean. THE WHITE BOOK (LE LIVRE BLANC)
Codrescu, Andrei, ed. EXQUISITE CORPSE READER
Cornford, Adam. ANIMATIONS
Corso, Gregory. GASOLINE
Daumal, René. THE POWERS OF THE WORD
David-Neel, Alexandra. SECRET ORAL TEACHINGS IN TIBETAN BUDDHIST SECTS
Deleuze, Gilles. SPINOZA: Practical Philosophy
Dick, Leslie. KICKING
Dick, Leslie. WITHOUT FALLING
di Prima, Diane. PIECES OF A SONG: Selected Poems
Doolittle, Hilda (H.D.) NOTES ON THOUGHT & VISION
Ducornet, Rikki. ENTERING FIRE
Duras, Marguerite. DURAS BY DURAS
Eberhardt, Isabelle. THE OBLIVION SEEKERS

Eidus, Janice. VITO LOVES GERALDINE
Fenollosa, Ernest. CHINESE WRITTEN CHARACTER AS A MEDIUM FOR POETRY
Ferlinghetti, Lawrence. PICTURES OF THE GONE WORLD
Ferlinghetti, Lawrence. SEVEN DAYS IN NICARAGUA LIBRE
Finley, Karen. SHOCK TREATMENT
Ford, Charles Henri. OUT OF THE LABYRINTH: Selected Poems
Franzen, Cola, transl. POEMS OF ARAB ANDALUSIA
García Lorca, Federico. BARBAROUS NIGHTS: Legends & Plays
García Lorca, Federico. ODE TO WALT WHITMAN & OTHER POEMS
García Lorca, Federico. POEM OF THE DEEP SONG
Gil de Biedma, Jaime. LONGING: SELECTED POEMS
Ginsberg, Allen. HOWL & OTHER POEMS
Ginsberg, Allen. KADDISH & OTHER POEMS
Ginsberg, Allen. REALITY SANDWICHES
Ginsberg, Allen. PLANET NEWS
Ginsberg, Allen. THE FALL OF AMERICA
Ginsberg, Allen. MIND BREATHS
Ginsberg, Allen. PLUTONIAN ODE
Goethe, J. W. von. TALES FOR TRANSFORMATION
Hayton-Keeva, Sally, ed. VALIANT WOMEN IN WAR AND EXILE
Herron, Don. THE DASHIELL HAMMETT TOUR: A Guidebook
Herron, Don. THE LITERARY WORLD OF SAN FRANCISCO
Higman, Perry, tr. LOVE POEMS FROM SPAIN AND SPANISH AMERICA
Jaffe, Harold. EROS: ANTI-EROS
Jenkins, Edith. AGAINST A FIELD SINISTER
Kerouac, Jack. BOOK OF DREAMS
Kerouac, Jack. POMES ALL SIZES
Kerouac, Jack. SCATTERED POEMS
Lacarrière, Jacques. THE GNOSTICS
La Duke, Betty. COMPANERAS
La Loca. ADVENTURES ON THE ISLE OF ADOLESCENCE
Lamantia, Philip. MEADOWLARK WEST
Laughlin, James. SELECTED POEMS: 1935-1985
Le Brun, Annie. SADE: On the Brink of the Abyss
Lowry, Malcolm. SELECTED POEMS
Mackey, Nathaniel. SCHOOL OF UDHRA
Marcelin, Philippe-Thoby. THE BEAST OF THE HAITIAN HILLS
Masereel, Frans. PASSIONATE JOURNEY
Mayakovsky, Vladimir. LISTEN! EARLY POEMS
Mrabet, Mohammed. THE BOY WHO SET THE FIRE
Mrabet, Mohammed. THE LEMON
Mrabet, Mohammed. LOVE WITH A FEW HAIRS

Mrabet, Mohammed. M'HASHISH
Murguía, A. & B. Paschke, eds. VOLCAN: Poems from Central America
Murillo, Rosario. ANGEL IN THE DELUGE
Paschke, B. & D. Volpendesta, eds. CLAMOR OF INNOCENCE
Pasolini, Pier Paolo. ROMAN POEMS
Pessoa, Fernando. ALWAYS ASTONISHED
Peters, Nancy J., ed. WAR AFTER WAR (City Lights Review #5)
Poe, Edgar Allan. THE UNKNOWN POE
Porta, Antonio. KISSES FROM ANOTHER DREAM
Prévert, Jacques. PAROLES
Purdy, James. THE CANDLES OF YOUR EYES
Purdy, James. IN A SHALLOW GRAVE
Purdy, James. GARMENTS THE LIVING WEAR
Purdy, James. OUT WITH THE STARS
Rachlin, Nahid. MARRIED TO A STRANGER
Rachlin, Nahid. VEILS: SHORT STORIES
Reed, Jeremy. RED-HAIRED ANDROID
Rey Rosa, Rodrigo. THE BEGGAR'S KNIFE
Rey Rosa, Rodrigo. DUST ON HER TONGUE
Rigaud, Milo. SECRETS OF VOODOO
Ruy Sánchez, Alberto. MOGADOR
Saadawi El, Nawal. MEMOIRS OF A WOMAN DOCTOR
Sawyer-Lauçanno, Christopher, tr. THE DESTRUCTION OF THE JAGUAR
Scholder, Amy, ed. CRITICAL CONDITION: Women on the Edge of Violence
Sclauzero, Mariarosa. MARLENE
Serge, Victor. RESISTANCE
Shepard, Sam. MOTEL CHRONICLES
Shepard, Sam. FOOL FOR LOVE & THE SAD LAMENT OF PECOS BILL
Smith, Michael. IT A COME
Snyder, Gary. THE OLD WAYS
Solnit, Rebecca. SECRET EXHIBITION: Six California Artists
Sussler, Betsy, ed. BOMB: INTERVIEWS
Takahashi, Mutsuo. SLEEPING SINNING FALLING
Turyn, Anne, ed. TOP TOP STORIES
Tutuola, Amos. FEATHER WOMAN OF THE JUNGLE
Tutuola, Amos. SIMBI & THE SATYR OF THE DARK JUNGLE
Valaoritis, Nanos. MY AFTERLIFE GUARANTEED
Wilson, Colin. POETRY AND MYSTICISM
Wilson, Peter Lamborn. SACRED DRIFT
Zamora, Daisy. RIVERBED OF MEMORY